EROTICON 4

The seduction of a willing young trollop by a gnarled old priest, a handsome young man generously showing a solitary woman the sociable path to pleasure, an elegant Victorian lady who loves to satisfy her insatiable appetites by slumming it, a glimpse inside the harem tent of a virile Egyptian nobleman, and a Roman slave at last granted the opportunity to slake his lust on the voluptuous body of his mistress – these and many others form part of this new sampler of the best in erotic writing thoughout the ages.

Also available in this series:

EROTICON
EROTICON 2
EROTICON 3

EROTICON 4

Anonymous

Introduced and edited by J-P Spencer

This book is a work of fiction.
In real life, make sure you practise safe sex.

First published in 1990 by
Nexus
Thames Wharf Studios
Rainville Road
London W6 9HT

Reprinted 1991 (twice)
Reprinted 1998

Copyright © J-P Spencer 1990

Typeset by TW Typesetting, Plymouth, Devon

Printed and bound by
Cox & Wyman Ltd, Reading, Berks

ISBN 0 352 32563 1

Contents

THE
AUTOBIOGRAPHY
OF A FLEA

In the hundred years since it first gripped the imagination of an eager readership, The Autobiography of a Flea has achieved a degree of notoriety known to only a handful of erotic novels. Though often banned by the authorities – as recently as the early 1980s an innocuous (and inept) video based on the book was regularly seized by the British police – like many other 'dirty' books this one refuses to die, indeed the novel is as difficult to eradicate as the robust vermin of its title. Yet its appeal is not obvious. Based firmly on anticlerical themes made popular in France in the eighteenth century in books such as Gervaise de Latouche's Dom Bougre and Mirabeau's Libertin de Qualité, it recounts the loss of innocence of a young girl at the hands of those who should be protecting her, namely her priest and her guardian uncle. Inevitably, in a book of this nature, the young lady takes to sexual excess like a drunk to free beer and a wild time is had by all. What distinguishes the story, and doubtless has earned it a permanent place in the affection of generations of readers, is the personality of the narrator. As indicated by the title of the book, the tale is told by a flea.

Blessed by a 'mental perception and erudition which placed me for ever upon a pinnacle of insect grandeur' our flea lives on the luscious flesh of young Bella – 'a beauty – just sixteen – a perfect figure, and although so young, her soft bosom was already budding into those proportions which delight the other sex.' Poised upon such an adorable meal ticket, the flea is in the perfect spot to recount every nuance of her exhausting adventures. The following excerpt finds Bella reporting for the first time to the formidable Father Ambrose as a consequence of losing her maidenhead to her sweetheart Charlie. The priest has fortuitously witnessed the adolescent tryst and, on pain of disclosure to her guardian, has commanded Bella to meet him in the sacristy the next day . . .

Curiosity to learn the sequel of an adventure in which I already felt so much interest, as well as a tender solicitude for the gentle and amiable Bella, constrained me to keep in her vicinity, and I, therefore, took care not to annoy her with any very decided attentions on my part, or to raise resistance by an illtimed attack at a moment when it was necessary to the success of my design to remain within range of that young lady's operations.

I shall not attempt to tell of the miserable period passed by my young protegée in the interval which elapsed between the shocking discovery made by the holy Father Confessor, and the hour assigned by him for the interview in the sacristy, which was to decide the fate of the unfortunate Bella.

With trembling steps and downcast eyes the frightened girl presented herself at the porch and knocked.

The door was opened and the Father appeared upon the threshold.

At a sign Bella entered and stood before the stately presence of the holy man.

An embarrassing silence of some seconds followed. Father Ambrose was the first to break the spell.

'You have done right, my daughter, to come to me so punctually; the ready obedience of the penitent is the first sign of the spirit within which obtains the Divine forgiveness.'

At these gracious words Bella took courage, and already a load seemed to fall from her heart.

Father Ambrose continued, seating himself at the same time upon the long-cushioned seat which covered a huge oak chest:

'I have thought much, and prayed much on your account, my daughter. For some time there appeared no way in which I could absolve my conscience otherwise than to go to your natural protector and lay before him the dreadful secret of which I have become the unhappy possessor.'

Here he paused, and Bella, who knew well the severe character of her uncle, on whom she was entirely dependent, trembled at his words.

Taking her hand in his, and gently drawing the girl to the same seat, so that she found herself kneeling before him, while his right hand pressed her rounded shoulder, he went on.

'But I am wounded to think of the dreadful results which would follow such a disclosure, and I have asked for assistance from the Blessed Virgin in my trouble. She has pointed out a way which, while it also serves the ends of our holy church, likely prevents the consequences of your offence from being known to your uncle. The first necessity which this course imposes is, however, implicit obedience.'

Bella, only too rejoiced to hear of a way out of her trouble, readily promised the most blind obedience to the command of her spiritual Father.

The young girl was kneeling at his feet. Father

Ambrose bent his large head over her recumbent figure. A warm tint lit his cheeks, a strange fire danced in his fierce eyes: his hands trembled slightly as they rested upon the shoulders of his penitent, but his composure was otherwise unruffled. Doubtless his spirit was troubled at the conflict going on within him between the duty he had to fulfil and the tortuous path by which he hoped to avoid the awful exposure.

The holy Father then began a long lecture upon the virtue of obedience, and the absolute submissions to the guidance of the minister of holy church.

Bella reiterated her assurance of entire patience and obedience in all things.

Meanwhile it was evident to me that the priest was a victim to some confined, but rebellious spirit which rose within him, and at times almost broke out into complete possession in the flashing eyes and hot passionate lips.

Father Ambrose gently drew the beautiful penitent nearer and nearer, until her fair arms rested upon his knees, and her face bent downwards in holy resignation, sunk almost upon her hands.

'And now, my child,' continued the holy man, 'it is time that I should tell you the means vouchsafed to me by the Blessed Virgin by which alone I am absolved from exposing your offence. There are ministering spirits who have confided to them the relief of those passions and those exigencies which the servants of the church are forbidden openly to avow, but which, who can doubt, they have need to satisfy. These chosen few are mainly selected from among those who have already trodden the path of fleshly indulgence; to them is confined the solemn and holy duty of assuaging the earthly desires of our religious community in the strictest secrecy. To you,' whispered the Father, his voice trembling with emotion, and his large hands passing by an easy transition from the shoulders of his penitent to her slender waist.

'To you, who have once already tasted the supreme pleasure of copulation, it is competent to assume this holy office. Not only will your sin be thus effaced and pardoned, but it will be permitted you to taste legitimately those ecstatic delights, those overpowering sensations of rapturous enjoyment, which in the arms of her faithful servants you are at all times sure to find. You will swim in a sea of sensual pleasure, without incurring the penalties of illicit love. Your absolution will follow each occasion of your yielding your sweet body to the gratification on the church, through her ministers, and you will be rewarded and sustained in the pious work by witnessing – nay, Bella, by sharing fully those intense and fervent emotions, the delicious enjoyment of your beautiful person must provoke.'

Bella listened to this insidious proposal with mingled feelings of surprise and pleasure.

The wild and lewd impulses of her warm nature were at once awakened by the picture now presented to her fervid imagination – how could she hesitate?

The pious priest drew her yielding form towards him, and printed a long hot kiss upon her rosy lips.

'Holy Mother,' murmured Bella, whose sexual instincts were each moment becoming more fully roused. 'This is too much for me to bear – I long – I wonder – I know not what!'

'Sweet innocent, it will be for me to instruct you. In my person you will find your best and fittest preceptor in those exercises you will henceforth have to fulfil.'

Father Ambrose slightly shifted his position. It was then that Bella noticed for the first time the heated look of sensuality which now almost frightened her.

It was now also that she became aware of the enormous protuberance of the front of the holy Father's silk cassock.

The excited priest hardly cared any longer to conceal either his condition or his designs.

Catching the beautiful child to his arms he kissed

her long and passionately. He pressed her sweet body to his burly person, and rudely threw himself forward into closer contact with her graceful form.

At length the consuming lust with which he was burning carried him beyond all bounds, and partly releasing Bella from the constraint of his ardent embrace, he opened the front of his cassock, and exposed, without a blush, to the astonished eyes of his young penitent, a member the gigantic proportions of which, no less than its stiffness and rigidity completely confounded her.

It is impossible to describe the sensations produced upon the gentle Bella by the sudden display of this formidable instrument.

Her eyes were instantly riveted upon it, while the Father, noticing her astonishment, but detecting rightly that there was nothing mingled with it of alarm or apprehension, coolly placed it into her hands. It was then that Bella became wildly excited with the muscular contact of this tremendous thing.

Only having seen the very moderate proportions displayed by Charlie, she found her lewdest sensations quickly awakened by so remarkable a phenomenon, and clasping the huge object as well as she could in her soft little hands, she sank down beside it in an ecstasy of sensual delight.

'Holy Mother, this is already heaven!' murmured Bella. 'Oh! Father, who would have believed I could have been selected for such pleasure!'

This was too much for Father Ambrose. He was delighted at the lubricity of his fair penitent, and the success of his infamous trick (for he had planned the whole, and had been instrumental in bringing the two young lovers together and affording them an opportunity of indulging their warm temperaments, unknown to all save himself, as, hidden close by, with flaming eyes, he watched the amatory combat).

Hastily rising, he caught up the light figure of the

13

young Bella, and placing her upon the cushioned seat on which he had lately been sitting, he threw up her plump legs and separating to the utmost her willing thighs, he beheld for an instant the delicious pinky slit which appeared at the bottom of her white belly. Then, without a word, he plunged his face towards it, and thrusting his lecherous tongue up the moist sheath as far as he could, he sucked it so deliciously that Bella, in a shuddering ecstasy of passion, her young body writhing in spasmodic contortions of pleasure, gave down a plentiful emission, which the holy man swallowed like a custard.

For a few moments there was calm.

Bella lay on her back, her arms extended on either side, and her head thrown back in an attitude of delicious exhaustion, succeeding the wild emotions so lately occasioned by the lewd proceedings of the reverend Father.

Her bosom yet palpitated with the violence of her transports and her beautiful eyes remained half closed in languid repose.

Father Ambrose was one of the few who, under circumstances such as the present, was able to keep the instincts of passion under command. Long habits of patience in the attainment of his object, a general doggedness of manner and the conventional caution of his order, had not been lost upon his fiery nature, and although by nature unfitted for his holy calling, and a prey to desires as violent as they were irregular, he had taught himself to school his passions even to mortification.

It is time to lift the veil from the real character of this man. I do so with respect, but the truth must be told.

Father Ambrose was the living personification of lust. His mind was in reality devoted to its pursuit, and his grossly animal instincts, his ardent and vigorous constitution, no less than his hard unbending nature made him resemble in body, as in mind, the Satyr of old.

But Bella only knew him as the holy Father who had not only pardoned her offence, but who had opened to her the path by which she might, as she supposed, legitimately enjoy those pleasures which had already wrought so strongly on her young imagination.

The bold priest, singularly charmed, not only at the success of his strategem which had given into his hands so luscious a victim, but also at the extraordinary sensuality of her constitution, and the evident delight with which she lent herself to his desires, now set himself leisurely to reap the fruits of his trickery, and revel to the utmost in the enjoyment which the possession of all the delicate charms of Bella could procure to appease his frightful lust.

She was his at last, and as he rose from her quivering body, his lips yet reeking with the plentiful evidence of her participation in his pleasure, his member became yet more fearfully hard and swollen, and the full red head shone with the bursting strain of blood and muscle beneath.

No sooner did the young Bella find herself released from the attack of her confessor upon the sensitive part of her person already described, and raised her head from the recumbent position into which it had fallen, than her eyes fell for the second time upon the big truncheon which the Father kept impudently exposed.

Bella noted the long and thick white shaft, and the curling mass of black hair out of which it rose, stiffly inclined upwards, and protruding from its end was the egg-shaped head, skinned and ruddy, and seeming to invite the contact of her hand.

Bella beheld this thickened muscular mass of stiffened flesh, and unable to resist the inclination, flew once more to seize it in her grasp.

She squeezed it – she pressed it – she drew back the

15

folding skin, and watched the broad nut, as it inclined towards her. She saw with wonder the small slit-like hole at its extremity and taking both her hands, she held it throbbing close to her face.

'Oh! Father, what a beautiful thing,' exclaimed Bella, 'what an immense one, too. Oh! Please, dear Father Ambrose, do tell me what I must do to relieve you of those feelings which you say give our holy ministers of religion so much pain and uneasiness.'

Father Ambrose was almost too excited to reply, but taking her hand in his, he showed the innocent girl how to move her white fingers up and down upon the shoulders of his huge affair.

His pleasure was intense, and that of Bella was hardly less.

She continued to rub his limb with her soft palms and, looking up innocently to his face asked softly – 'If that gave him pleasure, and was nice, and whether she might go on, as she was doing.'

Meanwhile the reverend Father felt his big penis grow harder and even stiffer under the exciting titillations of the young girl.

'Stay a moment; if you continue to rub it so I shall spend,' softly said he. 'It will be better to defer it a little.'

'Spend, my Father,' asked Bella, eagerly, 'what is that?'

'Oh, sweet girl, charming alike in your beauty and your innocence; how divinely you fulfil your divine mission,' exclaimed Ambrose, delighted to outrage and debase the evident inexperience of his young penitent.

'To spend is to complete the act whereby the full pleasure of venery is enjoyed, and then a rich quantity of thick white fluid escapes from the thing you now hold in your hand, and rushing forth, gives equal pleasure to him who ejects it and to the person who, in some manner or other, receives it.'

Bella remembered Charlie and his ecstasy, and knew immediately what was meant.

'Would this outpouring give you relief, my Father?'

'Undoubtedly, my daughter, it is that fervent relief I have in view, offering you the opportunity of taking from me the blissful sacrifice of one of the humblest servants of the church.'

'How delicious,' murmured Bella; 'by my means this rich stream is to flow, and all for me the holy man proposed this end of his pleasure – how happy I am to be able to give him so much pleasure.

As she half pondered, half uttered these thoughts she bent her head down; a faint, but exquisitely sensual perfume rose from the object of her adoration. She pressed her moist lips upon its top, she covered the little slitlike hole with her lovely mouth, and imprinted upon the glowing member a fervent kiss.

'What is this fluid called?' asked Bella, once more raising her pretty face.

'It has various names,' replied the holy man, 'according to the status of the person employing them; but between you and me, my daughter, we shall call it spunk.'

'Spunk!' repeated Bella, innocently, making the erotic word fall from her sweet lips with an unction which was natural under the circumstances.

'Yes, my daughter, spunk is the word I wish you to understand it by, and you shall presently have a plentiful bedewal of the precious essence.'

'How must I receive it?' enquired Bella, thinking of Charlie and the tremendous difference relatively between his instrument and the gigantic and swollen penis in her presence now.

'There are various ways, all of which you will have to learn, but at present we have only slight accommodation for the principal act of reverential venery, of that permitted copulation of which I have already spoken. We must, therefore, supply another and easier

17

method, and instead of my discharging the essence called spunk into your body, where the extreme tightness of that little slit of yours would doubtless cause it to flow very abundantly, we will commence by the friction of your obedient fingers, until the time when I feel the approach of those spasms which accompany the emission. You shall then, at a signal from me, place as much as you can of the head of this affair between your lips, and there suffer me to disgorge the trickling spunk, until the last drop being expended I shall retire satisfied, at least for the time.'

Bella, whose jealous instincts led her to enjoy the description which her confessor offered, and who was quite as eager as himself for the completion of this outrageous programme, readily expressed her willingness to comply.

Ambrose once more placed his large penis in Bella's fair hands.

Excited alike by the sight and touch of so remarkable an object, which both her hands now grasped with delight, the girl set herself to work to tickle, rub and press the huge and stiff affair in a way which gave the licentious priest the keenest enjoyment.

Not content with the friction of her delicate fingers, Bella, uttering words of devotion and satisfaction, now placed the foaming head upon her rosy lips and allowed it to slip in as far as it could, hoping by her touches, no less than by the gliding movements of her tongue, to provoke the delicious ejaculation of which she was in want.

This was almost beyond the anticipation of the holy priest, who had hardly supposed he should find so ready a disciple in the irregular attack he proposed; and his feelings being roused to the utmost by the delicious titillation he was now experiencing, prepared himself to flood the young girl's mouth and throat with the full stream of his powerful discharge.

Ambrose began to feel he could not last longer without letting fly his roe, and thereby ending his pleasure.

He was one of those extraordinary men, the abundance of whose seminal ejaculation is far beyond that of ordinary beings. Not only had he the singular gift of repeatedly performing the veneral act with but very short respite, but the quantity with which he ended his pleasure was as tremendous as it was unusual. The superfluity seemed to come from him in proportion as his animal passions were aroused, and as his libidinous desires were intense and large, so also were the outpourings which relieved them.

It was under these circumstances that the gentle Bella undertook to release the pent-up torrents of this man's lust. It was her sweet mouth which was to be the recipient of those thick slippery volumes of which she had had as yet no experience, and, all ignorant as she was of the effect of the relief she was so anxious to administer, the beautiful maid desired the consummation of her labour and the overflow of that spunk of which the good Father had told her.

Harder and hotter grew the rampant member as Bella's exciting lips pressed its large head and her tongue played around the little opening. Her two white hands bore back the soft skin from its shoulders and alternately tickled the lower extremity.

Twice Ambrose, unable to bear without spending the delicious contact, drew back the tip from her rosy lips.

At length Bella, impatient of delay, and apparently bent on perfecting her task, pressed forward with more energy than ever upon the stiff shaft.

Instantly there was a stiffening of the limbs of the good priest. His legs spread wide on either side of his penitent. His hands grasped convulsively at the cushions, his body was thrust forward and straightened out.

'Oh, holy Christ! I am going to spend!' he exclaimed, as with parted lips and glazing eyes he looked his last upon his innocent victim. Then he shivered perceptibly, and with low moans and short, hysteric cries, his penis, in obedience to the provocation of the young lady, began to jet forth its volumes of thick and glutinous fluid.

Bella, sensible of the gushes which now came slopping, jet after jet into her mouth, and ran in streams down her throat, hearing the cries of her companion, and perceiving with ready intuition that he was enjoying to the utmost the effect she had brought about, continued her rubbings and compression until gorged with the slimy discharge, and half choked by its abundance, she was compelled to let go of this human syringe, which continued to spout out its gushes in her face.

'Holy Mother!' exclaimed Bella, whose lips and face were reeking with the Father's spunk. 'Holy Mother! What pleasure I have had – and you, my Father, have I not given the precious relief you coveted?'

Father Ambrose, too agitated to reply, raised the gentle girl in his arms, and pressing her streaming mouth to his, sucked humid kisses of gratitude and pleasure.

A quarter of an hour passed in tranquil repose uninterrupted by any signs of disturbance from without.

The door was fast, and the holy Father had well chosen his time.

Meanwhile Bella, whose desires had been fearfully excited by the scene we have attempted to describe, had conceived an extravagant longing to have the same operation performed upon her with the rigid member of Ambrose that she had suffered from the moderately proportioned weapon of Charlie.

Throwing her arms round the burly neck of her confessor, who whispered low words of invitation, watching as she did so, the effect in the already stiffening instrument between his legs.

'You told me that the tightness of this little slit,'

20

and here Bella placed his large hand upon it with a gentle pressure, 'would make you discharge abundantly of the spunk you possess. What would I not give, my Father, to feel it poured into my body from the top of this red thing?'

It was evident how much the beauty of the young Bella, no less than the innocence and *naiveté* of her character, inflamed the sensual nature of the priest. The knowledge of his triumph – of her utter helplessness in his hands – of her delicacy and refinement, all conspired to work to the extreme of lecherous desires of his fierce and wanton instincts. She was his. His to enjoy as he wished – his to break to every caprice of his horrid lust, and to bend to the indulgence of the most outrageous and unbridled sensuality.

'Ay, by heaven! it is too much,' exclaimed Ambrose, whose lust, already rekindling, now rose violently into activity at this solicitation. 'Sweet girl, you don't know what you ask; the disproportion is terrible, and you would suffer much in the attempt.'

'I would suffer all,' replied Bella, 'so that I could feel that fierce thing in my belly, and taste the gushes of its spunk up in me to the quick.'

'Holy Mother of God! It is too much – you shall have it, Bella, you shall know the full measure of this stiffened machine, and, sweet girl, you shall wallow in an ocean of warm spunk.'

'Oh, my Father, what heavenly bliss!'

'Strip, Bella, remove everything that can interfere with our movements, which I promise you will be violent enough.'

Thus ordered, Bella was soon divested of her clothing, and finding her Confessor appeared charmed at the display of her beauty, and that his member swelled and lengthened in proportion as she exhibited her nudity, she parted with the last vestige of drapery, and stood as naked as she was born.

Father Ambrose was astonished at the charms which

now faced him. The full hips, the budding breasts, the skin as white as snow and soft as satin, the rounded buttocks and swelling thighs, the flat white belly and lovely mount covered only with the thinnest down; and above all the charming pinky slit which now showed itself at the bottom of the mount, now hid timorously away between the plump thighs. With a snort of rampant lust he fell upon his victim.

Ambrose clasped her in his arms. He pressed her soft glowing form of his burly front. He covered her with his salacious kisses, and giving his lewd tongue full licence, promised the young girl all the joys of Paradise by the introduction of his big machine within her slit and belly.

Bella met him with a little cry of ecstasty, and as the excited ravisher bore her backwards to the couch, already felt the broad and glowing head of his gigantic penis pressing against the warm moist lips of her moist virgin orifice.

And now, the holy man finding delight in the contact of his penis with the warm lips of Bella's slit, began pushing it in between with all his energy until the big nut was covered with the moisture which the sensitive little sheath exuded.

Bella's passions were at fever height. The efforts of Father Ambrose to lodge the head of his member within the moist lips of her little slit, so far from deterring her, spurred her to madness until, with another faint cry, she fell prone and gushed down the slippery tribute of her lascivious temperament.

This was exactly what the bold priest wanted, and as the sweet warm emission bedewed his fiercely distended penis, he drove resolutely in, and at one bound sheathed half its ponderous length in the beautiful child.

No sooner did Bella feel the stiff entry of the terrible member within her tender body, than she lost all the little control of herself she had, and setting aside all

22

thought of the pain she was enduring, she wound her legs about his loins, and entreated her huge assailant not to spare her.

'My sweet and delicious child,' whispered the salacious priest, 'my arms are round you, my weapon is already half way up your tight belly. The joys of Paradise will be yours presently.'

'Oh, I know it; I feel it, do not draw back, give me the delicious thing as far as you can.'

'There, then, I push, I press, but I am far too largely made to enter you easily. I shall burst you, possibly; but it is now too late. I must have you – or die.'

Bella's parts relaxed a little, and Ambrose pushed in another inch. His throbbing member lay skinned and soaking, pushed half way into the girl's belly. His pleasure was most intense, and the head of his instrument was compressed deliciously by Bella's slit.

'Go on, dear Father, I am waiting for the spunk you promised me.'

It little needed this stimulant to induce the confessor to an exercise of his tremendous powers of copulation. He pushed frantically forward; he plunged his hot penis still further and further at each effort, and then with one huge stroke buried himself to the balls in Bella's light little person.

It was then that the furious plunge of the brutal priest became more than his sweet victim, sustained as she had been by her own advanced desires, could endure.

With a faint shriek of physical anguish, Bella felt that her ravisher had burst through all the resistance which her youth had opposed to the entry of his member, and the torture of the forcible insertion of such a mass bore down the prurient sensations with which she had commenced to support the attack.

Ambrose cried aloud in rapture, he looked down upon the fair thing his serpent had stung. He gloated over the victim now impaled with the full rigour of his huge rammer. He felt the maddening contact with inexpressible delight. He saw her quivering with the anguish of his forcible entry. His brutal nature was fully aroused. Come what might he would enjoy to his utmost, so he wound his arms about the beautiful girl and treated her to the full measure of his burly member.

'My beauty! you are indeed exciting, you must also enoy. I will give you the spunk I spoke of, but I must first work up my nature by this lascivious titillation. Kiss me, Bella, then you shall have it, and while the hot spunk leaves me and enters your young parts, you shall be sensible of the throbbing joys I also am experiencing. Press, Bella, let me push, so, my child, now it enters again. Oh! oh!'

Ambrose raised himself a moment, and noted the immense shaft round which the pretty slit of Bella was now intensely stretched.

Firmly embedded in his luscious sheath, and keenly relishing the exceeding tightness of the warm folds of youthful flesh which now encased him, he pushed on, unmindful of the pain his tormenting member was producing, and only anxious to secure as much enjoyment to himself as he could. He was not a man to be deterred by any false notions of pity in such a case, and now pressed himself inwards to his utmost, while his hot lips sucked delicious kisses from the open and quivering lips of the poor Bella.

For some minutes nothing now was heard but the jerking blows with which the lascivious priest continued his enjoyment, and the cluck, cluck of his huge penis, as it alternately entered and retreated in the belly of the beautiful penitent.

It was not to be supposed that such a man as Ambrose was ignorant of the tremendous powers of enjoyment his member could rouse within one of the opposite sex, and that with its size and disgorging capabilities of such a nature as to enlist the most

24

powerful emotions in the young girl in whom he was operating.

But Nature was asserting himself in the person of the young Bella. The agony of the stretching was fast being swallowed up in the intense sensations of pleasure produced by the vigorous weapon of the holy man, and it was not long before the low moans and sobs of the pretty child became mingled with expressions, half choked in the depth of her feelings, expressive in delight.

'Oh, my Father! Oh, my dear, generous Father! Now, now push. Oh! push. I can bear – I wish for it. I am in heaven! The blessed instrument is so hot in its head. Oh! my heart. Oh! my – oh! Holy Mother, what is this I feel?'

Ambrose saw the effect he was producing. His own pleasure advanced apace. He drove steadily in and out, treating Bella to the long hard shaft of his member up to the crisp hair which covered his big balls, at each forward thrust.

At length Bella broke down, and treated the electrified and ravished man with a warm emission which ran all over his stiff affairs.

It is impossible to describe the lustful frenzy which now took possession of the young and charming Bella. She clung with desperate tenacity to the burly figure of the priest, who bestowed upon the heaving and voluptuous body the full force and vigour of his manly thrust. She held him in her tight and slippery sheath to his balls.

But in her ecstasy Bella never lost sight of the promised perfection of the enjoyment. The holy man was to spend his spunk in her as Charlie had done, and the thought added fuel to her lustful fire.

When, therefore, Father Ambrose, throwing his arms close round her taper waist, drove up his stallion penis to the very hairs of Bella's slit, and sobbing, whispering that the 'spunk' was coming at last, the excited girl straightway opening her legs to the utmost, with positive shrieks of pleasure let him send his pent-up fluid in showers into her very vitals.

Thus he lay for full two minutes, while at each hot and forcible injection of the slippery semen, Bella gave plentiful evidence by her writhings and cries of the ecstasy the powerful discharge was producing.

CONFESSIONS OF AN ENGLISH MAID

Like Bella, the heroine of The Autobiography of a Flea, *pretty young Jessie takes to the delights of sexual activity at an early age – so much so that her step-mother has her committed to a reformatory for wayward girls. There, needless to say, she learns a great deal more about sex and the way in which her fair face and form can earn her a profitable living on her eventual release. It is her even more experienced friend Hester who turns her on to the pecuniary advantages of not giving it away for nothing – quite apart from the obvious pleasures of going to bed with a lot of handsome fellows. Breathlessly Hester proclaims the pleasures of working in 'a sporting house' and inflames Jessie's over-wrought imagination with what she intends to get up to on the first night of her release. 'Guess what I'm going to have,' she says. 'A stiff cock?' suggests Jessie. 'No,' proclaims Hester, 'five of them, all at the same time!'*

With such an influence at work it is no wonder that Jessie is keen to tread the professional path on her release. Eventually Hester's pander, Madame Lafronde, posing as her aunt, collects her from her prison and takes her to her new home – 'a place of quiet elegance, soft plush carpets and tapestried walls. Thus did I cross the threshold of a new life and the doors of the past closed behind me . . .'

A small but furnished alcove with a tiled bath in connection was waiting for me, and after I had examined it Madame Lafronde left Hester and me together, saying that she would have a talk with me later in the afternoon.

A maid appeared with a luncheon tray and as I ate, plying Hester with questions between bites, I learned that Madame Lafronde's 'family' comprised eight other girls in addition to Hester and myself. I would meet them later, they did not get up until after twelve, which accounted for the silence and absence of movement I had already noted.

When Madame Lafronde returned, her first request was that I strip myself entirely so that she could examine my body. I did so with some embarrassment, for though I had often enough exposed myself to boys and men, the impersonal, appraising eyes of this strange old lady filled me with a nervous dread that I might be found wanting in some essential.

I was small of stature and feared that the absence of clothing might accentuate the possible defect. However, to my vast relief, she gave every evidence of satisfaction and nodded her head approvingly as I turned around and around in obedience to her indications. When I had replaced my clothing she shot question after question at me, until every phase of my early and subsequent sexual life had been revealed. To her questions I endeavoured to give frank and truthful answers, regardless of the embarrassment which some of them evoked.

'Now, my dear,' she said, when the interrogating had been concluded, 'I want you to know that we're all one big, happy family here. There must be no jealousy of friction or petty animosities between girls. Our gentlemen are very nice, but men are men, and a pretty, new face always distracts their attention from older ones. I have a plan in mind which fits you as though you were made for it. If you handle it rightly you'll be helping the other girls as well as yourself, and instead of being jealous of you they'll all have reason to be grateful. We're all here to make money and as it must come from the gentlemen our aim is to get them to spend it and then come back and spend some more. Never forget that.'

And Madame Lafronde explained the unique role I was to play, a role which to a more mature mind than mine would have at once revealed the astuteness and subtlety of the guiding genius behind this lucrative business and which accounted for its success, measured in terms of gold. Madame Lafronde was nobody's fool.

In brief, she proposed to dangle my youthful prettiness before the jaded eyes of the clientele as a sort of visual aperitif, much as water was placed before the thirsting Tantalus, in view, but just beyond reach, the psychological effect of which would be to so whet their passions that they would in the end, perforce, satisfy

30

themselves with such feminine fruit as was within their reach.

I was to tantalise masculine passion while leaving to others the duty of satisfying them. This with respect to the regular 'parlour' clientele. Exceptions would be made privately with certain special patrons who were always able and disposed to pay well for favouritism.

Things were not as they had been before the war, explained Madame Lafronde. Even this profitable business had suffered from the falling economic barometer, and too many of the gentlemen who dropped in were inclined to pass the evening sociably in the parlour. Of course, between liquors consumed, tips to the girls, and various other sources of minor revenues, their presence was desirable, but the real profits of the business were garnered in the bedrooms, not in the parlour. It was a case of a bird in a bedroom being worth five in the parlour.

As a sort of stimulant designed to inspire blasé gentlemen with an irresistible urge to make use of the bedroom service, I was to be rigged up in an enticingly juvenile fashion and paraded constantly before their eyes in a semi-nude state. Various pretexts and artifices would ostensibly account for my presence and movements. I would carry a tray of cigars and cigarettes, serve drinks, and be available for general services and accommodations with but one single exception. I would joke and chat with patrons, tell a naughty story now and then, even permit them to fondle me within certain limits, but, because of my youth (I was to pretend to be only fifteen years old!) my services were not to be expected in a professional capacity.

I gasped at hearing that I was to play the part of a fifteen-year-old, but Madame Lafronde insisted that it would not be difficult in view of my small body and the fact that certain artifices in costume, hairdressing and other details would be employed to help out the illusion.

The first step was to call in a barber who trimmed my hair so that it hung just below my ears. It was naturally wavy, and when the work was finished it was quite apparent that Madame Lafronde had not erred in assuming that short curls would lend a peculiarly childish effect to my face. I gazed in the mirror with genuine surprise at the transfiguration.

When the barber had gone Madame Lafronde ordered me to undress again, and after taking certain measurements left the room to return later with several garments and a box which on being opened revealed a safety razor, soap and brush.

'We could have let the barber do this, too,' she commented dryly, indicating the razor, 'but maybe you'd rather do it yourself.'

'Do what?' I asked, looking at the razor in perplexity.

'Shave the pretty little curls off your peek-a-boo,' she answered, with a gesture toward the dark shadow which was visible through the texture of my single garment.

'What!' I expostulated. 'Why ... even girls fifteen years old have ... !'

'Shave it off,' she interrupted. 'If you don't know how, I'll do it for you.'

'I can, I can!' I responded hastily. 'I've shaved the hair under my arms lots of times ... only ...' and I glanced around in confusion for, in addition to Madame Lafronde and Hester, several girls had appeared and were standing in the door watching me curiously.

'Go over by the window with your back to us and stand up, or sit down, whichever you wish, if you're afraid someone will see your love trap. You'll get over that before you've been here long.'

Without further protest I took the shaving equipment, turned my back on the smiling assembly and sitting on the edge of a chair with my legs apart I lathered and soaped the hair and shaved it off the best I could. I had to go over the ground several times before the last prickly stubs were finally removed, and when I stood up, much embarrassed, to let Madame Lafronde view the results she expressed her approval and suggested that I dust the denuded flesh with talcum powder.

The absence of the hair from its accustomed place caused me to feel peculiarly naked, and I turned my gaze downward. The two sides of my cunny stook out prominently like fat little hills, the crease between them tightly closed as I stood with my legs pressed together.

I was now to don black hose of sheerest silk and a pair of tiny slippers with exaggerated high Spanish heels. Around my legs, just above the knees, fitted narrow scarlet garters, each adorned with a little silk rosette. Next came an exquisite brocade coat or jacket of black velvet into which was worked fantastic designs in gold thread.

'What about my bubbies?' I asked, as Madame Lafronde handed me the garment. 'Will I have to cut them off, too?'

A gust of laughter followed and I slipped on the loose-fitting coat. It terminated at a point about half-way down my thighs, leaving a few inches of naked flesh between its lower edge and the tops of my hose. Fastening just below the breasts with three braided loops, it covered my stomach all right, but from there down the folds hung loose and a naked, hairless cunny would be exposed with any careless movement.

The last item of this bizarre costume was a tall, military style cap of astrakhan, fitted with a small brim of shiny black leather and a strap which passed under my chin. Madame Lafronde adjusted the cap on my head at a rakish angle and stook back to view the effect.

I glanced at my reflection in the wardrobe mirror. Without undue conceit I realised that I presented a chic picture, one which undoubtedly fulfilled Madame

Lafronde's expectations, as was attested to by the satisfied gleam in her shrewd old eyes, by Hester's enthusiastic felicitations, and by the half-admiring, half-envious looks of the other girls who were watching silently.

From beneath the edge of the black astrakhan cap my hair hung loose in short, crisp curls. The low bodice of the brocade jacket teasingly revealed the upper halves of my breasts, while its wide and ample sleeves displayed my arms to good advantage with every movement. The jacket itself, fitting snugly around my waist, flared out sufficiently to show my hips to good advantage. Further down, the sheen of glossy silk with the brief variation in colour provided by the scarlet garters gave just the right touch to my legs, and the high-heeled slippers completed the exotic ensemble.

The rest of the afternoon and evening Madame Lafronde devoted to coaching and instructing me. The doors were open to visitors at nine o'clock, but it was never until after eleven or twelve that gentlemen returning from their clubs or other nocturnal entertainment began to drop in in any considerable number, and from then on patrons came and went, singly or in groups, some to linger briefly, others to pass an hour or two, or to remain all night.

I made my debut at eleven o'clock. With inward nervousness at first, but with growing confidence as I observed the electrical effect my entry made upon the half-dozen gentlemen who were lounging about the salon in various attitudes of interest or indifference to the wiles of the feminine sirens about them. As I crossed the room with my tray of cigars and cigarettes and matches supported by a strap over my shoulders the hum of conversation ceased as if by magic and every eye was on me.

I approached a tall, well-dressed gentleman who was sitting on a sofa with a girl on either side of him, and proffered my wares in a timid voice. His startled gaze took in the picture before him and lingered a moment on my legs. Shaking himself free from the arms of his companions, he sat up.

'My dear, I never smoked a cigar in my life, but I'll take all you have, if you go with them!'

This was Madame Lafronde's cue. Entering the room from a side door where she had been waiting. she said:

'Dear gentlemen, I want to present a new member of our family to you. This is Jessie. Jessie is here under peculiar circumstances. She is an orphan and, strictly speaking, not old enough to be here in a professional capacity. Though as you see, she is nicely developed, she is in fact only fifteen years old and I am sheltering her here only because of her orphaned condition. She is to make her living selling you cigars and cigarettes, gentlemen, and serving you in all other possible ways ... except one.'

Madame Lafronde paused.

'In other words,' interrupted a tall, thin young man with a tiny moustache who was indifferently stroking the silk-clad legs of a damsel on his lap, 'she can be only a sister to us. I knew she was too good to be true the moment she came into this room.'

A burst of laughter followed and Madame Lafronde, smiling, answered:

'A sister ... well ... maybe just a bit more than a sister, gentlemen, but not too much more!'

From across the room Hester beckoned to me.

'This is my friend Mr Hayden, Jessie. He wants to know you,' she said, indicating her companion.

I acknowledged the introduction.

'Bring us two Scotch and sodas, will you, honey?' added Hester.

Mr Hayden spoke to me pleasantly and took a packet of cigarettes from my tray, courteously declining the change I tendered him. As I turned to execute Hester's order, the man I had first addressed detained me.

'Wait a moment, Sister. I've decided to take up smoking.'

I might add that the nickname 'Sister' was unanimously adopted and clung to me during the time I was in Madame Lafronde's house.

The gentleman took a handful of cigars and reached toward his pocket. As he did so, his eyes drifted down below the edge of the tray.

'Hold on! I'm making a tactical error!' he exclaimed, replacing all the cigars but one. 'I see right now that cigars should be purchased one by one. You may bring me another when you come back!'

Nothing else was needed to start the ball of my popularity rolling and soon the salon was echoing with hilarity and laughter as all called for cigars and cigarettes at once, each trying to keep me standing in front of him as long as possible.

If this kept up there would be substantial returns on the tobacco concession, for half the profits were to be mine, according to Madame Lafronde's promise, and this in addition to whatever was given to me in the nature of tips or gratuities. Flushed and happy, I ran from one to another, replying to jokes and quips in a half-innocent, half-cynical manner, calculated to fit the role of a fifteen-year-old ingenue.

As the evening wore on new arrivals appeared and I was instantly the first object of their attention. Before long the pockets of my brocade jacket were heavy with silver, I had replenished my tobacco stock several times and received several generous tips for bringing in liquor, and in addition, a gentleman had given me four shillings for being permitted to feel my bubbies, 'just in a brotherly way', as he expressed it.

What the effect of my presence was on the regular revenues of the house I could not judge, for though there was a constant movement of couples in and out of bedrooms I had no way to knowing whether this was a normal or an increased activity.

With the advancing hours the movement gradually diminished and by four o'clock the last guest had departed. The door was locked, the girls ate a light luncheon and prepared to retire. It was then that Madame Lafronde informed me that the bedroom service had showed a decided increase, which increase she was fair enough to attribute to my presence.

She was well satisfied and I surely had reason to be, for when the money was counted up and the tobacco sales checked there remained for me the sum of two pounds and eight shillings, which was duly credited to me and would be at my disposition on request.

I was tired out; I had hardly slept the previous night, yet such was my excitement that I did not feel sleepy and preferred to gossip with Hester for an hour in my room. I had a hundred questions to ask. I wanted to know about the nice-looking, gentlemanly Mr Hayden, and learned that he was one of Hester's regular and most favoured friends.

He had been much interested in me, and Hester had unselfishly confided to him that I might reservedly be at his disposition at some later occasion, to which he had gallantly responded that in such an event he would insist on having the two of us together. How good Hester was, I thought, to be willing to share this nice man with me and maybe risk my supplanting her in his affections. He had appealed to me greatly, and there had been several others whom I would not have been averse to doing something with.

'You made a tremendous sensation, darling,' said Hester. 'You could have a dozen roomcalls. I heard what everybody said. But Lafronde is right. The other girls would have been ready to scratch your eyes out. There's nothing makes them so mad as to have a new girl take their regulars away from them. Did you notice that fellow who went with me? He comes here every three or four nights. I guess every girl here has had him, but now he always takes me. He's got lots of money and he's kind of nice, but, gee, he never has a hard-on and it takes about half an hour of work to give

37

him a stand. Sometimes I even have to put the buzzer on him, but tonight, oh baby, it was as stiff as a poker. I jollied him about it and told him I bet it was thinking about you instead of me. 'My word,' he said, 'you're a deucedly clevah mind reader. That little tart did have a most extraordinary effect on me. Wonder what the chawnces would be to secure her company for an hour or two? I think that's all bally rot about her virginal estate, don't you know!' I told him to talk to Madame Lafronde and maybe it could be arranged. That's two of my regulars that have fallen for you already, but I'm not jealous. You can have Bumpy if you want him. It takes too long to make his cock stand up.'

I laughed.

'What did you mean, putting the buzzer on him?'

'The juice, the electric massage machine. Don't you know what an electric massage machine is?'

'Of course I do. They use them for facials. But how . . . what . . . ?'

'Facials! Oh baby, you don't know the half. Wait . . . you're tired out . . . I'll fix your bath water for you and after you're bathed I'll give you a massage that will make you sleep like an infant.'

Hester ran into the bathroom and turned on the water. Then she went to her room and came back with an entrancing little pink silk nightgown, face cream, perfume, and a large leather-covered box.

While I lay splashing lazily in the tub, soaking in the pleasant warmth of the foamy, scented water, she laid out the nightgowns and opened the box to show the apparatus it contained and which was, in effect an electric vibratory massage machine fitted with a long cord for attachment to an electricity outlet. There were several assorted pieces in the box and from these Hester selected one fitted with rubber lips which turned out in the form of a small cup.

When I had got out of the tub and dried myself I lay down naked on the bed. Hester dipped her fingers in the jar of cream and passed them lightly over my face, neck, breasts and limbs.

I thought suddenly of the peculiar aspect the shaving had given me in a certain place and flipped a corner of the sheet over it. Without a word Hester flipped it back and her hands were between my thighs, softly spreading the cold cream over them and down my legs.

'You're awful good to go to so much trouble for me, Hester,' I murmured.

'It's nothing. You can do as much for me sometime,' she replied.

When she had finished anointing my body she connected the massage machine. It began to hum and the next instant the rubber cup was buzzing over my forehead, cheeks and neck. My flesh thrilled to the refreshing stimulation and I lay still, enjoying it to the full. Gradually the rubber moved down over my chest, between my breasts, then up over one of them right on the nipple. I came out of any languid rest with a bound. That bubbling, vibrating cup over the nipple of my breast was awakening sensations quite remote to those of mere physical refreshment.

Both my nipples stiffened up, the sensitive area around them puffed out and radiations of sexua' excitation began to flow through my body, Laughing hysterically, I sat up and pushed the tantalising device away.

'Be still, will you? Lie back down!' expostulated Hester, giving me a shove which tumbled me back over the pillows.

'But, Hester! That thing . . . it's positively distracting! Don't put it on my bubbies again . . . I can't stand it!'

Hester smiled.

'You'll think it's distracting before I finish with you. Keep quiet or you'll wake the girls in the next room.'

Down over my stomach, in widening circles, around and around, and then back and forth moved the diabolical apparatus guided by Hester's hand. I had a premonition now of what was coming, and as it slowly but surely crept downward until it reached the upper part of the rounded elevation of my cunny, I clenched my fists and held my breasts.

No sooner was it close enough to impart its infernal vibration to my clitoris than tremors of sexual agitation began to shake my body. It was simply irresistible. I could not have forestalled its action by any conceivable exercise of willpower.

But I did not try. The fulminating intensity of the sensations which now had me in their grip nullified any will or desire to thwart them. I threw my head back, closed my eyes, and surrendered supinely. My legs parted shamelessly beneath the insinuating pressure of Hester's fingers, and the humming, buzzing cup slid between them. Up and down it moved, three, four, maybe half a dozen times, pressing lightly against the flesh.

My orgasm, wrought up to the final pitch of excitation and unable to withstand the infernal provocation longer, yielded, and in a second I was gasping in the throes of sexual ecstasy.

When I recovered my breath, and in part my composure, I exclaimed:

'Hester! You . . . you . . . I could murder you! Fooling me with that thing!'

'Make you sleep good, honey, and keep you from having naughty dreams,' she answered complacently, and she disconnected the device and restored it to its container.

'Does that work on men like that, too?'

'Yes; we use it on them sometimes to give them a stand when they either can't get one or are too slow.'

'Well,' I commented. 'I'll say it gave me a stand I wasn't expecting.'

She giggled, tucked the covers around me, kissed me on the cheek, and turned out the lights.

'Sleep tight, honey. I'll wake you in the afternoon.'

She departed, leaving me alone to drowsily review the stupendous transition which twenty-four hours had wrought in my life. Last night, a hard, narrow cot in the drab and comfortless ward of a reformatory. Tonight, the soft luxury of a beautiful bed with the seductive caress of silk and fine linen about my body and all around me the material evidences of a life of ease, gaiety, and luxury. Gradually my thoughts became hazy and I drifted off into a pleasant, dreamless slumber from which I did not awaken until nine or ten hours later.

A week slipped by quickly, each night a pleasant repetition, without any notable variations, of the one I have described. This was time enough to assure Madame Lafronde that the experiment was a success. The continued approval with which my seminude appearance was received by patrons, together with certain indications, was proof that I really constituted an attraction which was imparting a new popularity to the resort.

But it was not Madame Lafronde's intention to limit my activities to exhibitional purposes. She was already being importuned by gentlemen whose interest in me was not to be resigned to mere optical satisfaction and the subtle old procuress was but biding the time necessary for these gentlemen's inflamed fancies to get the best of their financial perspectives. I was being reserved for the most exacting and best-paying customers. To the rest, including the general run of parlour guests, I was to remain only a visual aphrodisiac.

Into the ample pockets of my brocade jacket these more or less credulous victims of my enticements and beguilings poured their silver, eagerly taking advantage of such opportunities as I permitted them to fondle me tentatively or superficially, bought my cigars and cigarettes, tipped me generously for every trifling ser-

41

vice, sighed, and generally visited a bedroom with one of my companions where, doubtless, evoking visions of my naked legs and other presumed charms, they ravished me by proxy.

Of the patrons I subsequently served in a more intimate fashion, five developed into 'steadies,' that is, became exclusively mine, and came with more or less regularity. A sixth, no other than the gentlemanly Mr Hayden, kept his promise to Hester and either by virtue of genuine affection for her or actuated by a kindly sentiment to avoid wounded feelings, insisted upon having both of us with him at the same time and maintained an attitude of strict impartiality.

I think Hester's generous spirit would not have resented a surrender of her priority to me, but though Mr Hayden was one of the nicest men I ever met, I was glad that his instincts of gallantry saved me from being placed in the light of having distracted his attention from one who was beyond doubt my best and sincerest friend. I have never found another such.

Patrons like Mr Hayden, unfortunately always in a minority, were the bright and redeeming features of a life otherwise vicious and degrading. They were the ones who, regardless of a girl's lost social status, always treated her with respectful consideration. Generous in recompensing the efforts which were made to please them, they never exacted arduous or debasing services, nor were they addicted to unnatural vices which went beyond the pale of those sexual practices ordinarily considered acceptable and legitimate.

To my lot fell the patronage of a Mr Heeley, a gentleman of this desirable category though with the minor disadvantage of being much older and less attractive physically than Mr Hayden. There was a Mr Thomas, middle-aged and wealthy, who had garnered his fortune in Ceylon and who always had some interesting story to tell. There was Mr Castle and Mr Wainwright, both of whom were addicted to eccentricities of a peculiar and disagreeable nature. At first I protested to Madame Lafronde that these two gentlemen were personages *non grata* with me and insinuated that I would not be loathe to dispense with their attentions. It was unequivocally impressed upon me that my inclinations were quite secondary to those of wealthy patrons. 'Do whatever they want within the limits of endurance. Satisfy their whims, fancies, even their aberrations if possible as long as they are willing to pay accordingly. Humour them, please them, get the money and keep them coming back as long as you can!' This was the unwritten law in the world of prostitution.

Mr Hayden was, I think, about thirty years old. I could easily have become really infatuated with this pleasant-spoken, educated, and cultured gentleman. We never knew exactly who he was with reference to his place in the outside world, nor even indeed that his name was really Hayden, for it was not unusual that gentlemen frequenting such places of entertainment as that provided by Madame Lafronde prudently concealed their identities under fictitious names. Nevertheless, there was no doubt that he was of the real gentility.

I liked him very much and I think the affection was reciprocated to an even greater extent than was ever manifested, but he was of that conscientious, kind-hearted type, disposed to go out of the way even at personal inconvenience to avoid causing pain to others and he knew that Hester adored him.

To Mr Hayden fell the honour, if such it might be styled, of initiating me into the real service of which I was now a recruit. My absence from the salon was noticed, but Madame Lafronde accounted for the numerous inquiries with the old alibi 'a bad time of the month, don't you know.' Hester and I and Mr Hayden enjoyed a little dinner by ourselves and thereafter repaired to Hester's room where we disported ourselves lightheartedly for an hour, romping and tumbling over the bed in good-natured abandon as the wine we had imbibed warmed our blood and attuned our receptive senses to lecherous ideas.

Mr Hayden was a healthy, vigorous young man, a splendid example of physical perfection. The sight of his clean-cut, well-kept body, and the magnificently rigid and well-formed member which was disclosed when he undressed sent the blood surging through my veins. I did not know by what procedure he intended to make use of two women at the same time, but imagined that he should probably take us in turn, maybe changing from one to the other at intervals.

I waited expectantly for Hester to take the initiative. Inside, I was fairly burning up. Though I had bathed most carefully but a short while before, my cunny was wet with anticipation, my clitoris swollen and pulsing. In excuse of this ardour was the fact that I had not been with a man for three long years and during this sterile period there had been no outlet for my passions except the one provided by my own nimble fingers, an occasional wet dream and, as I have related, the orgasm effected by Hester's so-called massage.

We lay down on the bed on either side of our male companion, Hester and I both naked except for our slips, hose and shoes, which we intended to leave on until done with our play and ready for sleep. Mr Hayden caressed us impartially for a while, passing his hands over our breasts, fingering the nipples until they stood up stiffly, and finally a hand drifted down over each of the two cunnies. The contact of his warm hand as it lay over mine with one of the fingers pressed lightly within the cleft produced in me an effect which was almost sufficient to put my orgastic mechanism into immediate action. I literally had to 'clench' my nerves and strain my willpower to keep from coming. Had he let his finger linger there a bit longer, or had he imparted the slightest friction, my efforts to restrain orgasm would have failed then and there.

But he removed it after a short interval without apparently having observed my delicate condition, and straightening out on his back he drew Hester across his body where, by urging her forward bit by bit, he eventually got her straddled across his chest with her knees doubled beneath her on either side of him. Her dark auburn curls were right at his chin and it required no great imagination to divine that her cunny was going to be licked French fashion.

'If he does that to her before my eyes I'll cream despite anything I can do to hold it back. I know I shall!' I thought to myself.

In the light of experience throughout subsequent years I confess this: that the sight of another woman being Frenched by a man, or a woman Frenching a man, reacts upon me more violently than any other spectacle of a lewd nature. My senses are excited to a frenzy at the sight of this act, and if I let myself go I can have an orgasm without even touching myself, but simply through the impulse conveyed to the genital system through the trajectory of the eye.

Having accommodated Hester comfortably on his strong chest, Mr Hayden reached over and took me by the arm, manifesting by his motions that I was to seat myself across his middle, impaled upon the turgid emblem of masculinity, behind Hester. Obeying his wordless indications I crouched over him, passing my arm around Hester and clasping her plump bubbies in my hand. Then, gently, breathlessly, I sank down until I felt the entire length of that glorious member throbbing within the living sheath I was providing for it.

But, alas, to my consternation, barely had I perceived the contact of his crisp hair on my naked cunny than my emotions, overriding all powers of resistance, as though deriding my futile efforts to hold them in abeyance, rebelling incontinently, loosed themselves and in a second I was gasping, writhing and suspiring in a regular paroxysm of passionate ecstasy.

As the reverberations gradually died away and my thoughts took on a semblance of coherency, I was filled with mortification. What would Mr Hayden think of such amazing lubricity and precipitation? Hester, surprised at first, had twisted around, and now burst into laughter.

'What happened?' she gasped.

'I don't know! I did it . . . I couldn't help it!' I answered, shamefaced.

Mr Hayden was also laughing.

'You're a fast worker, sister,' he said, his sides shaking, and realising that I was momentaruly, at least, exhausted by the orgasm, he added compassionately: 'Better get off and rest a moment while Hester and I catch up with you!'

I discharged myself and threw my still trembling body on the bed beside them. With his hands against Hester's knees Mr Hayden pushed her backward to take the place I had vacated and a moment later his cock slid in between her legs. Crouching over him, supporting herself on her hands, Hester worked gently up and down on the glistening shaft, alternating from time to time, with a twisting, rolling movement of her hips as she sank down upon his member, completely hiding it from view.

As I watched this sensuous play the tide of my own passions began to gather anew. Yielding to sudden impulse I inserted my hand between Hester's thigh and got my fingers around the base of the white column which was transfixing her. With each of her downward lunges my hand was compressed between the two bodies, and each time it was compressed my own clitoris throbbed in sympathy.

Hester began to moan softly. A delicate colour crept into her pretty cheeks, and her movements became more vigorous. As I perceived the more powerful pressure of her moist cunny crushing down upon my fist, and the strong, regular pulsations in the hard flesh about which my fingers were clenched, the fires of reawakened lust again glazed within me. My sexual potency was back in full force.

In this opportune moment Mr Hayden murmured something to Hester. Instantly she ceded the post of honour, slipped forward, and again crouched over his face. A second later I was on the throne she had vacated, and with my arms embracing her from behind, was quivering in response to the throbbing of the rigid shaft which penetrated me and filled me with its soul-stirring warmth.

To the accompaniment of Hester's low moans as a vigorous and active tongue teased her organism into expression I gasped out my own ecstasy and clung to her, half-fainting, while jet after jet of the hot balsam of life flung itself against my womb.

I was no longer a novice. I had graduated from the chippy stage of harlotry and was a full-fledged practitioner of the oldest profession. I was now a professional prostitute.

Mr Hayden came regularly, adhering faithfully to his programme of impartiality, and his visits were interludes in which both Hester and I forgot the sordid, commercialised circumstances under which we were prostituting our bodies and enjoyed ourselves like healthy, robust young animals.

GUS TOLMAN

A short but energetic piece of sexual bravado, Gus
Tolman *is of early twentieth century American origin.
Our hero Gus is a wonder of manhood, 'of commanding
physique' and 'strikingly attractive' who holds every
woman spellbound. More specifically (and like many a
hero of the erotic genre) he is blessed with prodigious
sexual equipment over which he is able to exert such
amazing control that any partner is guaranteed 'transports of the wildest joy and supreme ecstasy'. Added to
which, Gus is a musician – a pianist, naturally – of
such sensitivity and touch that he can play upon the
bodies of his lovers as skilfully as he can upon the
keyboard of a baby grand. In short, despite the anaphro-
disiac effect of his name – often rendered in moments
of supreme emotion as 'Gussie' – he is the kind of super-
lover only to be found in books.*

*His fictional confessions, however, make for some rol-
licking reading. As befits a true sexual opportunist, Gus
is a generous soul and here he is to be found saving
a neighbour from certain solitary vices – in order to
introduce her to more social ones. The boy's all
heart . . .*

Passing in and out of the house where I had a room, I frequently noticed a young lady of attractive face and figure with dark hair, who appealed to me very much.

At the very first I was not so much attracted to her until I noticed how she ogled me and the peculiar expression in her eyes whenever she looked my way. Then I began to get interested.

I began to study her. On closer observation I noticed that she was really quite pretty in a way, and that she possessed a tempting figure. One evening, as we were both returning to our respective rooms, I noticed her attire and discovered that she had the room next to mine, looking out onto a narrow balcony. She was attractively gowned in a light summer dress with short sleeves and the neck was cut low enough to reveal a plumpness of the bust. I tarried in the hall to let her precede me up the stairs.

Her rather short skirts displayed a pair of neat trim ankles and a pretty pair of shapely legs fitted in sheer smooth stockings. A pretty leg always made me long to see more, and I usually got a hunch as to whether or not I could feel of it. I managed to get a long look as she slowly preceded me up the stairs.

When we reached the top I spoke: 'Pardon my intrusion and boldness but I would surely like to know the girl with such a pretty figure. You are most attractive.'

She gasped and turned a frightened look towards me. I then got a good look at her face by means of the light overhead. I noted a peculiar, languorous look in her dark eyes. The face had all the marks of a nature which was more or less sensual.

I detected a look of lecherous longing as her eyes swept over me as if she were sizing me up. I made up my mind right then to get close to this beautiful girl. Her voice trembled and her bosom heaved with apparent emotion as she softly murmured: 'I am Miss Taylor – who are you?' I introduced myself in my usual debonair manner, which seemed to attract her. 'May I have the pleasure of calling on you?'

'Sometime,' she bashfully answered as she passed through her door and closed it.

I noticed that she did not lock her door, having probably forgotten in her confusion. I entered my room and for the first time noticed the very thin partition between it and Miss Taylor's room. I later heard strange sounds like moans from a woman in distress. Then I distinctly heard a one-sided conversation; she was apparently talking to herself and this is what I heard: 'Oh – Oh – if I could only have a lover like that man,' she said trembling. 'He – he – is so big and handsome.'

I could hear her voice shake, as if she was under some great strain or emotion. I remembered the sensual expression on her face as the dreamy, pathetic eyes swept over me. Surely, I thought, the poor girl is in heat and apparently craves relief. While I was preparing for bed, and removing my shoes, my eye caught sight of a register in the partition, evidently used in the winter to allow a circulation of warm air. Upon examining it, I found that it opened very easily and through the grill frame I had a wide view of Miss Taylor's room. In my range of vision I saw the bed and an upholstered chair of generous capacity. Opposite this was a bureau with a large tilting mirror.

Miss Taylor was standing before the mirror, slowly removing the belt from her waist and gazing intently with that same languorous look at some pictures on the wall on either side of the mirror. Peering intently, I discovered that they were pictures of men, three of a stalwart pugilist in different poses stripped, but with a sash to hide his bulging genitals. Other pictures were of actors, presumably matinee idols, but the girl's eyes lingered on the muscular figure of the pugilist.

I saw her full red lips move as if she were talking to the fighter. Lifting up a pair of pretty white bubbies out of her corset, she bounced them up and down, then spoke in a low hysterical voice: 'Oh, Jack, see my titties – come – to – me – and – fondle them.'

I was no longer puzzled. The girl was hot and she was calling to Jack, the pugilist, as an imaginary lover. Her thoughts were lustily centred on the fleshy pleasures such a body would impart if she could but hold it in her arms and feel the strong sexual embrace and enjoyment that might result. In her impulsive emotions the girl tore off her corsets and then slipped out of her dress and drawers. She stood there revealed in nothing but her stockings and under-vest, which she quickly removed. When I saw what a finely built young girl she was, that settled it. She had to be gratified. I lay on my back so I could better contemplate with ease what might transpire in the girl's room.

She was about twenty and I could plainly see her white nude body, rich in lovely contours and graceful curves, together with a very disturbing view of her

53

dark thickly haired pussy and her white cherry tipped bubbies. They made me rampant, and my tool was standing straight up. I doubtless would have made a rush through the door to the girl if my curiosity had not gotten the better of me. I gasped when I saw her press her hand to her pussy and insert a finger and again gaze at the picture of the pugilist as she vigorously rubbed and worked her finger in and out.

Her feelings were getting the better of her and as she worked herself up to a pitch of passionate frenzy, a wave of erotic emotion spread a lovely glow over her shapely charms. As if suddenly thinking of something, she unlocked the bureau drawers and extracted a book and a small packet from which she selected several pictures, evidently an obscene book, as I later discovered.

Reclining on the edge of the bed, with one leg hanging over the side, she switched on a reading lamp over her head, which gave me a brilliantly lighted view of the girl's tempting and sensual body in a voluptuous pose. The line of my vision took in every detail of a plump and well defined cunnie between a pair of lovely white thighs. The contrast of the dark thick curls made her belly and thighs appear like alabaster.

Adjusting her pillow, the girl began reading, holding two of the pictures on the edge of the book, leaving her right hand free. Occasionally she would gloat on her own charms reflected in the tilting mirror. At the same time she would pinch and titillate the stiff red nipples of her firm round bubbies.

The swelling, curly mound and pretty round belly began to rise and fall with convulsions and erotic longings as she gloated over the book and pictures. Inflamed to a frenzy the girl's hand slipped down and covered the restless pussy. Then with her middle finger she sought to appease her passions with a rapid nervous thrust and pressure on the burning clitty. Suddenly, apparently coming to a passage in her book

54

which inflamed the poor girl, she gasped aloud. I heard a smothered cry – 'Oh, how lovely – how I'd – like – to – be – in her place.' Then holding the pictures close she gazed with languorous eyes and clasped the whole of the plump curly cunnie in her hand with two fingers in it, squeezing it hard.

The heavy breathing and groans told me of her approaching crisis. Dropping the pictures, her head went back to the pillows. Her limbs twitched and quivered. The pretty bubbies trembled. Then with a convulsive heave and choking expressions of pleasure, as ' – Oh – Oh – how – good,' spasm after spasm of voluptuous ecstasy swept over her in a thrilling orgasm.

She trembled and shivered terrifically, holding her hand very tightly over her cunnie for a short while, and then seemed to die away in a languorous doze for a few minutes. When she finally picked up her book and continued to read she was so worked up that she was as frantic for relief as before. All the time she had held her hand on her moist cunnie, though without moving it at all. Occasionally she would pick up the pictures again and look at them and then go back to her book. This she kept up for some little time, for the book was apparently very interesting.

Finally, however, she threw down the book and began irritating herself in real earnest. Her magnificent bubbies she could just pull up so as to make her lips grasp the nipples and these she sucked hard, at the same time playing her fingers around her cunnie. Then she used one hand to inflame her clitoris and with the other hand she inserted a finger deep in her cunnie until, judging by her emotions, she was coming, she frantically drove three fingers deep into it and worked them in and out fast until she died away in a glorious spend.

This sight was too much for me. I was lying on my back and was naked. I had become so inflamed and highly sensitised that the scene was like a match to dry powder. My erect and well primed penis went off and shot stretches of pearly juice high into the air. It was all that I could do to withhold a cry of delight, for the spend and the sensations accompanying it were terrific. It fell in little puddles all over my belly as I watched the throes and last tremors of the gratified girl. She got up, put on her nightgown and replacing the book and pictures in the bureau drawer, retired.

I quietly closed the register and crawled into bed. In the morning I awoke with my usual morning hardon and lay awake planning how to have Miss Taylor and to get a glimpse of her book and pictures. I heard her go out at seven-thirty. Getting up and dressing I took the key to my bureau drawer, feeling sure that it would also fit her drawer. Going to her door I found it unlocked. Entering and closing the door I tried the key. It fitted. I found the book that the girl had been reading and the package of pictures. The book was called *The Education of Laura* and was intended to inflame passion and instruct girls in sexual pleasures. The photos were faithful pictures of men and women together in all the known positions of indulgence.

No wonder I thought that she was a masturbator. But why she resorted to it was a mystery to me for she was a girl to attract any man sexually. I made my plans to see her that evening when she would return from work. She returned and dressed for dinner in a most attractive dress, and for some unknown reason left off her corsets and put on a pair of those late fashionable hosettes coming just above the calf, leaving the knees bare.

Apparently she was prone to making herself attractive to men. On this occasion she wore very little under a thin organdy dress, through which could be seen the distinct outlines of a remarkably well-shaped leg and thigh. She also left off her drawers. It might have been that she wanted to make a hit with me, but that I didn't know yet. She was standing in the main hall before the open front door when I came out of the dining room. My alert eye caught the alluring view as the light showed through the girl's skirts, outlining the attractive curves and contours.

Passing out on the large veranda, where there were chairs, all occupied but one, which Miss Taylor took, I seated myself on a step below and facing her. Glancing up I had a tantalising view of the bare knees, which were crossed in careless girlish pose. Several times I caught glimpses of a dark brown tuft between the plump white thighs. I was getting too conspicuously uncomfortable and randy for comfort. Miss Taylor noticed the restless shifting and gloating eyes as I glanced up. She too, got restless. The fact that I was watching her with lustful longing aroused all the sensual fires in her passionate body. Did I really like her, was probably the girl's thought as she watched me out of half-closed eyes. Strategy was one of my strong assets. Suddenly I arose and asked her to take a stroll to get an ice-cream soda. At first she demurred, then bashfully consented. Once out on the street she became a little more sociable.

'If you don't mind, Mister Tolman, I'd like to have a gingerale highball,' she said as we walked along.

'Sure thing, my dear,' I answered, 'sodas are not much good when one is as uncomfortable as we are. By the way what is your first name?'

'Margery – Madge for short,' replied the girl. For an hour she conversed and showed absolutely no signs of the seething desires that were teasing her young pussy. Her nature was not revealed. On the way home I took her arm, delicately passing my hand up and down the soft cool flesh.

'Madge, dear,' I said to her in my tenderest way, 'mayn't I sit with you in your room tonight? I have something most important to tell you.'

The poor girl got so frightened and flushed she

almost collapsed, but answered in a low trembling tone: 'I – I don't know – would – would it be safe?'

'Why, my dear girl, I hope you are not afraid of me, and no one would know anything about it in your room,' I said reassuringly. She said nothing but I could detect a tumultuous storm in the heaving of her firm round bubbies and trembling steps. Reaching the house I begged her to remain on the steps until I got to my room, then when hearing her enter her room, I would call. She followed the instructions to the letter.

I knocked on the door. I then heard a fluttering voice: 'C – Come in.' When I stood before her in a white silk shirt turned down at the neck and short sleeves and wearing blue flannel trousers that displayed my muscular limbs, Margery gasped and almost fainted, but finally said:

'Oh, Mister Tolman, I have never allowed a man in my room before. Tell me what you want with a poor working girl like me? You are so big and handsome that you embarrass me.'

The door was closed and covered with drapery that smothered out all sounds of voices from within. Madge remained standing as I stepped up to her side, and anxious of my opportunity to begin, I said:

'My dear little girl, what I am going to say is for your own good and safety.' She again got frightened, her eyes usually so languorous and wide, her scarlet lips hung apart as she breathlessly waited.

'My dear Madge,' I said tenderly, 'do you know that you are doing yourself an awful injury and injustice every time you indulge your passions as you did last night?'

The frightened and surprised girl gasped, 'My God!' and then fainted. I caught her in my arms and picking her up, I sat down in a large easy chair and held the unconscious girl on my lap. The feeling of her soft corsetless body and pressure of the soft round bottom on my penis inflamed instantly.

My tool stiffened and assumed its splendid throbbing proportions. Reaching a bottle of smelling salts I saw on the bureau, I held it to her nose, then chaffed her hands. Pulling up her skirts I slapped and squeezed the plump dimpled knees. My other hand was moulding a lovely tittie. My lips were grazing a velvety cheek. Presently Madge showed signs of reviving. I fondled her bare knees with affectionate caresses and pressures on the nerves that I knew would excite sensations of passion, moving my hand always further up. Her flesh was like the softest velvet.

My rampant tool was moving and bounding against her little pussy. Of course she could feel it through her clothing. Her eyes opened, she drew a long breath and cuddled closer to me, then in a frightened voice she asked:

'Where am I? What has happened?'

'In your lover's arms, who thinks you are the most beautiful and sweetest little peach in the world. Kiss me, Madge,' I said. She didn't speak, but I could tell that she was gradually warming up from her restless breathing and squirming bottom, but she did not want me to know it. She was shy and somewhat frightened at the suddenness of the situation. Finally when she remembered what I had told her of the night before, she straightened out and putting on an air of injury from the liberty and accusation, she stimulated a resentment, but she knew that she was guilty.

'How do you know – how can you – say – such a thing? How dare you?' I was amused. 'Why my dear,' I replied, 'it was very easy. I was in my room and I overheard your moans and cries. I was alarmed and seeing that register I took a chance of looking through it to ascertain the trouble, and what I saw you doing to yourself made me feel terrible to think that a lovely young girl would injure yourself in that way. Tell me Margery, why do you do it, when you can have a lover?'

'Then with a trembling voice and tears in her dark

59

eyes, she related how she had been taught to gratify her passions, that all her life she had been a victim of uncontrollable passions – that because a girl friend had once let a man have her and she became pregnant and she was always afraid to let a man have her out of fear.

'Why, Gus, that same girl after that gratified herself with her fingers. She was like me, always hot, and it was she who taught me to do it to myself, giving me naughty books and pictures, she got from a man. Is it any wonder that I do it?'

'Not a bit,' I answered. 'But don't you know that you could have a man without serious results?'

'No! How?' cried the girl. I then explained if a girl indulged her passions with a man in the week before her periods or used a strong solution for a douche before and after each time, she would be perfectly safe.

The effect of my hand on her knees and my throbbing tool had so inflamed Madge she was in a tumultuous flutter. 'OO – oo, Gus,' she gasped. 'I must tell my friend Tessie.' Then winding her arms about me she kissed me with her moist red lips, clinging to me with ardent longing. Suddenly and with impulsive emotion, Madge parted her thighs and whispered:

'Fondle me – Gus – I – I'm – I'm so passionate.' I laid my hand over the curly plump nest. 'Oh, Gus – put your finger into it – and make me – spend.'

'Ah, no, my dear,' I said. 'I'm going to break you of that habit, it's not good nor healthy for you and besides it's not natural. Why can't we have the real pleasures together? It's so much lovelier.'

'Oh, Gus, I'd like to, but I'm afraid. I'd surely get caught and I've never done that in my life. I haven't even seen a real live thing, only the pictures that I have.'

'Well, my dear girl,' I said, 'do you want to see one and even have it in you and make you feel so good –

oh so good, better than you have ever felt when you did it with your finger?'

'Oh, heavens, yes, I'm just insane for it, but I'm too scared of it.'

I had been fondling her smooth round belly and tickling her highly sensitive clitty. I stopped and asked her to let me stand up and show her something that beat a finger or candle all to bits. Curious and eager with passion to see what she had seen in hot lascivious dreams, the girl stood leaning against a long library table as I lowered my trousers and released my prodigious tool. It popped out and stood proudly erect and flaming with fiery vigour.

The girl, with eyes aflame with wonder and interest, just stood and gazed. Her face was a study, first blushing a deep scarlet, then distorted with fear, her face lighting up with a hungry gleam of lustful passion. With a choking gulp Madge managed to speak in a half whisper:

'Heavens, Gus, it doesn't look anything like those in my pictures, but it's glorious – a monster. My God! How can a girl take it? I never saw a real live one before.'

I moved towards the girl and she almost shrank. 'Feel it, girlie,' I said. 'It won't hurt you.' Slyly and with girlish modesty Madge placed her hand on it, her fingers just encircling it. They slipped along until her hand held the turgid purple knob in its palm, she squeezed it, then gasped, her panting bubbies heaving and rising and falling in a tumult of erotic sensations.

Remembering some of the lewd acts shown in the photos and described in her book, Madge became very eager.

'May I kiss it, Gus?' she asked. 'Why, of course, if you'll let me kiss yours,' I replied.

'Oh – where? when? how?'

I quickly cleared the table and placed some cushions upon it.

'Now I'll show you for you are a real scout, Madge, and one of the most lovable and fuckable girls I ever knew,' I said. I picked her up and placed her on the table with her peachy bottom on the edge, and directed her to place her feet on the back of a chair I had drawn up behind me. It was my usual preliminary to this, my favourite position to win a woman over. Throwing her dress back and exposing Madge's delectable charms, I feasted my eyes on one of the prettiest bellies and pussies I had ever seen. Such lovely legs and thighs, such a plump and creamy bottom, spread out under the fluffy bunch of dark brown curls, through which the pulpy lips of her moist cunnie were pouting, opening and closing with hot longing.

A bright red clitty protruded stiff and pert. Altogether, Margery's pussy offered about as tempting a feast as any man would wish to see between a pair of shapely legs. I patted and caressed the round white belly and velvety plump inside of the girl's thighs, all the time gloating on the delicious morsel nestled in a thick tuft of silky curls, till I was hungry for it. 'Oh, Gus,' she said, 'will you do what the book calls – lapping the cunt?'

'Why, of course, Madge, and a lot more,' I replied as I proceeded to lay back the thick soft lips and opened up the red meaty interior, disclosing a small puckering orifice, with palpitant longing. I placed my mouth to the distended gap and the fragrant mellow lips closed about my mouth. At the first thrust of my tongue, Margery almost screamed from the new and novel sensation. The faster my tongue glided in and out, the tighter she clasped my head between her convulsed thighs. All she could utter was a trembling. 'Oh, how good – that – feels – Oh God, don't stop!'

I then began a lively tongue play on the stiff clitoris till the poor girl was almost insane with a desire to spend. 'For heaven's sake, bring it,' she pleaded pathetically.

'Yes, pet, I'll make you go off and spend more than you ever did before. When did you say you were last unwell?'

'Ten days ago,' replied Margery with quickened delight. 'Good,' I said, getting to my feet. I had placed the table in front of the mirror and I tilted it to reflect every detail. Taking a soft shapely leg under each arm, I opened Margery's moist and quivering cunnie and guiding my restless penis, I rubbed the purple knob all about the gap.

'Watch in the glass,' I said, as I titillated the sensitive clitoris. The girl was watching every detail, her eyes limpidly languorous, her crimson lips parted in a sensuous smile. When I began to force the head of the ferocious tool into the tight puckering orifice she gave a smothered groan: 'You'll never get that big thing into me. It'll kill me.'

'Yes, dear, it'll kill you with pleasure.' I got the head well in and then stopped to play with the creamy bubbies and tickle her clitty and wait for her to get accustomed to the stretched feeling. She began to sigh and squirm and then murmured softly: 'Oh, Gus it feels so good – I – I – think that you can go a little farther.' She closed her eyes and then gripped the table when I made a lunge that sent the turgid tool into the juicy depths till it bumped against her womb. She gave a smothered scream, her eyes were swimming and her bubbies heaving with a voluptuous sensation. Slowly and sensuously I moved back and forth now.

'There, Madge,' I said softly, 'isn't that nicer than your finger or a candle?'

'Oh, God, yes,' she exclaimed, 'it's heavenly. Do it faster.' I held her belly and with lively hip action, I twisted and screwed the lustful creature. 'OO – Oh, it's lovely – Oh – I'm dying – hold – me – it's – com – ing – Oh – how – good – now – now – Oh, darling.' I distinctly felt her throbbing womb as each spasm of her orgasm shook her inflamed body and made her breathe hard and stammer her expressions of voluptuous sensations. The amorous girl was so inflamed that her unappeased passion made her call out in her agony of erotic emotions, 'Don't stop, for God's sake, don't stop – I'm not half gratified – I never imagined – it – was half so – lovely to be properly fucked.'

Suddenly realising my immense tool was still stiff and in full vigour and believing that I had spent, Margery looked at me with amazement and dreamy eyes and said, 'Didn't you come?' 'No, my lovely little Madge, I'll not spend until I've made you go off again, and say – no more finger fucks for me.'

'I'll never do it that way after this,' she replied. 'I shall tell my friend all about it. Will you give her a treat like this some time, too?'

'Sure,' I replied, 'if she'd like me well enough to let me.' And then I continued to feast my fleshy appetite on the girl's lascivious charms. Margery indulged her own sensual nature and revelled in thoughts of lascivious pleasures in company with me and her friend Tessie. 'Oh, she will, Tess will go wild when she meets you and sees your lovely big thing,' she said. 'She is just crazy to have a big strong man. Can't we three make a party some night together?'

'Of course. We'll go to a hotel,' I answered, pleased.

'Oh, Gus, you make me so passionate, I could scream. Do it faster!'

I pressed the turgid bursting head against her womb and made it throb and tickle her, sending thrills of lustful emotions over her trembling body. 'Oh, Gus! Oh!' she moaned, as I worked my tool in and out with a lustful spiral motion.

'How's that, girlie?' I asked.

'Oh, it's great – it's – com – ing – fuck me – fuck me hard – Oh, my God!' And her eyes rolled and sank back into her head, showing only the whites.

I groaned. I had held back as long as I could. 'Oh, baby,' I hollered. 'I'm coming, too – suck it – so – so

– ' I cried, as Margery's nipping cunnie closed with convulsive spasms. 'Ah, – there – there,' as I shot a charge of hot balsamic juice into the girl's belly. She lay still and received the balmy delirious juice in ecstasy.

Before the last sensuous thrill had passed, I picked up the half-conscious girl and carried her to the bed with my reeking stiff still in her. Getting off my shirt, I managed to divest Margery of her clothes and then we lay for some time in a languid sea of blissful content, till I got eager for another orgasm.

Getting on top of her, I placed it in her with frenzied frictional thrusts till we both died away again in a voluptuously complete finish. I got up and returned to my room to let the poor girl sleep off the effects of our dream of pleasures such as she had never experienced before.

Two days later I met Madge and she passed the word to me: 'Tessie will be here to meet you at eight o'clock in my room. Come at that time and knock.'

I made a careful preparation for conquest and a night with mylatest finds. First engaging a room at a hotel of unquestioned privacy and then completing a toilet that would prove the way to conquest. I wore a Palm Beach suit over a sheer silk shirt with no underwear. I had, without a doubt, an attractive figure and my close-fitting trousers displayed my muscular limbs and abnormal sexual development to good advantage.

Promptly at eight o'clock I heard Madge in her room, and then a cheery voice: 'Gee, Madge, I'm just wild to meet your friend. How do I look?' asked Tessie as she threw off her cape. 'Say, Tess,' said Madge, 'he will go wild and eat you alive when he sees your bare back, it's lovely.' She had left her entire back exposed to her waistline with but a narrow line over each shoulder, the front being so thin that even the stiff red nipple points of a pair of the prettiest bubbies stuck out alluringly. Tessie was taller than Madge, with remarkably pretty arms and legs – not large but tempting in form and shape. She possessed a bottom that was ravishing in contour and agility. She wore nothing else but a lace petticoat and black silk stockings, gartered well above the knees.

When I answered the call to enter, the vision that met my gaze, startled me. 'Miss Tessie Bangs,' said Margery, introducing us, 'this is Mr. Tolman.' I bowed low as I took Tessie's hand and kissed it. She shivered for she felt a thrill go through her. 'Surely,' I said, 'this is a refreshing pleasure.' Tess was speechless as her eyes swept over my figure and when she could speak, her voice was low and musical, 'I am equally delighted,' she said, 'I do hope your pleasure will be equal to mine.'

'Well,' I said, 'judging from appearance, when I see more of you, I know that my pleasure will know no bounds. You are the peachiest looking and most delectable looking chicken I've met in years.' She resented the term I gave her. Her big blue eyes flashed and with a vivacious but injured dignity she retorted: 'I beg your pardon Mister Tolman, I'm no chicken and you needn't think that because Margery Taylor fell for you and you happen to be a handsome brute, I shall fall, too.'

I saw that she meant every word and that I would be obliged to trim her claws as I had often done with others. I replied, looking steadily and smilingly into her flashing eyes, 'You are a chicken and a deucedly tempting bird to broil, and with proper seasoning you will make fine eating.' Tessie gasped, for she knew well what I meant.

'I never met up with such nerve before,' she said. Her practised eye caught sight of the bulging outlines of my abnormal sexual charm, already showing signs of vigour and life. She jumped back with a twist of her pretty shoulders and shaking her pendulous bubbies. 'My God, man, but you are immense,' she said, still gloating on my tool and balls, which showed plainly through my light trousers.

'Pshaw, Tess,' spoke up Margery, 'you ought to see it out and stiff. Take it out, Gus.' It was my plan to work Tess up until she was at the point of begging for it, but as she seemed curious and willing, I unbuttoned my trousers, but first I stepped up to her and without warning clasped her lithe and willowy form in my arms and pressed her mound to my rapidly stiffening tool by placing a convulsive hand on her plump bottom.

She tried to wriggle loose, but the more she wriggled the stiffer my penis became till it throbbed against her pussy. The sensation was so exciting to her that she just hung limp in my arms and shivered. I kissed her and then when my mouth closed over her ruby lips, I thrust my tongue into her mouth and squeezed her soft bottom with both my eager hands.

She returned my kisses almost unconsciously as she gazed at me with limpid, languorous eyes. Once or twice she half clung to me and when I began to run my tongue between her lips, it was too much for her. She just hung onto me enough to keep from falling.

All of a sudden, tearing her mouth loose, she cried out in a frantic appeal:

'Stop, I don't mean to let you get fresh with me!'

My hands and touchings were doing their work, however. I slipped one hand all over her smooth bare back, tickling her spine at the same time and running my tongue around her neck under her chin and ears. Her eyes flushed, her bottom wriggled – she laughed and then began to scratch. I realised I had an unusually spiteful chicken to deal with. Shaking my trousers loose, my rampant penis came forth in all its passionate splendour.

'Oh, look Tessie,' said Margery, laughing. In her excitement and struggle one of her hands came in contact with it. Like oil on troubled waters, her flush of injured dignity subsided and she melted in my arms like jelly in a mould, and hung limp from surprise and suddenly aroused emotions. At first she couldn't speak, she seemed so dazed. Then with sudden curiosity, her hand went to the prodigious, throbbing weapon, her long tapering fingers closing about it. Gasping she drew back to look: 'Good God,' she exclaimed, 'what is it, a bone or a club?'

'The stick that you are going to be broiled on, my dear,' I said.

'Never, never!' cried the astonished girl, looking at it and squeezing the long hard shaft. 'Why that thing would kill me.'

'Aw, go on,' laughed Margery.

'I'll be,' said Tess to her, 'you never had that brute of a thing in you. You told a fib. I never heard of a man having a tool like that.'

'Ah, Tess, just you wait until it's in you, and you'll see all the stars in creation and go off like you never did before, and I'll bet that you'll never want anything else. Why Tess, it beats a finger or a candle a thousand ways. To be broiled on that darling cock is a treat you'll never forget.'

Then turning to me, Margery kissed me and said: 'Strip, Gus, and let Tessie see.' 'I will if she'll do the same,' I replied. Margery led the way and began to undress. She hadn't much on to be taken off. Tessie was now gay and festive, lively as could be. She and Margery were soon stripped to their stockings and I gazed with lustful enthusiasm on two of the most charming and fuckable damsels I ever laid my eyes on. Tessie was perfect in symmetry and shapeliness. Tall and graceful, she was exquisitely rounded with a pair of luscious, slightly drooping bubbies, not as large as Margery's but just as lovely to play with and mould in the hands. She had a prominent, protruding mound covered with a profusion of thick blonde curly hair like silk, through which the pretty deep slit of a plump pussy could be seen.

I was now more than rampant to get at it. I stripped naked, to my socks. When Tessie's eyes swept over me, she gasped with carnal admiration, her eyes almost popping out of her head as she gloated on my penis, which she expected to be broiled upon.

'My God, Madge,' she exclaimed, 'I don't wonder that you fell for him, he is magnificent, but I'll have to see you take that tool before I'll believe you had it in your little cunnie,' she said, as she again felt of it with trembling hands, trying to pull it away from my belly, where it stood stiff as a bar of iron. It slipped from her hand and sprung back with a thud. Tessie giggled and continued to enjoy the unusual vigorous elasticity of the perky, obstreperous penis.

'Let's get busy,' I said. 'I'm getting too hot for comfort and I'm anxious for a drink. We'll have a round, go out for a highball, and then go to a room I've engaged for the night. You two lovely chickens have to broil on both sides thoroughly, so let's get busy while the bone is in good form.'

'I want to see Madge take it first,' said Tessie with a mischievous and lustful thrust of her naughty handsome bottom. I arranged the table with cushions and directed Margery to lie on it as on the first night when she was initiated.

Margery looked most tempting and desirable as she lay with her legs wide open and her peachy, salacious pussy ready for the stick. Two firm milky bubbies, with their stiff red nipples pointing straight up and out, invited kisses.

'Now, Gus,' laughed Tessie, 'do exactly what you did to her the other night. I want to see how you got that awful thing into her tight little cunnie.'

I seated myself directly in front of the voluptuous little pussy with Margery resting her pretty fat legs on each shoulder. 'My God,' exclaimed Tessie, all curious and getting hotter every minute, 'I've had some fun in my life but I was never kissed there.'

I began my feast with hot kisses on the pretty rounded belly and on the soft white insides of her thighs to arouse keener sensations of desire. I then titillated her with lively tongue play on her perky, red clitoris.

Madge began to moan, but when the ardent sweep of my tongue along the pouting slit penetrated the puckering orifice, she trembled and cried out: 'Oh – Tess – ie – wait – till he does this to you – Oh, it's so good – Oh.' When I thrust my tongue into the salacious meaty depths of her pussy and tickled her womb, Margery suppressed a scream, shook all over and cried: 'Oh, Tessie – suck my titties, quick – I'm – I'm – com – com – ing.' Tessie quickly took a big red nipple in her mouth and tickled the other one with her finger-nails. As nothing excites a woman to spend as quickly as that, Margery just moaned and heaved and clutched at her friend and cried out: 'Oh, Tess! There – there – Oh – how good – OO – oo – Oh!'

I received her sweet, creamy spend on my tongue and sucked it up as it flowed freely. She being thoroughly lubricated, I got to my feet, and taking the bursting red tool in my hand I worked the swollen inflamed head all about in the juicy slit, while Tessie stood by holding apart the fat lips and watching the all-absorbing and lascivious act of broiling Madge. Her eyes wide, almost popping out, her snowy bosom heaving with excitement and her pussy itching and twitching, Tessie saw me plunge my frenzied penis into Margery to the hilt. Madge stuffed her fist into her mouth to smother her cries and screams of lustful pleasure. I worked my tool back and forth with sensuous effect and Tessie, watching it as it went in and out, almost screamed herself.

'Hurry, Madge, I'm just dying for a piece,' Tessie again tickled the quivering red nipples. Madge cried out: 'Oh, God! It's coming – what a lovely – fuck.' Her voice died away. I pulled out my inflamed tool reeking with her pearly spend and lifting Madge up I laid her on the bed, telling Tessie to get on the table. I had not spent for I wanted to save it for the excited Tessie.

The table was before the mirror and when Tessie discovered that she could watch herself being fucked, she laughed in glee. I stood for a moment to gloat on the exquisitely lovely charms of this delectable girl, fondling every part of her. Then taking my place again in the chair between the prettily shaped legs out-stretched for the kisses, I gazed lustfully at one of the prettiest and alluring pussies I ever saw. Profusely covered with silky blonde hair, it stood out plump and impudent. Tessie had what might be termed a real hardon, for the outer lips were hard and horny and her clitty stuck out its red nose stiffly. I noted the delectable, sweet scented, savoury condition of her private parts. Holding the soft cheeks of her fat bottom apart, I gazed fondly at all her beauties when she anxiously wound her fat legs around my neck and exclaimed, 'My God, what a lover you are!'

I now buried my nose in her slit and worked my tongue deep in. She bit her lips and exclaimed with a deep moan: 'Suck me.'

I then gave her the same tonguing I had just given Madge, but I fairly ate the mellow meaty interior with lively tongue thrusts.

I gathered all the ripe parts on her cunnie into my mouth and sucked like mad, with my tongue rubbing her stiffened clitty. Tessie was trembling and quiver-ing all over. 'Wow! Oh! Ouch!' she cried. Her cry aroused Margery from her languor, and she came smil-ing to the side of the table.

'Oh, Madge,' she cried, 'he's sucking the life out of me – oo – oo – Oh, how I'm spending!'

'Isn't it great?' asked Madge, patting Tessie's titties and pinching the little stiff nipples.

'Oh, it's heavenly,' replied Tessie as she died away in another swoon of voluptuous ecstasy. I jumped up then with a terrible hardon that was actually painful. It was forbidding in appearance. Tessie had never seen nor dreamed of a penis like it before. Handsome it was, to say the least, with its splendid appendages like ripe fruit bursting with a wealth of rich juices.

Tessie's eyes, languorous with the sensual after effects of a copious spend, looked with fear as I stood beside her. In a voice trembling with apprehension, she said: 'Let – let me feel it, Gus, it's awful.'

I stepped closer to her, and she felt the awful thing from the balls to the tip of the turgid knob as if testing and measuring its size and power. I took it in my hand and moved the knob around in her neck, under her chin and ears. She murmured:

'Oh, you beauty. Now I'm ready – Oh, Gus, be careful, won't you?'

'Yes,' I answered.

'Then broil me and do it good, I'm hot as a blister,' and to Madge she said, 'don't leave me, Madge, and give me a handkerchief.'

I took a pretty leg under each arm and Madge stood by to assist. She pulled the inflamed fat lips apart, revealing its red meaty interior and puckering orifice from which oozed traces of her recent spending. I moved my tool up and down and rubbed the quivering inflamed clitty. 'Oh, God! that's exciting,' she cried out suddenly, 'put it in quick,'

I placed the almost bursting knob at the entrance and pushed. She gasped and stuffed the handkerchief into her mouth to smother a cry of pain. With the head just inside, I waited for her to get accustomed to the stretching. The nipping stricture was maddening to me. Tessie relieved her mouth long enough to say, 'All of it, Gus – I – I – want it all!' Replacing the wad of handkerchief in her mouth, she grabbed Margery. I braced myself and clutching the girl's squirming hips, I crammed my penis into the tight hot depths till it was completely sheathed. How she did squirm and writhe. I hollered myself with sensuous delight, exclaiming:

'Oh, Tes – sie – what a perfect cunt you have .'

Her pain had subsided, she removed the cloth from her mouth, her crimson lips parted in a smile of joy. Margery bit and sucked the stiff red nipples whilst I tickled her navel. 'What a pretty belly. What pretty legs. You two girls are the peachiest chickens to fuck that I ever knew,' I whispered as I moved my straining spear out and in, producing a fury of erotic thrills in us both. Tessie could not prolong the delightful indulgence long enough.

'Gee,' she gasped, 'I wish that it could last all night.'

Once her tongue was loosened she became obscene as her erotism increased. I was getting a royal feast of voluptuous sensation. The climax was approaching us both. Tessie's curly blonde head rolled from side to side – she clawed at her stomach and her milky panting bubbies as they rose and fell faster and faster with her quickened breath. I put my most masterful strokes to the frenzied girl with agonising thrills.

She hollered in smothered gusts, 'Oh, God! I'm coming!' Her arms dropped to her side.

'Somebody kiss me! Hold me! I'm dying! Oh – oo – oo.' Margery giggled. I grabbed the exploding girl in my arms, crushed a soft tittie in each hand and smothered her gasping cries with a tonguing kiss. She sucked the tongue almost out of me.

'There, you hot little cunt, take my sap, it's – good for you,' I said as I poured hot streams of delicious juice into the trembling girl, the jets piercing her like needles and bringing a secondary spend in which Tessie's eyes rolled back in erotic delirium. I laid her gently back and completed my own double spend in a blinding orgasm which shook me to my toes.

'Heavens,' cried Margery, 'you've got me so hot I can scarcely wait for another piece.' Tessie wriggled off the and staggered as if drunk to the bed, where she lid in a half-faint from the effect of the frenzied orgy.

I quickly got a bottle of brandy. We all had a stiff drink and prepared to go out. After Tessie had had two drinks she was as lively as a cricket and ready for a frolic. Like a contortionist she writhed and displayed her enticing charms to excite the lewdest passions. Her sensual nature was thoroughly fired after getting a generous taste of my powers and my skillfully manipulated tool. She was wanton to the core. Before I had completed my toilet, Tessie kissed my penis. Being now soft and normal she drew it into her mouth and cuddled it with her tongue. 'Gee,' she exclaimed, 'I'd like to suck you off.' We were all hotter than blisters and ready for anything. We left the house unseen and were soon in the room I had engaged for the night. I ordered highballs with plenty of ginger. Both girls stripped, and jumping onto the table, they did a most exciting and lewd dance. Tessie was more agile than Madge, but Madge's movements were far more suggestive and voluptuous.

They had often practised together when under the influence of lecherous desire to indulge their wanton passion and to induce a spend would press their pussies together and rub and twist with their titties crushed together till a frenzied orgasm would reward their efforts. I watched the lascivious performance till I was so hot my turgid gun was standing cocky and purple and almost ready to go off. I grabbed both girls and fell with them on the bed. I was about to mount Tessie when she cried out:

'Hold on Gus. I'm hot, too hot for an old-fashioned fuck. I want a hootchie cootchie diddle.'

'How's that?' I asked.

She then directed me to lie across two chairs with my head on the bed and my knees hanging over the edge of the farthest chair while Madge was to straddle my head and press her cunnie to my mouth. This was a new trick but I liked the idea and at once arranged for it. I first drew both girls to the edge of the bed, with their plump bottoms on the edge, with their legs wide apart and knees drawn up.

The quivering swollen cunnies were then gaping open, the orifice of each pouting for something stiff. I took a highball and holding Madge's little hole well open, I poured into it a goodly portion and then held the lips together so it wouldn't spill, to let it soak in and heat up the tight little box. Dropping to my knees, I deftly placed my mouth to the lips and sucked out the warmed up liquor. She screamed and wriggled her fat bottom. She was consumed with longing. I gave Tessie the same treat and when I had sucked out the last drops she writhed and screamed.

'My God, that was brutal. I was hot enough without that. Hurry up and get on the chairs and I'll screw the balls off you while you lap Madge.' I got awful randy as Tessie took her position while I lay as she directed, with my erect penis standing straight and rigid, ready to burst. Tessie cuddled it in her soft bubbies and kissed it again with thrusts of her tongue in the little orifice.

Our passions spent, we fell back on the bed. I was asleep as was Tessie. Madge, in her state of erotic feelings, began working her fingers in her moist slit, but was so passionate and eager for another piece, she knew that she had first to get it stiff. Following descriptions she had read, of a way to get a man's penis to stand, Madge hung over me and lifted my seemingly dead penis into her mouth with her tongue after tickling the wrinkled balls. When she got half of the soft mass into her mouth she slipped her tongue around and around the head as she gently chewed the soft root. I stirred, woke up and not thinking which of my partners was at me, clutched Tessie and kissed her, feeling and moulding her titties, now firm after a rest. She, too, awoke.

'Oh, Gus, do you want me again so soon?' I then perceived that it was Madge who was eating it up.

'Look Tess,' I said. 'Madge wants it. Poor girl, she's hungry.' When Tessie saw Madge frantically chewing the mouthful, she rolled the splendid reservoir of sap in her one hand. 'That's right, Madge,' she said. 'That'll make it come up if you want a piece. I'm ready for one myself.' Tess tickled me, sucked my hard nipples and between the two amorous girls, I began to get stiff. My penis got too big for Madge's mouth. Letting it languidly out, she said:

'I do want a piece. I'm hot from my toes to my hair.'

I handled both quivering cunnies, sticking a finger into each. This would always make me hot. My tool swelled and stiffened to grand proportions till I had one of my characteristic morning hardons.

'Give it to Madge first,' cried Tess. 'She found it first.' I got on top of the plump, passionate girl and gave her the liveliest, hottest fuck I ever put to a girl, till she groaned and screamed in an ecstatic satisfying orgasm. I finished her off and left my rigid tool in her till she swooned off in a sensuous die-away, having restrained my own desire to spend.

I preferred my morning feast between Tessie's soft, shapely legs in her tight excitable little box. I wanted to feel Tessie's long lithe limbs wind about me and once more experience the ecstatic spend by her wriggling bottom and toe curling, sucking cunnie.

'Heavens, you're bigger than ever,' she exclaimed. 'It's just grand. Oh, Gee, how lovely, umm.' She groaned with each straining thrust and throb. Tessie twined her pretty legs around me and thus braced, she not only met my thrusts with effective bucking up motions but could wriggle and twist with a screwing motion that thrilled me with lustful zeal.

Her cries and shuddering frame told of the delightful spends she was having. When I could no longer restrain myself to prolong the voluptuous feast, I gathered the trembling plump form of Tessie in my arms and gazing down in her misty rolling eyes, groaned out:

'Oh, Tessie – there – it – comes – Oh, God! how exquisite!'

Our delicious feeling was ravishing after I shot a long charge of creamy spend into the hungry depths of Tessie's cunnie.

She quickly jumped off the bed and let the stuff escape in a morning pee. Returning to the bed we all had a nap. At six o'clock we all arose and went our way. Tessie remarked: 'Oh, Gus, I never had such a treat in all my life. Madge picked a star performer when she picked you.'

THE WANTONS

It is London in the mid-50s, the era of the Teddy Boy. Sixteen year old Linda is both appalled and fascinated by these flamboyant young tearaways — she'd like to know them better but she doesn't dare. Her home life, however, provides no safe haven. Her mother hates her — or so she feels — and her new step-father ogles her opulent young body in a funny way. On the night her mother stays at her aunt's house the reason for that funny look becomes all too clear as the step-father forces his way into her bedroom and into her bed. This experience, unwanted and repulsive though it is, awakens a rampant sexual curiosity in Linda and when she tells her friend Betty she is no longer a virgin, Betty can't help feeling a little jealous. Thus the two of them are in a receptive mood when they attend a dance and make friends with two swaggering Teds, Des and Jim. The boys whisk them off to a party in Hampstead and introduce them to a whole new world . . .

The atmosphere was pungent and smoky and the softly-tuned jazz from the record player mingled like an aural incense.

Linda and Desmond lay on the floor listening to the music and he stroked her bottom through her dress.

'Let's have another drag,' she breathed, moving her hand slowly towards the thin cigarette between his lips. They had told her not to expect anything from the first one and she had gone on smoking while they smoked, quietly inhaling, taking in a lot of air with the smoke as they suggested. Now she felt tranquilly wonderful. The room around her seemed a world in which she would live forever. She had no idea of the time and didn't care. All around her were friends, all those couples lounging and lying in the big room, hardly speaking, fondling a little, talking quietly. Betty was over there lying on the floor looking up at the ceiling with a smile on her face and Jim was lying with her, looking at the ceiling too.

She felt a great liking for Des and a great intimacy with him. He was stroking her bottom gently, feeling its round bulge lingeringly and he had a kind look on his face. She felt she was safe and at peace with Desmond. She never wanted to go home. Home! She smiled happily. It didn't bear thinking about.

She drew in on the cigarette and the smoke passed in a dry relief down her throat; the sweet, exotic aroma floated to her nostrils and she breathed deeply, with concentration. Then she relaxed and passed the butt end back to Desmond and the music enveloped her softly in an erotic wave of peace the way his arm and his gently stroking hand enveloped her.

Sam was sitting next to the record player. It was he who made possible this peace, this discovery. She felt tender towards him and to his mistress whose money had provided this Hampstead flat.

The record slid to an end and after a while someone put on another. Most of the girls were young – about eighteen and the men a few years older except for Sam who looked about thirty. His mistress was supposed to have a lot of money.

'Linda.' It was Betty's voice. She moved her head and looked over. Jim had undone the top buttons of her dress and had his hand inside. 'I feel good.'

Betty was going to have it tonight. Linda knew that for sure as she smiled back. This marihuana, "pot" they called it, was great stuff.

She listened again to the record. It was very clear. Everything was very clear, even the sound of Desmond's hand stroking her buttocks and Jim rustling Betty's dress.

'How do you feel?'

She looked up at Des.

'I feel wonderful.'

Her heart overflowed with tenderness for him and she knew that she could tell him anything if she wanted to, that he felt the same for her. She leaned up and kissed him suddenly, tenderly, on the cheek and he moved his hand from the full flower of her buttocks down between them over the dress, sharply aware of the sudden cleavage into separate orbs. His fingers between her legs pressed through the dress and briefs to the fleshy line of her labia. The tenderness she felt flushed in a tender, warm desire to give herself. Desmond felt soft warmth under his hand.

'Any room outside?' he asked Sam softly. It seemed to Linda that his voice rang clearly through the room.

Sam jerked his head absently towards the door and resumed his glazed concentration on the music.

'Let's go,' Des whispered to her, pressing his fingers meaningfully against the hot, giving ridge between her legs.

'All right.'

They rose quietly and she was suddenly aware of a floating unsteadiness in her limbs. Nobody took any notice of them. She was vaguely aware that Jim was kissing Betty and that Betty had one breast bare and protruding from her dress. Around the room everyone seemed to be necking or lying still.

With an arm around her, steadying her, they left the room quietly. Outside, the air was cooler, the thickness of the atmosphere cleared and for the first time she felt slightly dizzy and gave a giggle.

'What's the matter?' Desmond grinned at her.

'Nothing – I felt a bit dizzy that's all.'

He caught hold of her then and kissed her, pressing her hard against a wall so that she felt dizzy again as if she were sinking slowly through turns and turns of a spiral staircase.

His hands cupped her buttocks, pushing her hips out from the wall against his hips. She heard the loudness of his breathing. She put up her hands and caught his face and pushed her tongue into his mouth and rubbed her lips against him, murmuring little sounds all the time.

He released her suddenly and drew her along the passage and through a door into a bedroom. Moonlight came in through a window beyond a glass partition which cut the room in two. It all seemed hardly real. She was vividly aware of a number of objects which seemed to come toward her suddenly and unexpectedly and have no relation with one another.

Des pushed the partition back a little without switching on the light and they passed through into the small room beyond. Thankfully she sank down onto the bed, pulling him down with her. The sensation of lying down and the roaming in her head was a delicious combination and she felt tender and generous and her body seemed like an acutely strung instrument ready for ecstatic sensual use.

'Take your clothes off,' Des whispered, in the moonlight.

'Take them off for me,' she whispered back, settling snugly on the bed.

She felt his hands pulling her dress gently up over her hips, her breasts, felt him move her arms and pull it off over her head. The cool air and the cool counterpane refreshed her skin like a shower. She felt him fumbling with her brassiere and he pulled her half up, holding her against him. Her face came up against his loins and she rubbed her cheek against him. But something kept her at a distance from his body, a great, hot bulge in his trousers. She turned her face towards it, looking at it. She felt a tenderness towards it, a desire to caress and fondle. Slowly she moved her hand on his leg as he held her, still-fumbling. The bulge was farther away than she'd anticipated, but her hand reached it and closed over it, creasing the trousers around it. Far above her she heard him gasp and against her hand she felt the flexing of bulge and hips behind it.

Gently she squeezed it through the cloth, trying to

fell its length. She kissed the bulge tenderly and on an impulse bit it gently through the clothing.

She saw his hand come whitely down between her face and the bulge and, fascinated, watched it pull at buttons which jerked undone one after the other.

She pushed his hand away and, with her movement, felt her bra slip down off her breasts. There was still a wild floating in her head, but she focused on the opening and pushed her hand through it. Her hand was assailed by the heat of his loins. She searched around with her fingers, pulling aside his shirt, eventually finding the slit in his pants while he strained impatiently against her. She felt the hot, hard length against her hand – hard; but with a soft, delightful surface. She pulled and it shot out through the opening. Des grunted above her.

It felt beautiful in her hand; a long, white, hot, soft-textured length of stiff Plasticine to play with and mould.

She could see it white, almost luminous in the moonlight. He let her feel it, breathing heavily, pressing against her as he held her up on the bed.

The length of white substance was almost the whole range of her vision. Beyond that was only the vague floating and the clear sound of his breathing.

She stroked it and slowly pulled back the skin from the end-knob which glowed redly at her in contrast with the soft folds of the drawn-back whiteness. Gently she moved her fingers on it and held it in her hand, squeezing slightly and then harder to see how hard he could stand it. The object was hot and slightly pliable under her hand – a beautiful thing.

His hand came down over hers at last and he moved her hand up and down with his over his penis. She began the gentle massage and continued when he let go and pushed his hips out at her with a gasp.

He began to squirm and rock on his feet. She could feel the rocking movement against her and it seemed to make her float farther away with her white penis in her hand.

The sound of his passion was like a rushing sea above her and again his hand came down and pulled her hand away. She released him reluctantly and then he had caught hold of her face and was jabbing his penis gently against her soft lips. For a moment she didn't understand what was going on, but the pressure was there, heavily, on her mouth and automatically her lips opened and the white flesh plunged into her mouth. For a moment she fought against it, afraid she would choke, but he held it there and reached down to stroke her breasts. Floating, hardly aware of what she was doing she began to move her mouth against the soft velvet which filled it.

She was aware of a trembling behind her breasts, almost as if it had nothing to do with her directly and she sucked at the heat between her lips, trying to cool it.

Above her was the moaning, rushing from his lips; his hand pressed hard against her hair, forcing her against his loins. She licked the knob with her tongue, enjoying its smoothness. It was like a big, velvety lollipop which she would eventually swallow. She caught it in her hand, holding it against her mouth while she sucked the end; nothing seemed strange in her activity; she sucked as if she did it every day of her life in a normal routine.

In her floating, spiralling mind it seemed that the great thing was expanding, that it would fill her mouth and plunge down her throat, perhaps to emerge through her vagina. She felt a giggle deep inside her and sucked harder.

Above her, his moaning had reached a frenzied pitch and he was no longer rocking, but had locked his thighs together and was rigidly flexing his hips at her while he leaned slightly backwards with the top part of his body.

She heard the moaning break into little barks, coughing barks of sound and he pushed into her mouth, grazing the velvet organ along her teeth, choking her. And she felt her mouth flooded suddenly with a hot, sticky wetness which encircled her tongue and lodged on her palate and oozed down her gullet.

He sank against her and she realized vaguely that it was finished, found the knob, slight and limp now, still in her lips and gave it a few little sucks and licks before letting it flop out against his trousers.

She lay back on the bed, aware of its whiteness, like the whiteness of him. Through the window there was only the silver space of the sky washed in the moonlight. It seemed to envelop her; she felt a great delight in it.

After a little while she felt him against her, naked, warm and soft-skinned and his hands ran fluidly over her bare breasts and pulled her briefs down over her thighs and off her feet. He was sitting up looking at her. He kissed her belly, her breasts, moved his lips moistly over her soft body. He kissed her knees, her thighs and she was tenderly excited.

His lips moved up her thighs. He turned her over and kissed her buttocks, her back, running his lips down her spine. She shivered delightedly and he turned her on her back again and opened her legs. She felt his face there, slightly rough between her thighs. She was floating happily, sensually, and all she had to do was lie there and he would give her joy.

And suddenly his mouth had moved up between her warm thighs to the long lips between her legs, his tongue had darted out and into her vagina. She pulled up her legs, gasping and then reached down to grasp his head as she actively began to move into a rhythm with him, unable just to lie, wanting to float and writhe and twist, unearthly and above the world in a torment of strange passion.

Desmond buried his face in her crotch and sucked

her clitoris. He was fairly high, but nowhere near the way she was. What a find! he was thinking. What a hot little bitch! And now he was going to fuck the daylights out of her. God, how she was writhing and wriggling and clutching at him and moaning! It was going to be a real kick hearing her moan all the time as if she were in agony.

Against his lips he felt the soft, ragged moistness of her nether lips, the hard slipperiness of the clitoris and then he withdrew and slithered up onto her, wriggling up between her legs, crawling onto the slim strength of her body.

He lay along her and she lay under him with her eyes closed and her lips moving like prayers in the moonlight. She was pretty, damned pretty. God, what a kick! And her pretty face and excellent body were tormented now in a marihuana maelstrom which was making sex seem like the end of the world.

He was sent by the pot he'd had and the sight of her puckered face and the feel of her body underneath him and he covered her mouth passionately with his, sucking at her moist, lost lips and tongue the way he'd sucked at her clitoris.

Her breasts were like soft, pointed cushions beneath him and her hips like a pillow. He strained against her, crushing his prick against the little lawn of hair down there at the point. She wriggled against him and moaned.

Slipping down on her a little, he guided his prick at her cranny with his hand. It was throbbing with a certain feeling of frustration.

He moved a hand against her thighs and she pulled them higher – and then he had crushed slowly, agonisingly through the labia up into the vagina, high up towards the cervix and was beginning to undulate his behind between her legs. His frustration disappeared on the first entry and all his high excitement zipped down through his body to that one penetrating rod of sensation lost in her fleshy passage.

Up and down, up and down, gently, gently and growing stronger his hips played, while his penis drove in and out, in and out and an explosion of sound escaped his lips on every stroke.

The girl grasped his shoulders and then put her arms tightly around him as if she were hanging onto some whirling machine at a fair; her mouth hung open letting out a stream of low sound. His penis, cleaving into her, had a permanent acute sensation as if he wanted to pee and couldn't. Her tight little passage sucked pains of joy out of his lost flesh with each thrust.

God, oh, what a kick, oh, oh; the words danced in a vague *pas de deux* with a plethora of feeling in his head. Her skin caught and brushed and battled with his as she wriggled against him. Her thighs squeezed and released and as he explored farther and farther, letting the knob lead on into the welcoming tunnel, she swung her legs up and wrapped them around his waist, crushing him in a vise as she gasped out.

She was gone, really gone, with eyes closed, just a body abandoning itself. What a sexy little bitch! And he was half gone and it was wonderful, out of this world, that great sucking pool of joy down there where they met and mingled and he dominated and she gave and begged for more.

He put his hand around her buttocks. What delightful mounds they were – a little too big for his hands, they overflowed and he could lose his fingers in them as they relaxed. When they tautened he pushed his fingers between them and felt the little anus. It was a tiny little slit, like an unopened vagina in a small child. She squirmed, squirming with squirms as he touched it. She contrived to press it against his fingers as with her arms she pulled his hips at her loins. He dug his finger at its resistant surface and felt the little, glossy crack give and his finger worm in a little.

'Oh Des, oh, Des,' she moaned as his finger moved into the soft hole. He moved it around within the tight cavity to bring more passion from her limbs as he shagged her.

As his hips writhed and squirmed, impelling his rigid member up between her hot, flailing thighs he rubbed his chest across her breasts, feeling the hard nipples brush his firm flesh, feeling the full, solid flesh of the breasts resist and give and suck against him.

She brought down her slim thighs from around him and spread them out on either side, horizontally so that tendons showed between thighs and crotch. He rammed into the greater depth that that gave him and she jerked with the sudden excruciating expanse of his filling.

She reached around him with her arms and pulled his head onto hers, biting his lips, thrusting out her tongue, licking him, biting and licking and sucking his neck. When he bit her neck, she cried out and hugged him closer, swinging back her thighs to press him into her.

His rhythm which had grown farther and almost brutal began to slow as he felt the end drawing ecstatically near.

She too began to wriggle all the time, clamping her buttocks together on his hands, pushing her hips flat into his and then relaxing, moaning and gasping and waving her tongue in his mouth.

God, this time he would die! It was too excruciating to bear! He soared slowly, crushingly into her, up and up, never ending, a feast of sensation all the way.

He was vaguely aware that she was almost delirious, rocking and moaning against him and flexing her loins with every stroke. He heard her gasp in a long drone of excitement and pain, felt her wriggle in a sharp, furious movement as he pulled her behind at him and then she was pressing her hips at his off the bed for several seconds as she cried out her fulfillment.

She continued to hold him tightly, with her lips moving in a prolonged ecstasy while he forced his staff up and up in great, grand, final movements, feeling the tissues of her passage clutching at him, drawing the lifeblood from his penis which would surely shatter into total destruction.

'Oh God, God, you lovely bitch, ooh, oh!' His knob seemed to be growing and growing, heavy with its imminent discharge. His whole length of penis seemed to expand, to hurt, to have a needle running sharply down its centre. He dug his nails into her, felt her hands around him, digging, urging, asking for his sperm. His penis had grown to an enormity and she was groaning again. It was going to suddenly turn inside out, it would burst. He gasped, caught his breath and then lost it in a great surging of his lungs as needle after red-hot needle of ecstatic pain shot hotly and wetly from him to her in a culminating blaze.

He wriggled his prick into her even when it was growing limp and empty. He didn't want it to be over, that delight which was better than he'd had before.

At last he lay still on her hot, rounded body, which was still as death, but with a heart he could feel pumping at a declining fury of speed.

She opened her eyes at last and smiled at him, kissing his cheek.

'God, that was wonderful,' she whispered.

'You said it.'

He felt a great contentment and satisfaction; a temporary euphoria in which he wanted to lie for as long as possible.

'You're heavy,' she said after a while, and he rolled off and lay beside her with one arm across the peaks of her breasts.

He felt now the full effects of the pot. He wanted to lie absolutely still and take delight in the fact of being warm and still and able to watch the moonlight and have his arm across her warm, smooth breasts.

They lay for a long time without speaking, perfectly still.

The opening of the outer door and a shaft of light flooding the outer room and cutting across the wall beyond the foot of their bed disturbed them slightly, but not even enough to make them turn their heads. They remained still, looking at the long yellow shaft lighting up the yellow wallpaper and the top of a chest of drawers. They heard the door close.

'Nobody here,' came Jim's voice, hazy and strange, from the other room.

There was the sound of footsteps across the outer room followed by that of someone falling on the bed.

'Oh, I feel as if I'm not really here.' It was Betty's voice, slow and careful as if she was having difficulty in speaking.

Linda stirred, attempting to sit up, but Desmond held her down, putting a finger to his lips.

'Perhaps we'll see something amusing,' he whispered with a wink.

Linda stifled a giggle. What a joke. Betty was about to be fucked for the first time and she and Des would probably be witnesses. How funny!

'Get down on the other side of the bed,' Des whispered. They slid nakedly off the bed and crouched down on the side away from the partition. Des reached up and pulled their clothes down with them.

There was a murmur of voices from the other room. Linda was trying to stifle her growing desire to laugh.

The light flashed on in the other room and filtered dimly through the partition. They heard Jim moving and then his voice saying: 'Looks as if someone was in the other room, but it's empty now. You want to go in there?'

Linda held her breath.

'No, I can't move off this bed. Let's stay here.'

There was silence with a few muffled noises for a time and then Betty's voice.

'Why don't you turn the light off?'

'No, I want to see you. God, you're beautiful.'

Gently Des and Linda eased themselves up. The light came through very dimly. They climbed softly onto the bed and lay out flat facing the partition, watching.

Betty was lying on her side, her back towards them, unclothed and Jim, in a similar state of nudity, was leaning over her on the bed.

'Jees, she's almost as good as you,' Des whispered.

She looked pretty good, Linda admitted to herself. Slim shoulders which curved down in a long line to her hip, exaggerated by her reclining position. Her bottom was bigger than Linda's, each separate buttock seeming to belong to the other, cast in an embracing, oval mould. Her thighs were shorter, more muscular – that was what gave her the dumpier, slightly more sexy appearance; her calves were slim and strong.

She saw Jim's body, too, with its hair. It seemed to be almost covered with hair: on his chest, his shoulders, his thighs, his belly and in a great fuzz around his fat, white erection. Linda felt a thrill of excitement to think that a few days ago she'd been a virgin and now she'd seen three pricks and been fucked by two men.

They watched Betty, saw her put out her hand and touch the giant rod. All her nervousness, her inhibitations had disappeared, Linda noticed. That was the pot.

Jim slid down beside her and they saw him kiss her, watched Betty roll back so that she was flat on the bed and her breasts pointed to the ceiling. They were whoppers, Linda thought. She remembered how they had developed before hers and how embarrassed Betty had been about them at first.

Their faces were fused and Linda saw Jim's hand

stray away and flow over first the right breast and then the left. She could hear Betty's breathing quite clearly.

'She's a virgin,' she whispered to Desmond.

'No kidding!'

Desmond looked through the partition into the clearly-lit room with an interest that approached envy. What a feeling of power that was to be initiating someone into the ways of sex. He wondered how long it would take Jim to find out.

They saw Jim's hand stray away over her ribs down over the belly and the film of hair that was just visible. Betty kept her legs together for the moment, but as he fingered her around the sweating vault of her crotch, she opened them for him.

'He's lucky,' Linda whispered. 'If it hadn't been for the pot she'd have been terribly embarrassed – she might not even have wanted it at all.'

'She'll be a damn good fuck once she knows how,' Des murmured. 'D'you see the flesh on those hips.'

'How about me?' Linda pouted.

'Oh, you're tops already.' He risked the rustle to rub his hand over her rump and she hid her face because she wanted to giggle again.

Jim, meanwhile, had pushed his fingers into Betty's vagina. She had cried out at first, but now she was wriggling around with her thighs half open and her head moving from side to side as he kissed her neck.

Jim took her hand at last and placed it around his prick, squeezing it round him. They saw his organ shooting out over Betty's hips as he lay alongside her.

'She's learning,' Des whispered, as Betty began to squeeze and caress the rigid flesh and Jim began to breathe heavily and push his hips and thighs against her side.

Jim moved his mouth down and they saw the outermost angle of her breast with its cherried nipple disappear into his mouth. Betty gave another shriek and clutched his head after having moved as if to push him away.

'I wonder what they'd say if we burst in on them now,' Linda whispered with a grin. 'I don't think I can stand much more of this.'

'Nuts,' Des whispered back. 'Nothing more exciting than being a Peeping Tom. I want to see how she looks when she's having it for the first time.'

By now Jim's penis was flaming red, turning almost purple. He moved as if to climb onto Betty, and they heard the words falter from her lips: 'No, not yet, not for a bit.'

Jim sank down again and they could see his wrist jerking about between her thighs.

'I – I didn't tell you – but I'm a virgin,' Betty said softly.

At first they could see that Jim hardly believed her.

'God almighty,' he said at last. 'Where you been all this time – and with a body like that?'

Linda hid her face in the counterpane again and Des followed suit. Jim had looked comically surprised – almost hurt that she'd never known a man before.

He recovered eventually, while she lay with eyes closed, wriggling quietly against the wrist between her muscular, white thighs, and he began his digital penetration with greater care and relish. He actually looked down towards her slit as if he wanted to see what a virgin's hole looked like. Des, watching, felt a fresh pang of desire.

Kissing her breasts, mauling her, Jim was gradually getting her more and more excited. She'd spread her legs wide, now, and was squeezing his penis so hard that he had to tell her to ease off.

'Do you think we can try it now?' he panted.

There was a moment of hesitation. Linda knew just what fear, excitement and desire for complete abandon were battling in Betty's head.

'Yes, all right.'

Jim knelt up and climbed between Betty's legs. Her knees came up chest high on either side of him. Linda, seeing his fat thing stabbing out like a spar at an angle of 75 degrees with his belly felt a sudden desire to be filled again, but she couldn't take her eyes from the drama of devirgination. Des, too, lay transfixed.

Gently Jim stretched out on Betty, who gave a little whimper of anticipation as she felt his thighs move out under hers, his knees against her upturned buttocks.

They almost lost sight of his prick, as he guided it with his hand, but they heard Betty's sudden shrill gasp and saw her jerk as if she'd been stung.

'Ooooh, oh!' she gasped. 'Oh, please.' Her head was flung back and in spite of her gasps she made no effort to push him off. She was taking it very well after the preliminary fingering.

When Jim's hand came away they could see where his prick had made a bridgehead. Just the knob and a bit more inside her; the rest they could see, white and somehow tense-looking. Betty had a look of strain about her for the moment. They could see the delightfully voluptuous line of her buttocks, tensed, slightly lifted in the strain, waiting for further shock. It hollowed in like a piece of moulded clay.

'What I wouldn't do to have those buttocks in my hands,' Des was thinking. 'I'd give her something she'd remember for her first time.'

'Stop moving, they'll hear you,' Linda squeaked.

He realised he'd been moving his hips on the bed. He grinned and put his hand between her legs. In answer she pushed her hand under him, searching for his prick. He turned over towards her, still watching the others through the partition. She saw his prick had fattened again into its burden of desire. She caught it and began to move the skin softly up and down. Trying to stifle his breathing, Des let her start to toss him off. The pulsation in his penis was the more acute from his watching the spectacle.

Linda, too, turned her eyes back to the partition while continuing to massage the stiff mast of flesh at her side. It gave her a vicarious thrill to be filling Des with sensation, to be able to feel his great, hot doughy thing in her hand, between her deft fingers.

Betty was giving a series of little shrieks back in the other room, while Jim gently edged into her. His face was an open key to his passion. His mouth hung open, panting and his face was screwed up, tense. He won't hold himself back much longer, Des thought, watching and feeling his own passion rise as he followed their movements and felt the relentless hand on his penis.

Jim had placed his hand under Betty's bottom and pulled her hips up towards him a little, ranging his organ. Betty, with her eyes closed, the corners screwed up in a pain which was still half anticipation, was trembling and gasping.

Suddenly, with a firm thrust of his hips, Jim surged into her. They saw his white prick tear right in, disappearing, inch by inch, smoothly and quickly, from their view.

His head went back as he thrust. The tight, resisting passage gave him a sensual joy which was almost unbearable. Betty's head strained back into the pillow and her body arched up in shock as she gave another little scream.

'Oh, oh, oh, you're hurting me!'

But there was no quarter now. Jim had lost his prick in her and there was no going back. He couldn't even if she really wanted him to.

After several slow strokes which brought his penis almost right out into their vision and then plunged it right back again so that they could see where his black bush of hair met the raw flesh of her love lips, Betty's cries of pain calmed and settled into groans which could be a mixture of pain and passion.

Jim lowered his head and they saw her lips move

round toward his, as she felt his breath on her cheek. Her face was screwed up with a torture which was exquisite. They were making so much noise now, that they couldn't hear the laboured breathing from the next room.

In, in, in. Betty's virgin body was rifled, her channel scourged by a great, foreign body which marihuana had made her want more than ever. And now she knew the pain and ecstasy of it, the completion of herself, the end of those nights of wondering, fearfully desiring, unknowing.

Linda and Des watched gluttonously, following every movement as the two crushed bodies became one and sank into a single rhythm, sometimes faster, sometimes slower, according to the lead which Jim gave.

They watched the muscles on her thighs contract as they pressed him, saw her buttocks tense and relax, her breasts flattened slightly under his weight. Above all they watched that source and centre of the joy, that strangely naked section where his piece of protrusion fitted into her hollow and their hair mingled and moisture began to run and slide around her crotch and over his prick as it withdrew. Linda watched, fascinated as Jim's balls swung slightly, skinnily with their movement. Her hand moved, still on Desmond's penis, and in her mind it was moving on Jim's.

Desmond was straining. In *his* mind his prick was plunging into Betty, giving her the first experience she'd ever had of sex; his hands held those buttocks, his teats weighed on hers, his mouth on hers, his face hotly against her moist, helpless lips in her hot face.

Jim was gasping for breath as he buried himself in the soft suction of Betty's virginal tautness. He wanted to be brutal now and he pushed her thighs back towards her breasts leaning up from her, pushing with his hips, giving them a last flick into her so that some of his hairs were also sucked in with his flesh and reappeared moistly dripping. Betty writhed slightly, gasping, helpless, lost in herself, hardly aware that it was he, Jim, doing this to her, aware only that her body, that aching channel in her belly, was filled with a strange object which seemed to split it and rub it with an exciting, titillating rhythm which seemed to be growing to a white heat in the wandering haze of her mind.

Desmond, gasping quietly, one hand over his mouth, stared fixedly at the wet, raw area into which Jim's prick was slipping and then fixedly at Betty's tormented face, the face which that raw area was producing, which Jim's raging organ was producing. He watched, stared, fixed his eyes, concentrating until they bulged from his head because he could feel himself coming, and he wanted to be almost feeling that flesh when he came. Beside him Linda was breathing heavily, too, excited by his excitement and by the furious winding up of her friend and his friend in the other room. The air seemed to be filled with gasps and vague, sensual movement.

'I'm coming, I'm coming!' Desmond moaned softly.

Linda wriggled quickly in towards him, surprised that she should think of the counterpane. She turned over onto her back so that she could get her hip under his soaring flesh without changing her grip. He stared and stared through the partition until suddenly he tensed, seized her and bit her neck in a long roar of breath, and she felt a stream of hot liquid make a wet, punctuated path all the way across her belly.

In the other room the locked couple were coming to their climax. That was obvious from the animal noises they were making. Taking advantage of the noise, Linda slipped off the bed for her handkerchief. She wiped the sperm from her belly and wiped Desmond's penis before getting back onto the bed to watch the final throes.

Betty was wriggling like a worm suddenly come into

the light. Her face was contorted with a sort of pain. While they watched they saw her lips move very quickly and then her mouth open very wide as she suddenly convulsed against the body above her and inside her.

The pot's pretty good to get a climax for a virgin, Desmond thought.

Now it was only Jim and he was very near the end. He'd moved his hands to her shoulders as if pinning her to the bed against her will and was leaning up, putting the whole of his weight on her drawn-up thighs. His face, too, was wracked with passion, and his teeth seemed to be gritting together. They saw him slow suddenly, thrust, thrust, thrust and then push hard against her as he choked and then again, choking again and so several times until he'd emptied all into her.

When they'd been lying quietly for a while Desmond and Linda went laughing in to them. The pot made it all very funny and Jim and Betty weren't at all offended that they'd been watched.

MORE EVELINE

Eveline is one of the most interesting of Victorian erotic heroines, a lady of quality whose obligatory nymphomania is accompanied by a wicked sense of humour and a thoroughly masculine approach to sexual activity. Her story is told in two volumes, the sequel – More Eveline – being initiated by the crude but effective device of rewriting the ending of volume one (which had consigned her to the virtues of motherhood with her wicked ways behind her). The beginning of the second book sees her spurning the advances of the strapping peasant who impregantes her in the first book and taking off for the delights of London. There she sets about corrupting her rather wet cousin Emma and continuing to assuage her ever-abundant appetite for the flesh.

In pursuit of her amours Eveline is as single-minded and as cunning as any Casanova and she has a particular penchant for tumbling with those lower down the social pecking order than herself. When boredom sets in she is inspired to disguise herself as a working girl and set off on an adventure such as the following . . .

I entered the hotel's dowdy reception hall. The clerk was bemused at the appearance of someone as well-dressed as I. It mattered not. The room I was given was evidently their best. It was small and tasteless, but I intended not to stay too long within it. Scarce had the door closed than I stripped to my boots and stockings and drew out an old dress and bonnet that I had found long before in the attic. How they had got there did not matter. They were sufficiently shabby for my purpose.

The clerk, being engaged, did not see me go out, nor would have recognised me from the back. Down the long street I walked towards Pimlico. I needed the exercise. The late afternoon was warm. Houses alternated with small, poor shops. Women leaning in dark doorways disregarded me. From all appearances I was one of their kind. Several men stared at me. I ignored them just as I did one who drove a cart slowly past and stared into my face.

'What a lovely one! Cor, Miss, want a ride?'

I did indeed, but not of the sort he first intended. I knew not my way in this district and clutched my purse tightly. It was a ragged one. No one would expect to find more than a few pence in it. As I approached the Pimlico district, the houses became a little better. Steps had been cleaned and doorknockers polished. A carriage stood outside one, from which a man of about thirty-five descended. Paying the cabman, he stared at me and then walked quickly across my path.

'Pardon me, but you are exceedingly pretty. Allow me to introduce myself. I am Edwin Pickles, photographer.'

'Indeed? And how would that interest me?'

I placed a nasal Cockney twang in my voice, but my vocabulary evidently puzzled him. He was of neat attire and wore a sporting jacket and modishly tight trousers with black silk bands running down the sides. His shirt was open. Like the corset designer, he wore a cravat.

'I seek models. You would make a perfect one. I would pay you, of course.'

'Oh! ain't you a lark! Naked I suppose?'

'Would you like to talk about it? I pay a guinea for first poses – more later.'

I sniffed. I was remembering the manners and speech of some of the maids we had had. To imitate them amused me.

'As you like.'

We mounted the steps of the house. The hallway was clean within. I was led into a sitting room, as it is called in such dwellings. Scarce had I sat than a woman appeared. She was much of the man's age and had a slightly common but attractive face. He introduced her as his sister, Edwina. Her eyes cast up and down upon me.

'This one will do, yes. A pretty one.'

I affected to look pleased, pretended a bit of sharpness and tried to bargain for thirty shillings, but they would not have it. A glass of cheap sherry apparently assuaged me. I was led up two flights to the studio which had a large roof light. Couches, armchairs, and drapes of various shades lay about. On the floor were cushions. A painted cloth back-drop showed a rural scene. There was even a Penny Farthing, propped in one corner. In the centre of the room stood a large brassbound camera of mahogany on a sturdy tripod. The back of it was covered with a black cloth. A big brass lens gleamed at the front.

'Take your clothes off and I will pose you.'

I had little enough to take off. My dress followed my bonnet. I stood naked in my stockings and boots.

'What a beauty! I swear you are the loveliest girl I have had here!'

'Then you should pay me more, eh? How about it?'

He was close upon me. Poor girls did not struggle very much, I imagined, if there were money in the offing. He made bold to caress my naked bottom. I wriggled it a little and cast my eyes down.

'Will you pay me more if I do?'

His erection was evident already. He pressed it to me, raised my face and kissed me. His hand sought my breasts. It was two days since I had been mounted and I still had visions of Emma in her transports.

'Another guinea, by God, you shall have it!'

'Promise? You got to promise! Oh my gawd, what a whopper, what a big one!'

We were on the cushions. Their purpose was obviously twofold. A shaft of impressive size quivered in my grasp. His mouth smothered mine. I absorbed his tongue. Breeches sliding down, he prepared himself for the assault. I would have preferred some preliminaries, but my lust was as great as his. I panted. I guided the knob to the orifice. It sank within. A gasp of pleasure escaped us both.

'My, you're lovely! What breasts, what a bottom – it's as round as a peach! Put your legs up over mine!'

I obeyed. It would not do to be too forward with my skills. His cock sank in me to the root. I squeezed.

'Oh! you're hurting me with it! Don't go too fast!'

'There, there, you'll like it in a minute. Hold it in. Can you feel it throb? No one ever brought it up so quick, I swear. What a perfect fuck you are!'

'Suck my tits, then – I likes that.'

He began to thresh. His piston moved in my spongy clasp. I closed my eyes and felt a complete delirium. There are occasions when I can be mounted three times in a day and then feel that the fourth is the first I have had for weeks. It was so now. I bucked my bottom to encourage him.

'Do it fast – I like it! Make me come!'

'You beauty! Oh, what heaven!'

His knob seemed to be thrusting up almost into my womb. His balls made a fine smacking sound. Beneath the cushions the floorboards squeaked. I was wet already with my spendings. The perfect, simple glory of the act overcame me. Those who scorn such 'wanton pleasures' know nothing of the richness of experience such as only the truly initiated can enjoy. My pleasure was twice and thrice his own, had he but known it. Lithe in his movements he pumped it back and forth, his cock well oiled by my juices.

'Don't come in me! Suppose I 'as a child?'

Too far gone, he did not care. I pretended of a sudden the same abandon. I heaved to his heavings. Our pubic hairs rubbed together. My nipples were stark against his chest.

'You like it? Have I got a big one? Is it nice?'

'Oh, I loves it! Do it more!'

He shuddered. His words had been meant only as a prelude to his climax. Jets of warm come streamed from his prick and flooded me. The sensation was delicious. I alone, it seemed, could enjoy such pleasures and remain free of complications. I absorbed him like a sponge. He groaned in my velvety depths. Our bellies squirmed. Then he sank down. He panted mightily. We lay soaking until at last he decided to withdraw and rise. I rose and flopped into an armchair, feeling a little pool of sperm issue itself under me where it spilled from my cleft.

His eyes were somewhat rapturous as he covered himself and gazed at me. Indolently I let my thighs fall apart.

'You didn't 'arf fill me up, you did!'

'You'll come again tomorrow? I can photograph you then. The light isn't good now.'

'Tomorrow? I ain't got nowheres to go tonight.'

He looked bewildered. He ruffled his hair. His eyes could not take themselves from my muff.

'Very well. I will speak to my sister.'

He was gone. I looked around, saw a bottle of wine that had been newly opened, sniffed it and drank a little. My throat was parched. I replaced the bottle hastily when he ascended again.

'There is a spare room. You may sleep there.'

'You said as you would pay me two guineas, remember, and I 'as to get my supper.'

'All right. See, I have a half a crown on me. Take that and we will settle in the morning.'

I took it quickly and placed it in my purse where I had otherwise placed only notes so that they would not click together. He would think it otherwise empty. Having put my dress and bonnet back on I went down. His sister waited for me in the hall.

'I suppose he had you? He does that with half the girls. It's disgusting!'

'I don't know what you mean – I'm a decent girl, I am. Don't you go besmirching my name or I'll make ructions about it, that I will!'

I pride myself as an actress. She could not help but be convinced. I take care always with the expressions

107

in my eyes as well as the words that come from my lips.

'Nothing intended. After you've got your supper you can come back. Second door on the left, first landing, is your room. Has he paid you?'

'No. I ain't done no posing yet, 'ave I?'

Perhaps she thought to catch me out. I gave her a stare and departed. I had no need to return. The thought that I had earned two shillings and sixpence by enjoying myself was extremely amusing. I had learned something at least about the economics of copulation among such people. Entering an eating house I had passed on the way I saw a young girl standing there. She had dirty golden hair, a ragged skirt, and worn-down shoes on. I imagined her sixteen or seventeen. Our eyes met.

'Got a penny to spare, Miss?'

'Are you hungry?'

'Yes, Miss. I ain't eaten only but a scrap of bread since morning.'

'Come in with me. I will buy you something.'

I was moved by her prettiness and her poverty. She could scarce believe it when I ordered mutton chops. The grease ran through her fingers. She was in heaven. I gathered she lived in Stepney. Her mother beat her and she had run away from home. There were thousands of such poor homeless on the streets. Her name was Alice.

'Would you like to earn money, Alice?'

Her eyes were as bit as saucers when I explained. No, she didn't mind taking her clothes off. Her brothers had seen her often enough like that, and her father. They all lived in one room. When her mother was asleep she had played with their 'diddles,' she said. They called it tickling. She liked being tickled. It was a rare lark, she said.

I took her back with me, her tummy full. Before leaving I got the man who owned the eating house to

wrap some cold meat and pickles for us in a piece of
paper. It would serve as our supper or breakfast. Alice
danced along beside. I think she was sure I was a lady
but would not dare say so.

Edwina received us at first haughtily but changed
her mind when she had had a good look at Alice. In the
sitting room she lifted the girl's dress and displayed a
perfect, chubby bottom, handsome young legs and a
fine down of curls.

'She'll do. Edwin can photograph you both together.'

I guessed what that meant. We slept together in a
narrow bed, huddling close. I gave her a little 'tickle'
before going to sleep. It made her feel nice, she said.
My finger worked smoothly in her soft cleft. She
hugged and kissed me, then straightened her legs and
gave a sigh.

'Did you come?'

'Yes. I like that. Ain't it lovely?'

She would not confess to having had any cocks in
her, but I guessed she had. She was a warm little
thing, fully amorous when started up. Bread and drip-
pings and a mug of tea sufficed for our breakfast. At
nine Edwin began photographing us. We assumed
various poses, but it was necessary to remain perfectly
still for each one while Edwin counted solemnly. Little
by little he encouraged us until Alice lay on her back
with her legs in the air and I held my tongue close to
her slit.

'I mean to have a young fellow to pose with you girls
now. Would you like that?'

I said nothing. Alice stared and giggled. The young
man was presented. He was scarce more than a year
older than Alice. His eyes would have eaten me up.
I wore black stockings and nothing else. Edwin had
provided gaudy garters which clipped my thighs
tightly. Undressing as if embarrassed, the newcomer,
who was named Charlie, presented a slender figure to
our view. His penis looked equally thin.

109

We took our first pose with Charlie between us, he kissing me and Alice holding his cock. In a trice it was up. Though of small girth it was of reasonable length. At Edwin's command I lay on my hip and took it in my mouth. The long seconds passed while Edwin counted. I sucked seductively upon the pear-shaped knob.

'Let him do it? Would you?'

'Half a crown extra for that if I do.'

The photographer frowned. He regarded me obviously as a hard bargainer. By any working girl's standards I would be coming into riches.

'Very well. Kneel up. Have Alice lie under you. Keep your bottom up. I want you and she kissing while he holds it in.'

I presented a bottom as perfect as any that Charlie or Edwin would ever be likely to see. A thought had seized me that I could not resist. Passing my hand under me I took Charlie's stiff little penis and guided it – not in my slit but against my rosehole. Whether he had ever entered it in a girl before I know not, but he made no ado about presenting it there. Edwin, busy with his focussing beneath the black cloth, was at the wrong angle to see what was happening. Charlie groaned. I do not blame him. I was still then a trifle tight there, yet he proved a perfect size to initiate me in this respect.

A sob of pleasure escaped my mouth as it settled upon Alice's. The minx, excited, thrust her tongue. I moved my bottom back carefully on the doughty little rod whose knob was already pressing beyond the puckered rim of my rosette.

'Be still!' Edwin commanded.

Charlie's hands clapsed my hips. I dared not move. I wanted it too much. Fortunately at that moment Edwin fussed again beneath the cloth. He was forever rearranging his focussing and twisting the lens about. Quite beside himself meanwhile, Charlie inserted himself a further inch . . . another! Ah! the sensation was beyond description. My tongue twirled about Alice's. If I had measured the corset designer, then I measured Charlie's piston much more sensitively. I had reason too. There was a slight burning and itching, yet the pleasure was immeasurable. A sensation that the breath was being expelled from my body overtook me and then passed. I had absorbed five inches of his tool when Edwin again sternly bid us be still.

We froze our postures – externally at least. Within my bottom Charlie's prick pulsed its pleasure. A gurgling sound escaped him though he managed to keep perfectly still. Within seconds – the very seconds that Edwin was devoutly counting – I experienced the long shoots of Charlie's sperm that for a blissful moment seemed to throb endlessly and appeared to jet right up into my bowels.

The pleasure was rapturous. Too often in my delights I had failed to feel the spurting of the male liquid in my slit. Now in my narrower, tighter passage I could feel it all – ALL.

The photograph was taken. Charlie withdrew as slowly as he could. His sperm trickled armly from my bottomhole. Falling back, he appeared to grow pale, his cock oozing. Edwin – not knowing exactly what had passed – thereupon berated him. The further poses which should have included Charlie's young manhood, were ruined, he said.

'I am tired anyway. You must have taken enough.'

I made my tone clipped and certain. I rose to put on my dress. I wanted to absorb in my mind the experience I had received as much as I had done in my bold bottom.

'Is he going to pay us now, Evie?'

'Yes, he is. Are you not, Edwin?'

I had forgotten my Cockney accent for a moment. All stared at me. A certain furtive look came into his eyes. Overtones of false geniality entered his voice.

'No time to go to the bank today, you see. I tell you

111

what – come back tomorrow morning and I'll have it ready.'

'You must have some money. Ask your sister. Does she not keep your purse?'

'She is out.' His face was sullen.

'Very well –, we will return as you say.'

Alice looked bewildered. I believe she thought that both the photographer and I had conspired to welsh on her. I gave him no more of my time and let her down.

'He aint' going to pay us, Miss, I knows it.'

'Oh, he will pay us, Alice. You know I am not as you believed?'

'Oh yes, Miss – I guessed you was a lady. I knowed you was doing it for a lark, but now I aint' got a penny and nowheres to sleep or go.'

I hailed a carriage. It was the first one that Alice had ever been in, she said. In a few minutes we were at the hotel. The clerk, perceiving my face and then my clothes, nearly fell off his stool.

'This young lady will stay the night here instead of myself. It is paid for and therefore it does not matter. See to it that she gets what she wants and I will reimburse you.'

He nodded in a surly manner. I threw a note down before him. His expression changed. He stood up.

'Yes, Miss.'

I changed again and settled Alice in, giving her the half crown that I had received from Edwin. She would be able to buy food a-plenty with it.

'You will come back, Evie?'

Her gaze was solemn and anxious. I assured her of my word. She was a charming creature. Papa would appreciate her once she was bathed and cleanly clothed. I felt certain we could find a place in the household for her. She and Mary would get on no end.

I made my way down to the street. Cabs were a-plenty at that hour. One stopped expectantly beside me.

'Anywhere to go, Miss?'

'Yes. Scotland Yard, please.'

'Inspector Barkey is not here, Madam. Would you wish to see someone else? Can you tell me what the matter is about?'

The policeman who received me regarded me so closely that I imagined my dress had become transparent.

'It is a matter of some confidence. Who is the other senior officer?'

'Chief Inspector Ramage. I dunno whether he can see you now or not.'

The matter, however, was swiftly arranged. The Chief Inspector was a man of some physique. He accommodated me in his office. His eyes scanned my figure with more than passing interest. I affected my quietest manner as one who is deeply shocked. I had chanced upon a young girl, I told him, who had fallen into the hands of pornographic photographers. Not only had they made devilish use of her, but had refused to pay her and thrown her out of the house into the bargain.

'The devils! There are a number of these people about now that photographic work has taken on. We shall have them, Madam – I swear on it. Can you explain the nature of the photographs to me?'

His gaze was somewhat expectant. As if summoning himself up for some ordeal he partook of a glass of whisky and offered me one. I sipped my own delicately.

'The photographs were of an extremely intimate nature. I do not know whether or not I dare speak of them to you. In one, for instance, the poor girl – quite naked save for stockings, was bent over a chair. . . . Oh! but I cannot describe it!'

His look was immediately solicitous. He rose and came round his desk.

'Do not fret yourself. I believe I know well what you

113

mean. Allow me to show you. Perhaps if madam could stand a minute?'

I stood. My breasts made somewhat intimate contact with his chest. A slight hoarseness entered into his voice.

'I has to be certain, Madam, that the postures were within the meaning of the Act, if you catch my meaning. She was bent over, you say, right over, and all showing.'

I lowered my gaze. My breasts rubbed across him.

'If I show you, will it clear the matter up for you?'

'Indeed it will. If you turn round now – so. Take no fright now for I am just going to bend you over and draw your skirt up a shade. You say she was naked?'

'Yes. You will have to arrange my skirt higher, I fear, to get the full effect. Oh dear! am I showing all now?'

'All that is perfect. And another scoundrel were right behind her, if my guess is right. Putting it up her?'

'AAAH! OOOOH! Is that your truncheon, Inspector?'

'Not the one I use on the villains, ma'am. This one is to pleasure the ladies. Still now – jut your bottom up a bit. Ah, what lecherous likenesses they must be indeed, yet none would show as pretty an offering as yours. Steady now and we will get the posture perfect. Like so, was it?'

'In . . . In . . . In . . . Inspector, AAAH! Oh my goodness, it is in! You are stretching me! No more, Oh I beg you!'

'We'll never know otherwise, ma'am. Legs apart was it?'

'Yes! A bit more! Be careful of my stockings! Oh, you rogue, you are slipping more of it in. It's too big! Ah, what a thrust! Oh goodness, what a feeling it is!'

'Straddle your legs – keep your ankles firm. Another couple of inches does it. There – steady now – bend a little more. I love a girl who offers it up like this. Younger than you, is she?'

His cock was superb – a genuine ramrod of stiff flesh and muscle. With the last effort of his forcing it all in I felt his balls swing under me. A final squelch and nine inches of his weapon were within. I all but fainted with the delicious sensation.

'Ah, you naughty man, you are making me do it! Do you like my cunt? Is it tight and soft for you? Unbutton my dress – caress my breasts! OH! Yes! AH! Pump me hard!'

Our pretence had ceased. We were in the full throes of it. The buttons of my corsage flew apart. His big palms cradled the gourds of my tits. Bent over well as I was, it is a posture I adore. All propriety left me. I moaned and twisted. My bottom rotated lewdly against his belly. The warm silky orb enraged his lust further. His strokes, powerful and deep, quickened.

'Give it to me! Push it in! Oh, what a monster you have! Do you get many young ladies to do this to?'

'None as you. The working class lassies is easy. Many a one I've had in a dark passageway if she was afeared I were going to arrest her. Little devil! You know how to work your bottom, don't you?'

I was beyond reply. The friction of his big thick cock had already made me spill my libation twice. I was on the brink of another. The room seemed to swim about me. His loins were lusty. I suspected he could run a second bout in as quick a time as any man. And so it proved. Having inundated me, he uncorked and sat me upon his lap.

'Was it true, your story?'

'Of course! I will lead you to the young girl herself – and then to the den of vice. Promise me only one thing. The latest photographs taken must be destroyed. I do not wish them to appear before the courts.'

'I shall find no trouble in doing that. Move your bottom on my cock a little. I never knew a girl to stir me so!'

My nipples attracted his lips. He sucked them greedily. His hair was thick and dark. I stroked it encourag-
ingly while he was about his task. Beneath me the
thick worm stirred and transmuted itself into a small
pole that almost lifted me off his lap. I groped and felt
the girth of it, slimy with love's spendings.

'Do you want to again?'

'Clear your desk. I will lie on it with my legs hanging
over the edge. It will be nice that way. Do not soil my
dress. Oh, you rogue!'

He was upon me again in a minute. A second bout
is often the best. They take longer about it. Their cocks
are less feverish, but even more willing. We panted,
kissed and murmured our delights. After three or four
minutes he inundated me anew. My thighs were wet
with his come. I wiped them as best as I could with
my kerchief while he watched and grinned. I truly
believe he expected me to stay long enough for a third
injection.

'What a lot you do in me!'

I could not help but smile. His pride was obvious.

'And shall do again, ma'am, if the pleasure takes
you. As to the whereabouts of these rogues, now.'

'I would like to accompany you, Inspector. I wish to
assure myself that the photographs of Alice – the girl
I spoke of – are truly destroyed. Unfortunately at the
moment I have another engagement. Can you not
secure the villains tomorrow?'

'As you wish. A few more hours will make no difference. And the young girl concerned? I have to take her
statement down, you understand.'

I hesitated, but it would do no harm for Alice to
have a little company. He would take more than her
statement down, I felt sure. I gave him the name of
the hotel. His eyebrows raised. I hastened to explain
that I had paid for her accommodation as an act of
mercy.

'You are a good 'un, all right, ma'am.'

'I try to be, Inspector.'

He would not leave for an hour or two, I guessed. I hastened back to Alice who sat looking rather forlorn. I apprised her of events. Her first thought was of her money. I opened my purse and gave her a guinea. She clutched it as though it were the last coin in the world.

'The Inspector will call soon to see you, Alice. You will tell him everything and show him what you did. You won't be shy?'

'Oh no – I like a bit of company. When shall you come back?'

'In the morning.'

The next day I repaired immediately to the hotel where I had left Alice. There – not unexpectedly – I found her abed with the Inspector. Or rather he in his shirt-tails was sitting on the bed quaffing coffee while Alice lolled beside him like the princess she undoubtedly felt.

She grinned but showed little dismay at my entrance. The Inspector's doughty tool lolled rather limply. It had done much inspecting evidently. His pleasure at seeing me again at such an early hour was exceeding. With pleasing tact, however, he did not attempt to embrace me.

'What's afoot, Inspector? Do you intend to catch the rogues today?'

'No doubt on it, ma'am. I has six stout officers at the ready to pounce, and a cart to take away the photographic plates. They will be needed in evidence, of course.'

'Of course – save those of this dear girl. It would be a terrible thing if they came to light. May I propose a plan to you?'

'As you wish, so long as it don't impede our entry today.'

'No, it will not do that. In fact it will aid it. I intend to visit there. I shall take care to leave the door unlocked. That way your men may enter quietly and take them by surprise. Meanwhile I will ensure that Mr and Miss Pickles are caught in an unguarded moment.'

He gazed at me with admiration. So much did it show that his penis began to thicken. Its bulbous nose peeped from beneath his shirtfront.

'You've given thought to this matter, I can see that, ma'am'

'I do to all things, Inspector. It is now but nine A.M Allow me until eleven. All shall be ready then. Come, Alice, get dressed and we shall depart.'

'Yes, Miss. Will I gets my money?'

'Of course.'

The little wanton was quite naked. Getting off the bed she drew out the chamber pot from beneath it, squatted, and piddled loudly. She being then out of sight of us, I passed my hand beneath the Inspector's shirttail and held his penis for a moment in my gloved hand.

'You have been most accommodating, Inspector.'

'You, too, ma'am. Perhaps we shall co-operate again.'

His penis stirred. It began to assume alarming proportions. The tousled state of the bed afforded me lewd ideas, but I knew better than to succumb to them then. I gave his weapon a last squeeze.

'It will not be forgotten.'

'Nor yours, ma'am. We fitted 'em together nicely.'

Alice was up and wiping herself with a corner of the sheet. I had stepped away from the Inspector. She had not seen my movements. His risen baton appeared as a tribute to her charms. In a moment her clothes were on. Bustling her to the door I looked back at the policeman who lay extended on the bed, his cock upthrust. It was a farmyard invitation. I smiled and shook my head.

A quick breakfast at the eating house where I had previously taken Alice and we were ready for the fray.

I told her all that I intended. Her eyes were aglow with complicity and excitement.

'We have come to photograph again, if you want us.'

Edwina Pickles, who opened the door, looked more disappointed that pleased at our return. We were ushered in. Edwin appeared, looking rather pale.

'I had not expected you yet.'

'It does not matter. The light is good, is it not? If you promise to give us some likenesses of ourselves we will do this one free. But you must pay us for the others that we done.'

My speech was still an amusing mixture of cultivation and Cockney, but it did not matter. He appeared bemused at the invitation.

'Very well, then, but the young man is not here.'

'We will pose together, Alice and I. You will have plenty of sale for such pictures. I know a few people who would buy them – well-to-do ones.'

Their interest was immediately captured. The mystery of my identity added salt to the offer. Edwina accompanied us up to the studio.

'You are not a common girl, are you? Who are these friends you know?'

'Better to ask no questions, Miss Pickles, I am told they sell for two or three guineas a set – a fortune to some, a small amount to others. There are thirty or more men who would give a lot to see me naked in such pictures. First, though, you must pay us.'

The money came immediately to hand. Edwina could not contain herself for curiosity. The idea of quickly selling thirty sets was obviously uppermost in her mind.

'Who are you really? Are you making a market of us?'

'Shall we have wine first? Let me pour it. I find it quite amusing to serve people instead of constantly being waited on.'

There was no disguising my tone of manner now. I had them entranced. I expounded my themes. I was a high-born young lady of the best Society, I told them. The escapade amused me. I knew other young ladies of rank who would be equally daring, given the chance. Alice remainêd dumb with wonder. I satisfied them entirely as to my credentials without giving away a single name. While talking I refilled our glasses and passed into those of Edwin and his sister a few drops from a small phial that I had in my reticule. Papa had brought it back from India with him. I knew its power.

I continued my lecture, amusing myself no end. I reclined upon the floor cushions, so bringing them to follow suit. I had no doubts about the many poor girls they had cheated as they would have done Alice and I.

In a moment Edwina's features grew somewhat flushed, as did her brother's. Forewarned as she had been, Alice affected not to notice. The eyes of the pair assumed a glazed look. Their glasses lolled in their fingers. In a moment both sank back inert.

'Quickly, Alice!'

Edwina appeared conscious but incapable of resistance. We stripped her to her stockings. Her figure was firm and full. Arranging her neatly on her back, we spread her legs. Edwin was next. He attempted a faint resistance but was beyond strength to affect it. A slight dosage of an aphrodisiac in the drug had made his penis distend to a fine length and girth.

Edwina – unable to move – uttered a strangled moan as we rolled him upon her. Excited herself by the effects of the potion, the lips of her vagina were puffy, and moist. To a hollow groan from Edwin his stiff weapon was neatly inserted. The knob disappeared slowly and was engulfed. Their loins stirred restlessly as if each were in a dream. Fetching some rope which I had spied earlier I bound him tightly upon her beneath their arms, rolling Edwina about until he was couched upon her again. Raising her legs, I brought them to his hips and – with the help of Alice – bound her ankles in such wise that her legs could not slide down.

I rose and gazed upon the spectacle. Had I known how to effect a photograph I might have taken a fine one then.

'Shall we leave them like this, Miss?'

'Look for the plates he took of us, Alice. They will be in those metal slides, I suspect, in the corner.'

A neat pile stood there. Undoubtedly they were the ones. Edwin had not developed them yet. Removing them from the slides we shattered each one into several pieces. The evidence that most concerned us was now destroyed.

I gazed at my watch. There were yet six or seven minutes to go before the Inspector and his men arrived. I hastened down and unlocked the door. A carriage passing outside halted at my wave.

'Wait, cabbie.'

I returned to the studio upstairs. Unable to resist temptation, Edwin had begun to agitate his loins. With her legs bound up about him, Edwina was in no position to say no. Her bottom began to bump merrily on the cushions.

'Quickly, Alice!'

We had just time to effect our escape before the policemen arrived. Inspector Barkey approached with his contingent. I waved and pointed to the front door which hung open. His expression was one of dismay that I was departing . . .

A GALLERY OF NUDES

Like a previous excerpt in this volume A Gallery of Nudes *takes us back to London in the 1950s – though the protagonists of this particular episode are rather more sophisticated than the gauche teenagers of* The Wantons.

Anthony Grey is a well-known roué, a dyed-in-the-wool bachelor whose reputation as a lady-killer is wearing just a little thin now that he has reached the age of fifty. His interest has been piqued, however, by a woman of half his years whom he meets at a rather grand dinner party. Grey perceives Casilda Vandersluys to be 'a sleek young beast, full of surprise' and naturally his curiosity is further aroused by the knowledge that she is the lover of his hostess, the society heiress Helen. It soon transpires that Casilda's interests are not exclusively homosexual and that she is fascinated by all kinds of behaviour – 'meaning,' as she puts it, 'Sex with a big snaky capital S.' In short, Casilda is keen to indulge in any kind of sexual antics, the more outrageous the better. She arranges for Tony to watch Helen making love to her, she picks up a swarthy young Spaniard in a restaurant and beds him at Tony's flat, she turns the tables on Helen with Tony to that lady's utter horror – the more public the act and the more complex the emotions involved, the happier she is. And so, when Tony renews his acquaintance with an old girlfriend and her husband, Cassie is only too keen to make the most of what turns out to be a very uninhibited occasion . . .

It was at an exhibition of paintings by a young Austrian artist, one wintry February evening, that we ran into Janet, whom Casilda had not met before, though I, needless to say, had related to her many memorable incidents from the annals of our tempestuous, jaunty-blithe, dingdong engagement, which had lasted on and off for nearly seven years and broke up in final disorder, to our immense mutual relief, on the way in her car to the registry. I have a weak ankle still as a result of that thousand-and-first fracas, while Janet wears two wedding rings, a false front tooth, and a big white streak in her dark mane as reminders of what she calls 'the public wars' or 'my grim Grey period.' We were now fond friends, sharing the curious jocular charm that passions spent acquire as a patina with age, but I had not seen her, either, nor her inoffensive Scottish husband, Andrew, since 'the evening you vamoosed halfway through dinner,' as Janet reminded me rather tartly. She shrugged off my apologies. 'I only hope she was worth it,' she said, 'I assume so, as we haven't heard from you since.'

We were standing under the shadows of an elongated Battersea Bridge at sunset, and Casilda drifted in from the next room at that moment, catalogue in hand, looking for me.

'I rather like that,' Janet declared, waving a glove at some bathers on a canal bank and narrowly missing Casilda's nose as she approached.

'Me too,' I said. I introduced them. 'This was the reason why I owe you and Andrew an especially good dinner.' I explained, 'to make up, Janet dear, for my rudeness in leaving you that night a trifle abruptly.'

'Janet, the famous Janet!' Casilda exclaimed. 'Knowing Tony as we do, I needn't tell you how often he drags your name into the conversation. It's a household word with us, if you'll forgive me saying so.'

'Oh, my God, yes, I'm sorry for you,' Janet laughed. 'He's such a tireless reminiscer, isn't he? You must know all – but everything – about me in the most lurid detail, I'm sure. How dismal of you, Tony!'

'Let me give you the lowdown on Casilda in return,' I offered. 'When can you have a quiet, gossipy lunch with me?'

'I insist on getting my word in first,' Casilda stated. 'We girls have a lot in common. What do you say, Janet? Unless we let him come along as well – just to eat, shut up, and listen.'

We took a stroll round the gallery, discussing Klaus Ritter's quite commendable stuff, and gave Janet a few drinks at the pub on the corner before she dived into the Underground for Hampstead, where we were to dine with them the following Thursday. My two darlings, past and present, had taken to each other in a big way, and I was completely ignored in the frowzy saloon bar while they got on like a row of houses on fire, chattering and giggling so gaily that I noticed several staid customers regarding them with greater interest and more frankly amused admiration than any freak or foreigner can normally count on arousing among the British at home. They made a striking pair of beauties, even for the West End, I will admit, in that dowdy setting, though there was nothing bizarre about Janet's lean English looks and Casilda was so un-American an expatriate that she could happily refer to herself as a crossbred mongrel, instead of just taking it for granted.

'I'm nuts about that Janet of yours,' Casilda informed me as the station swallowed my ex-fiancée down its fetid gullet. 'She's loads of fun – and madly attractive, in a famished style of looks. Not much of her, is there?'

'If Janet were ever to shed an ounce of weight off her spare frame, skinny would be the only word for her. But that isn't feasible because there ain't no flesh on her anywhere that she could lose, as I used to tell her, without the light showing through. You'd have to scoop to hollow out even a sliver of Janet. My cronies used to describe her as scrawny, but dressmakers call it 'slenderly built.' She's a sylph – irremediably thin, or, as she says herself, 'thin with knobs on.' That's more accurate. The knobs are all there, and the curves – long and slight and sinewy as a greyhound's, but perfectly in proportion and finely drawn, like a streamlined, sensitive piece of machinery, a shiny steel instrument of some sort. Janet, stripped, presents a far less gaunt appearance than the fashionable self you saw in her clothes. A bit lanky, of course, but a damned sight more human in shape when she's naked.'

'So I would imagine,' Casilda commented with a smile. 'You and your nudes! You analyse and compare every woman's body you come across. Wouldn't you do better to photograph us all for the record, instead of trying to remember a whole jumbled mass of mental notes?'

Where Janet was concerned, if I wished to be critical,

I would set against her undoubted good points two anatomical flaws that are often found in this tall breed of Englishwomen. Her tits were appealing, firm and excellent, although of course too small – but they also were placed too low and rather too far apart, pointing outwards, which gave her a flat chest at first sight, and yet, almost as a pleasant afterthought, a distinctly feminine bosom. This was charming enough in itself, once discovered; but it seemed to have little, if any, connection with the strongly marked, splendid pectoral muscles that could scarcely be needed to lift those sweet, prancing, miniature breasts. Secondly, under her fork, at the top of her long, lean shanks, though she was not bow-legged, there was an empty space, an unsightly, inverted triangular gap between the thighs, which were devoid of any fat, so that, here, at the vital intersection itself, you got more room for manoeuvre than is usually provided for a man's comfort or the woman's ease in accommodating a visitor's retinue, however bulky. It always struck me that this fault – I would hardly call it a drawback – detracted from the obvious merits of Janet's smooth, pretty concave belly and proud, very prominent mount of Venus, which were among her best features, to my taste.

The Mackenzies lived on the far side of Hampstead. Andrew wore glasses, an incipient paunch, and a canny, good-natured expression, as though all three attributes were as congenial to him as the pink complexion which was a shade darker, if anything, than his now greying carroty hair. Physically he was not prepossessing, but he had the proverbial Scottish traits of dry humour and reserved gravity, though he carried neither to that excess which amounts, in many of his race, to unwarranted conceit and taciturn boorishness. The martinis, after a hard day's work at his printing office, loosened his tongue before we sat down to the delicious, unorthodox sort of meal in which both our hosts, and hostess, as butler and cook, were right to take great pride, for its succession of exotic specialities was typical of the house. Casilda could not conceal her admiring envy and thereby won Andrew's heart, so that no stranger joining us at table would have been able to guess who among the assembled company were intimate friends or had never met before in their lives.

Andrew assured me, when I complimented him on the choice variety of his food and wines, that above all else he had a passion for his trade as a typographer, which took up every moment of his time, he said, apart from weekend gold, because he had allowed it to become his hobby as well. He too was a collector – of books. 'I have a very small library,' he told me, 'but most of the items in it are prize specimens, and some are unique. You'll see – though they may not be much up your street. I only go in for fine bindings and perfect examples of print.'

Andrew kept his cigars also in the cosy little room off the hall, where we retreated with a decanter and plenty of coffee to inspect the shelves that glowed, like a tapestry, with rich tones of leather and gilt. He showed me a wealth of magnificent volumes, among them half a dozen that I had not merely seen before in booksellers' lists or behind glass, and though I did not doubt his word it occurred to me that sometimes perhaps he let the merits of subject matter outweigh the intrinsic value of the production. There was a priceless Aretion, the *Decameron*, Crebillon's *Sofa* and other curious works that may have owed their presence there to outward beauty, but, rubbing shoulders with them, I found a tome or two – a smudgy, tattered copy of Rochester's *Sodom*, for example – whose rarity alone would rate them worthy of inclusion, whereas the few modern editions, maybe a score, in a separate section, belonged to the same single class of illustrated master-pieces intended solely for perusal by adult and dis-criminating readers.

I was pouring over the pages of Sade's *Justine* when

the telephone pealed out beside me, and the bookworm Andrew answered it. An agitated voice spluttered at length into his ear, eliciting no more than an occasional gruff query or dour affirmative in reply. Finally he snapped: 'Well, all right then – I'll have to go down and cope with it myself, I shan't be long.'

He turned to me. 'I'm sorry,' he said. 'A call from that fool of a head printer. Apologise to the girls on my behalf. I might get back, with luck, before you go.'

He started to ring for a taxi, but I insisted on driving him at least as far as the station. It was a dirty night, and I was glad to let myself into the warmth with his latchkey. *En passant* I picked up another cigar and some brandy from the study before joining the ladies.

There they were, on the sofa together, in front of the drawing-room fire, but I could not say that I caught them in a compromising situation, because they showed no sign of heeding my intrusion in the least. Janet was almost lost to view in Casilda's arms, but both were still fully clothed. Casilda was kissing and fondling my former love, who very evidently relished her attentions, for her head was thrown back, her eyes were shut, and she was sighing and squirming in that abandoned way she had, which I remembered so well. This went on for some time, until Casilda, becoming aware of my diffident presence, looked up and gave me a wink of the most entrancing vulgarity. If she did not wave in recognition, it was because both her hands were deeply engaged, at first on a roving mission and then in a definite pincer movement that appeared to rouse our hostess from uneasy slumbers to a vocal and increasingly active share in the proceedings. Janet's staring peepers opened like a doll's, she suddenly found a great deal to say – all of it highly flattering to her newly acquired friend – and her arms, linked about Casilda's neck, dragged the happy, wide, scarlet mouth down to her own, silencing them both, to some extent, for neither one of the excited pair could speak again for a while in coherent terms, though the language they used was an expressive universal *lingua franca* sound beyond the limits of speech, as they kissed, mumbled, panted, gasped and sighed . . .

I was sitting back in a large armchair, quietly puffing at my mellow Larriñaga, as utterly at ease as a millionaire impresaria watching a deliriously popular stage turn from the wings. The success of the act did not exactly surprise me, though it had never crossed my mind, earlier in the evening, that the girls would fall for each other in such startling earnest, practically on first sight, or that their mutual attraction could produce this happy harvest, before one could say Tallulah Bankhead. Casilda, I realised, might perhaps have been feeling a trifle starved for this special form of love, which no doubt meant more to her than she was prepared to admit. Bless her wicked heart, I couldn't blame her for getting up to her old tricks again so soon, at the drop of an eyelid! But, casting my mind back over Janet's case history, I did not recall that she ever showed much liking or aptitude but rather, on the contrary, a natural distaste for any hint of these naughty digressions, which I would, I confess, have been only too ready to encourage and approve. It was obvious that Casilda had taken the initiative tonight, and was calling the tune, but I was equally fascinated to see that Janet must have welcomed her overtures without the faintest hesitation of demur, judging by their present harmonious pitch of enthusiasm. There had not been time, after all, for any lengthy process of persuasion, and Casilda, with her unfailing sixth sense in sexual matters, had clearly neither delayed nor rushed the pace unduly. They seemed meant for one another – and both were bent on proving it.

I crossed over and sat on the arm of the sofa. Casilda's black jersey dress was off one shoulder. She had undone Janet's shirt and removed her bra. Between them they struggled to get her out of her tight tartan trews. Casilda signalled to me for aid. She had slithered on to the floor and delved deep into Janet's lap at once, leaving the upper half of the long, slim body in my care. Janet's rosy limbs were flung wide across the cushions, like a starfish stranded helpless on the shore. Hers was the emaciated, abandoned carcass, we the plundering crows that swooped on her in unison to gnaw her vitals. Neither of them at last could bear the strain another moment. Leaping to her feet, Casilda wrenched off her sombre plumage, quickly cast the layer of downy silky beneath, and, launching the full force of all her naked weight into the saddle, bestrode the eager mount that bucked, quivered, reared, bounced hard up to meet her with a wild, savage will of its own. I was thrown off my perch and was forced to relinquish the tiny, tender, dancing tits to Casilda's strong grip, as she seized them for reins and clung to them also for support while she rode the cleft of Janet's crotch, hitching it fiercely to her own, twisting and writhing against it, plunging, pressing, thrusting more and more closely, more deeply into the devil's dripping mouth, the open breach, the entrance to the loins' dark, leafy-locked, mysterious cave, to dig within its folds on a hot quest for hidden treasure . . .

I could have sworn that the violence of this encounter made the roughest moments of the frenzied frolic I had witnessed between Helen and Casilda seem like child's play. Among several reasons for this distinct impression were the fact that here was a new and unexpected challenge, that it was largely a novel thrill for Janet, whose physique was particularly well constructed to ensure that she should get the utmost enjoyment out of such an awkward method of fornication, that both girls were conscious of their appreciative audience,so may have been tempted to play up accordingly, and not only had Casilda lately been deprived of this pleasurable outlet but probably she felt that, given the chance to cuckold me a little into the bargain, she must trespass on an ancient light-o'-love of mine with an extra vengeance. She did not stint herself, certainly, nor pull her punches. But Janet was never one to take things lying down – at least not in any metaphorical sense. She gave as good as she got, on principle – and in this case she put up such a gallant show that she succeeded, with all her wiry might and by a swift, wrestling ell-like motion, in turning the tables completely on her more solid opponent. I did not see how it was done, but in a tangled flash, after a brief upheaval of flailing legs and humped muscle, the lightweight came out on top, like a bantam in the cockpit, amid a triumphant flutter of wings, spurs and waving crests. It now seemed better so. She held Casilda in the scissor grasp, and their joint movement, fast and furious, grew, rose, galloped, pounded, swelled to Valkyrian speed . . . when the door behind me opened, and Andrew walked in.

He must have used the back way. He stopped dead in his tracks and stared at the scene that confronted him, but said nothing. I handed him a drink off the mantlepiece, which one of our women had sipped and left. We stood side by side in front of the fire, watching with all eyes. Still he did not speak. I was glad. Only brute force could have separated them. It would not take long . . . suddenly there was a single loud, sharp cry from both their throats – followed, seconds later, by a choking, breathless rattle of joy that fell away in the lost, heavy silence. Languidly Janet withdrew, as a man does, quitting the flattened body that has received the gift of his sperm. She staggered slightly and dropped into a chair. I passed her the rest of my cognac. We gazed at Casilda, lying motionless and spent, lax and spread-eagled on the sofa, as uncovered and starkly indecent as a corpse. When she moved at last, and looked at us, it was to clutch at her fork, her throbbing parts, with a quick shiver and a broad, quiet smile; but not to shield the wound or hide her trembling flesh from view. Her playful fingers parted it in fact, lightly toying with the matted curls, stroking the flushed red rim all round, as though applying an oily balm to soothe a gently tickling sore, and skimming down its blatantly bare, gaping length, as in a quick canoe between bushy banks, she sighed, arched her back lazily, with yearning, and rolled her tousled head upon the cushions. We knew what she wanted – a different, immediate and deeper solace. She had made that plain enough.

'Take pity on her,' I said to Andrew, 'since she's asking for it. You have my permission.'

He glanced at Janet, who nodded. 'And mine,' she said.

'No – that won't quite do.' It was Casilda who spoke, to our surprise, as though she could not yet have revived sufficiently to communicate with us directly by word of mouth, but must continue to emply her more expressive sign language.

'Both men – I'll have you both,' she said, sitting up. 'That's it, that's what I want – and always did. Hurry, can't you – get undressed! One in front and one behind. We can manage that if we try . . .'

It took some managing. Andrew had already torn off his clothes, before I could work out what Casilda meant or how she proposed to set about it. She sat huddled demurely on her tail now, a caricature of modesty, waiting. She studied us carefully although of course she didn't need to examine me, it all depended on Andrew. He was enormous. The tool he carried was a long, gnarled, hefty great club – a bludgeon. I was astonished. Casilda's eyes opened wide. She wet her lips. For such a little fellow, upon my soul, you would scarcely believe it possible – the most lavish endowment, and considering that it did not show up to advantage, under that bulging stomach, frankly excessive, an outsized monstrosity. How women can contemplate such repulsive objects without flinching in horror at the sight, they alone know! It had a curve on it like a rhinoceros horn or a hockey stick – and no less vast were the balls, slung in a hideous, wrinkled sack, as big as a cantaloupe. The corona itself was a dark, bursting ripe red plum, stuck on at the end of a thick, knotted bare branch – nothing short of grotesque. There we were, standing to attention, with weapons at the ready, presenting arms for Casilda's inspection. She leaned forward, putting out a hand to each of us, in an unconscious, ribald parody of a royal command soiree, assessing our offers – medium and immoderate – with judicious concentration on the big problem that faced or otherwise intimately concerned her.

In point of fact the choice was obvious; but she anointed us both for her own ends, when Janet's sisterly perception had sent her post-haste from the room, to the medicine chest, on an errand of mercy. The sofa looked a bit cramped, I thought, for the three of us, but Casilda shook her head when I beckoned her to the wide, woolly hearthrug, and, firmly drawing the two members of her party towards the couch, she lay down on her side, without letting go of us, as we loomed above her, wondering what to do next. There was only one solution, which Janet, the idle spectator, promptly advised, though it probably dawned on us all simultaneously. We turned Casilda on to her back. Andrew got up into position with some effort and misguided vigour, yet not so precipitately as the pawing stallion who needs assistance to put him into a proper fix, oddly enough, rather than to pull him out of a hole – and they settled down to it straightaway, going great guns, hard on the job with everything they had.

It was a sight to see, and thrilling to overhear, for they made the deuce of a noise, rootling like stoats, though neither of them said a word. None of us had a stitch on. A lurid light shone in Janet's eyes, as she hovered and circled around the inebriate pair, like a referee. I hopped, in sheer torture, from foot to foot, torn between fiendish impatience and jealousy. My turn would come to repay this lewd, hot-slotted nympho in kind, and I hoped it would hurt the crazy, cock-struck whore – hell take her grinding guts, I'd give it to the bitch till she laughed on the wrong side of her foul, fat fanny, damn it. I'd shoot some decent good sense up her leching, bawdy bum and fill my lovely lady with a jolt from a prick every bit as rich and randy as his ... but when? Would they never stop? She was carried away completely, curse her, she had forgotten all about me. He'd spend, and spoil half our fun in a minute, if she didn't watch out ... ought I to take the risk and cut in? Where was Janet? She'd serve, at a pinch. It was then, praise be, that Casilda rolled over, pushing the chap with her, jabbing him in the ribs, shoving them around, both of them, to lie, still copulating like monkeys, on their sides, with him facing out towards the fireplace, his back against the sofa, and she, in reverse, showing me her buttocks, the white, milky full moon of her bottom turned to me. There it was at last, beaming, big, broad and beautiful, in all its innocence or insolence, bland or crass, according to how one looked on it, delivered into my power as a hostage, meat indeed for the slaughter, rakish and docile, the sinful flesh ...

It was worth a further fleeting delay, a moment's scrutiny. I bent over the two-back beast, ran my hand along the steep ravine between the smooth, cool cheeks, which jounced about distractingly under stern orders from in front, though Casilda thrust her tail outwards as far as she dared while I probed the pursued little brown buttonhole, like the bud of a tiny wild-flower, with my fingertip at first, and then, flinging myself on the sofa behind her, and prising the massive mounds apart, with an inch or so of the old codger himself. Easy does it, in he goes – just as slippery and sweet as you please ... no trouble at all –

for a couple of split seconds, that is, until we got the warhead in place, truly embedded, streaking up her fundament like a dentist's drill through a temporary stopping, an express train roaring full-on into a tunnel, a bull-dozer boring a trench in a stiffly packed squelch of clay. But then, ye gods, what a to-do! What shrill yelps and yells, what wriggling, tugging and dodging, what tearful entreaties, elbowings, fisticuffs, and ghastly oaths! I held on to her grimly by one hip, with the other arm around her neck, and ploughed on, regardless of the cloudburst, which passed and was gone in a few more shakes at the crucial base of the triangle . . .

The last of this trio, however, was the first to quit. It wasn't my fault. I had shot my bolt a little while before the others finished – which apparently they did, bringing it off very adroitly, together. I might have lasted out, too, if Janet had not seen fit to chip in as an auxiliary to our already somewhat overcrowded act by prodding me from the rear and swiping at my backside with her open palm, just when we were all approaching the terrific climax of our intricate three-fold exercise. It's true that I was teetering on the sofa's edge the whole time, and nearly got butted off on to the floor once or twice, because there simply wasn't room for three on it: Casilda had her arms and legs coiled around Andrew in a ferocious hug to keep him in place, the couch was far too short, we stuck out in every direction like a cactus patch. But Janet's well meant intervention hastened my undoing.

I started to dress, and Andrew was about to follow suit, but his wife would not hear of it. She had snuggled up next to Casilda, cooing affectionately, but her hackles rose on the instant when she saw what was afoot.

'Hey, no you don't!' she cried with comic indignation, although quite seriously. 'That's all jolly fine – but what about me? You two stay right where you are, until I'm given just the same treatment as Casilda here. How frightfully ungallant of you, Tony, to try to sneak out on me, again! Really you're both absolute bounders, I do think. But I shan't allow it! I won't have you make such cads of yourselves. Come here!'

'Janet, honey,' I pleaded, 'have a heart! With the best will in the world . . .' I pointed to my cock. It was shrivelled and limp.

Andrew's, as she could see for herself, was in an even more pitiful plight – shrunk to a third of its former size, it hung down only a quarter of the way to his knees, like a discarded old rope end, frayed and soggy. Ugly enough at the peak of its rampant grandeur, now, in this tatty, slack, bedraggled state, it was simply revolting.

'I'd be no lousy use to you, my sweet,' he protested mildly. 'Another day – '

'Come here!' she repeated. 'We'll look into this . . .'

We were leaning against the mantlepiece, side by side, warming our backs at the fire. We did not budge – so Janet dropped on her haunches between us on the hearthrug. She refused to lose faith. She was not going to take no for an answer. We swayed, drooping before her very eyes, our crinkled, deflated organs dangling under her nose. She set to, an ardent revivalist, tackling the desperate, double task with both hands. I got the left, her better one – and she took us to task with both hands at once. She was making a lovely job of it, quite like old times . . . soon it was better still: I got her undivided attention, when Casilda flopped down beside her, and took over half the work. Now Janet could devote herself wholeheartedly to doing one thing at a time – too beautiful for words . . . her undivided attention was nothing if not widespread . . . she flag-wagged signals to Casilda, reporting progress, while simultaneously she massaged my scrotum and slid a hand between by legs, to visit warmer regions, where a venturesome middle finger went on an expedition to explore the interior ... Janet was never so rash and clumsy as to frig a fellow at all strenuously until it was required of her. In my present condition, any but the most gradual first aid would have proved fatal. She rubbed and kneaded my testicles, pinching and playing with them, while merely brushing and stroking my phallus, as though to chafe and polish it, with a certain curious maternal fondness, for its own sake. Comparing by results – which are, after all, what counts- I'd have said she ran rings round Casilda; but I may have been biased by gratitude in her favour – especially when she went the whole hog and adopted heroic measures, with her tongue at first, then her lips, and finally her mouth, that other vulva, a cavity as scorching-hot and spongy but twice as clever ...

We were the more advanced; Casilda was finding it an uphill, gruelling chore to strike a spark into that dormant, mouldy member, so she consulted me with an air of punctilious servility. 'May I? she asked. I gestured dumb assent. She clapped her kisser like a leech to his gross organ, which had begun to swell and stretch by infinitely small degrees, like some slow-waking giant. There, she had something to be going on with! Personally, my cure was almost complete ... we looked like queer bookends, the four of us, like heraldic supporters or carved figures, flanking the chimney piece, although the caryatids knelt, shoulder to shoulder, while the quaking male pillars could barely stand upright, but had to be propped and girded, fore and aft by sustained, intimate pressures from below. We were lifted and wired underneath, Andrew and I, to make a peculiar nude frieze and our two ministering angels, the fairer and the darker, identical in their position yet so different in build, the one full-bodied and shapely, the other spare and lithe. With heads bent over their labours, noses to the grindstone their agitated mops of hair were hoisted on our joysticks at half-mast, as though luxuriant, extra fleece

139

had sprouted from his protruding paunch, and my pale belly. Casilda linked the circuit by lending a hand to fiddle with Janet's pussy – a bonus which Janet promptly requited in kind. Andrew's arm lay, lightly touching mine, along the mantleshelf.

Casilda took command as mistress of ceremonies, but Janet jibbed at the sofa, like a horse at a hedge, so our tricky threesome was accomplished this time, in the end and with equal or even greater difficulty, after various vain attempts on the rug, when Andrew was shored up with pillows on the edge of a large armchair, Janet impaled herself upon his prong, to sprawl face down on top of him, crushing him against the springs and hitching herself high up into the air for me eventually to perforate at my leisure, though not with some jabbing and incitements from Casilda, who skipped around the simmering stewpot like a witch doctor. My orgasm was the last – a feather in my cap, I thought – and for a few moments after we were through with the smothered underdog, Janet and I shunted to and fro in ecstasy, a toppling pile of flesh, like a three-decker sandwich, that sagged to rest where it lay, until Casilda called us to get a bit to eat in the kitchen, which Andrew aptly compared to a nudist's canteen.

'Whenever you feel like a return match,' said Casilda brightly as we left, 'just let us know.'

THE ROMANCE OF LUST

The Romance of Lust, or Early Experiences *is one of the world's most notorious erotic texts. Here is a veritable cornucopia of lubricity from the Victorian era featuring possibly the most precocious and prodigious of sexual heroes, young Charlie Roberts. His remorseless pursuit of a thorough sexual education is spread over the course of four volumes, leaving the reader panting with exhaustion and our hero – incredibly – panting for more. It is the youthful Charlie's greatest delight to lure his elders and supposed betters into compromising positions and scarcely a member of his family can resist his phallic charm. However, in this excerpt from the opening of Volume Four, we see the indefatigable Charlie spreads his net beyond his own relations and undertakes the wholesale seduction of his landlady's family . . .*

I had taken lodgings in Norfolk Street, Strand, for the convenience of being near King's College. It was at the house of a Mrs. Nichols, tall, powerfully built, masculine, but a kind and motherly looking widow of fifty-two – an attentive and bustling landlady, looking herself to the better cooking, and having a plain cook, who was also a general servant, to help her downstairs, and two nieces to do the waiting and attendance on her lodgers upstairs. The younger was there alone when I entered the lodgings; her elder sister had had what they called a 'misfortune,' and was then in the country until she could be unburthened of it. She was expected back in about six weeks. Meanwhile, as the winter was not the season, I was the only lodger, and the younger had only me to attend to; her name was Jane; she was but a little thing, but very well made, good bubbies and bottom, which I soon discovered were firm and hard, projecting fully on both sides. She was fairly good looking, but with a singular innocent manner of freedom about her that made me imagine she had as yet had no chance of a 'misfortune.' In a week we became intimate, and after often praising her pretty face and figure, I snatched a kiss now and then, which at first she resented with an attractive yet innocent sort of sauciness. It was in her struggles on these occasions that I became aware of the firm hard bosom and bottom.

Up to this time my flirtations were without ulterior object, but the reality of the attractions of these hidden charms raised my lustful passions. I gradually increased my flatteries and caresses, squeezed her bubbies, when I sometimes drew her on my knee and was kissing her, and as at first she resisted my drawing her to my knee, I took occasion to lay hold of her buttocks, which I found more developed than I could have supposed. Gradually her resistance to these little liberties ceased and she would quietly sit on my knee and return the kiss I gave. Her dress was a little open in front, so from feeling her bubbies outside, I gradually got to feeling their naked beauties inside. I now thought I could attempt greater familiarities, so one day when seated on my knee with one arm round her waist, I pressed her to my lips, and while so engaged, whipped my free arm up her petticoats, and before she had become aware of the movement, had got my hand upon her mount, a very nicely haired one, She started up to a standing position, but as I held her close clasped round the waist she could not get away, and her new position enabled me the easier to get my hand between her thighs and thus to feel her charming pouting little cunt. I began attempting to frig her clit-oris, but stooping she drew her cunt away, and looking at me with a droll innocent expression of alarm, and with a perfect unconsciousness of the import of her words, cried, – 'Oh! take care what you are at. You don't know how a lodger this last summer suffered for seizing me in that way and hurting me very much. I

144

screamed out, aunt came up, and, do you know, he had £50 to pay for his impudence.'

I could not but smile at the extraordinary innocence of the girl.

'But I do not hurt you, dear Jane,' said I, 'and don't mean to do so.'

'That was what he said, but he went on in a most horrible way, and not only hurt me very much, but made me bleed.'

'It would not be with his hand, you see I only gently press this soft hairy little thing. I am sure that don't hurt you.'

'Oh no! if that was all I should not mind it, it was when he pushed me on the sofa, and pressed upon me, that he hurt me terribly, and you must take care what you are about, or you too will have to pay £50.'

There was a curious air of innocence in all this; it was evident to me the fellow had got into her, and broken her hymen with violence, and then her screams had prevented his finishing his work. Her manner convinced me that she was really not aware of the consequences, or rather had not as yet really had her sexual passions aroused.

'Well, my dear Jane, I neither intend to hurt you or make myself liable to pay £50, but you will not refuse me the pleasure of feeling this nice little hairy nest, you see how gentle I am.'

'Well, if you will do me no more hurt than that I shan't refuse you, because you are a nice kind young gentleman, and very different from the other rough fellow, who never chattered with me and made me laugh as you do – but you must not push your fingers up there, it was something he pushed up there that hurt me so.'

I withdrew my finger and as, at my request, she had opened her thighs a little, I felt and caressed her very nice little cunt, and with a finger pressed externally above her clitoris, I could see that she flushed and shivered on feeling me there. However, I did no more than gently press and feel all her hairy mount and fat pouting cunt; she said I must let her go, or her aunt would be coming up.

The first step was now gained. Gradually I progressed further and further; felt her charming bare arse as she stood before me, got her to let me see the beautiful curls she had got on her cunt, then came to kissing it, until at last she opened her thighs and let me tongue it, to her most exquisite delight. I made her spend for the first time in her life, and soon she came to me for it. I had gradually introduced a finger up her cunt while licking her clitoris and exciting her so much that she was unconscious of my doing it; then two fingers, and after she had spent deliciously, I made them perform an imitation of a throb, which made her jump and ask what I was doing. I asked if she did not feel that my fingers were inside of her sweet Fanny.

'You don't say so. It was there I was so hurt.'

'But I do not hurt you, dear Jane?'

'Oh, dear no, it makes me feel queer, but it is very nice.'

'Well, now you know that I have two fingers inside, I will use my tongue again against your charming little clitoris, and work the fingers in and out.'

I did so, and she soon spent in an agony of delight, pressing my head down hard on her cunt, and crying – 'Oh! oh! it is too great a pleasure!' and then died off, half insensible. Another time I repeated this she told me not to forget to use my fingers. Having made her spend twice I took her on my knee, and told her that I possessed an instrument that would give her far more pleasure than tongue or finger.

'Indeed?' said she, 'where is it? I should so like to see it.'

'You won't tell.'

'Oh, no!'

So pulling out my stiff-standing prick, she stared in

amazement. She had really never seen a prick, although it was evidently a prick that had deflowered her, for with my fingers I had explored her cunt, and found no hymen there. I put her hand upon it; she involuntarily grasped it firmly.

'This enormous thing could never get into my body, look, it is thicker than all your fingers put together, and only two fingers feel so tight.'

'Yes, darling, but this dear little thing stretches, and was made to receive this big thing.'

I was exciting her clitoris with my finger, she grew evidently lasciviously inclined, so saying, 'Just let me try, and if it hurts you I will stop; you know I am always gentle with you.'

'So you are, my dear fellow, but take care not to hurt me.'

She lay down on the bed, as I desired, with feet up and knees laid open. I spat on my prick, and wetted the knob and upper shaft well, then bringing it to her cunt, well moistened by my saliva in gamahuching her, I held open the lips with the fingers of my left hand, and half buried its knob before getting to the real entrance.

'Don't flinch, dearest, I shall not hurt,' And I got it well over the knob, and buried it one inch further.

'Stop!' she cried, 'it seems as it would burst me open, it so stretches me.'

'But it does not hurt you, dearest?' I had immediately stopped before asking the question.

'No not exactly, but I feel as if something was in my throat.'

'Rest a little, and that will go off.' I slipped a finger down on her clitoris, and as I frigged it she grew more and more excited, giving delicious cunt pressures on my prick, it gradually made its way by the gently pushing I continued to make without other movements. It was more than half in when she spent, this not only lubricated the interior, but the inner muscles

147

relaxing, a gentle shove forward housed it to the hilt, and then I lay quiet until she recovered from the half fainting state her last discharge had produced; soon the increased pressures of the inner folds showed that her passions were awakening afresh. She opened her eyes and, looking lovingly, said I have given her great pleasure, but she felt as if something enormous was stretching her inside to the utmost. Had I got it all in?

'Yes, dearest, and now it will be able to give you greater pleasure than before.' I began a slow withdrawal and return, frigging her clitoris at the same time, for I was standing between her legs. She soon grew wild with excitement, nature prompting her, her arse rose and fell almost as well as if she was mistress of the art. The novel combination of prick and finger quickly brought on the ecstatic crisis. I, too, was wild with lust, and we spent together, ending in an annihilation of all our senses by the extreme ecstasy of the final overpowering crisis. We lay panting for some time in all the after-joys. Dear Jane begged me to give her some water, as she felt quite faint. I withdrew, still almost in a standing state, got her some water, helped her up, seated her on the sofa and kissed her lovingly as I thanked her for the exquisite joy she had given me. She threw her arms round my neck, and with tears in her eyes told me I had taught her the joys of heaven, and she should always love me, and I must always love her, for now she could not live without me. I kissed and dried her eyes, and told her we should in future enjoy it even more when she got accustomed to it.

'Let me see the dear thing that gave me such pleasure.'

I pulled it out, but it was no longer at the stand; and this surprised her. I explained the necessity of its being so, but said she would quickly see it rise and swell to the former size if she continued to handle it so nicely. It rose almost before I could say as much. She fondled it, and even stooped and kissed its ruby head. We should quickly have got to another bout of fucking if the ringing of the call bell had not brought us to a sense of its imprudence; so after arranging her hair and dress, she hastily descended with some of the breakfast things.

Of course, so good a beginning led to constant renewals and Jane quickly became extremely amorous, and under my instruction a first-rate fucker.

As all my dear friends were not in London, I was fortunate in having such a *bonne bouche* to comfort me. My sisters passed every Sunday with me, and both got some good fucking out of me in every way, without raising any suspicions in the house.

A month after I had taken up my residence at Mrs. Nichols's, Jane's sister arrived. She was a much finer woman than Jane, broad shouldered, wide-spread bosom, which, in after-days, I found had not suffered by her 'misfortune,' but then she had not suckled it. Her hips were widely projected, and she was grand and magnificent in her arse. Naturally of a very hot temperament, when once she had tasted the magnificent weapon I was possessed of, she grew most lasciviously lustful, and was one of the best fuckers I ever met with. Her power of nip almost equalled my beloved aunt's. Jane was fair, Ann was dark, with black locks and black hairy cunt – a very long cunt, with a small tight hole in it, and above it a wide-spread projecting mount, splendidly furnished with hair. Her clitoris was hard and thick, but with little projection. She also became madly fond of arse-fucking, and particularly liked me to spend therein. This was partly to prevent any consequences leading to a second 'misfortune.'

On her first arrival Jane was much afraid she would discover our connection and we took every precaution, although I, in my heart, wished this might occur, for as she occasionally waited on me, I grew lecherous upon one whose charms, even covered, excited me greatly. I always flattered and praised her magnificence of figure whenever she came alone to me, but as Jane generally was running in and out, I did not attempt further action. One morning I overheard Mrs. Nichols tell Jane to put on her bonnet and go to Oxford Street on some errand; I knew thus that Ann would attend on me, and there would be no chance of interruption from Jane, so I determined to come at once to the point. We had become on friendly, chatty terms, and when she had laid breakfast I asked her to help me me on with my coat, which done, I thanked her and with one arm round her waist drew her to me and kissed her. 'Hallo!' said she, 'that is something new,' but did not attempt to withdraw, so giving her another kiss, I told her what a glorious woman she was, and how she excited me – just see. I held one of her hands, and before she was aware, placed it on my huge prick, that bulged out of my trousers as if it would burst its way through.

She could not help squeezing it, while she cried -

'Goodness, gracious! what an enormous thing you have got!'

Her face flushed, her eyes sparkled with the fire of lust that stirred her whole soul. She tried to grasp it.

'Stop,' said I, 'and I will put it in its natural state into your hand.'

So pulling it out, she seized it at once, and most lasciviously gazed upon it, pressing it gently. She evidently was growing lewder and lewder, so I at once proposed to fuck her, and thinking it best to be frank, and put her at her ease, I told her that I knew she had had a 'misfortune,' but if she would let me fuck her I should be on honour to withdraw before spending, and thus avoid all chance of putting her belly up.

She had become so randy that she felt, as she afterwards told me, she could not refuse so splendid a prick of a size she had often dreamt of, and longed for.

'Can I trust you?' said she.

'Safely, my dear.'

'Then you may have me – let me embrace that dear object.'

Stooping, she kissed it most voluptuously, shivering at the same time in the ecstasy of a spend produced by the mere sight and touch. She gave one or two 'ohs,' and drawing me to the bed by my prick, threw herself back, pulling her petticoats up at the same time. Then I beheld her splendid cunt in all its magnificence of size and hairiness. I sank on my knees and glued my lips to the oozing entrance, for she was one who spent most profusely, her cunt had the true delicious odour, and her spunk was thick and glutinous for a woman. I tongued her clitoris, driving her voluptuously wild. So she cried -

'Oh! do put that glorious prick into me, but remember your promise.'

I brought it up to that wide-spread, large-lipped, and immense cunt. I fully expected that big as I was I should slip in over head and shoulders with the greatest ease. So you may imagine my surprise to find the tightest and smallest of entrances to the inner vagina I almost ever met with, it was really with greater difficulty I effected an entrance than I had with her little sister, whose cunt presented no such voluptuous grandeur. It was as tight a fit as Ellen's was to me on our first coition. Tight as it was, it gave her nothing but the most exquisite pleasure, she was thoroughly up to her work, and was really one of the most voluptuous and lascivious fuckers I have ever met with, excellent as my experience has been. I made her, with fucking and frigging, spend six times before I suddenly withdrew my prick, and pressing its shaft against her wet lips, and my own belly, spent deliciously outside. Shortly after it rose again, and this time after making her spend as often as before, for she was most voluptuously lustful, when I withdrew, she suddenly got from under me, and seizing its shaft with one hand, stooped and took its knob between her lips, and quickly made me pour a flood of sperm into her mouth, which she eagerly swallowed and sucked on to my great delight.

We should have had a third bout but for the necessity of her going down to her aunt.

I breakfasted, then rang to take away. Again we had a delicious fuck, and a third when she came to make the bed and empty the slops. This third time I begged her to kneel on the sofa, and let me see her gloriously grand arse, and when I had to retire I would show her a way that would continue both our pleasure. So after fucking her from behind, and making her spend far oftener than me, I withdrew, and pushing it up between the lips over the clitoris, with my hand round her waist. I pressed it tightly against her cunt and clitoris, and continued to wriggle my arse, made her spend again as I poured a flood all over her belly. She declared it was almost as good as if inside.

After this very shortly I proposed to push its nose into her bottom-hole, and just spend within.

With reluctance at first, it ended in her not only liking the point there, but deliciously enjoying my whole prick within, and eventually it was always the receptacle of a first discharge induced by fucking, and a second fuck completely carried on in that more secret altar of lust. She became a first-rate *enculeuse*.

It soon happened that both sisters knew of the other enjoying me, and it ended in their slipping down from their attic, where both slept in the same bed, to my room, and we had most delicious fucking and double gamahuching.

Ann was by far the finest and the most lascivious fuck, but little Jane had a certain charm of youth and also of freshness, which got her a fair share of my favours.

We carried this on for several weeks until use made us careless and noisy.

The aunt, when no lodgers occupied the room, slept

overhead, and, probably being sleepless one morning, when it was early daylight, heard our voices, came down and surprised me in the very act of fucking Ann and gamahuching Jane, who stood above her and presented her cunt to my lecherous tongue. A loud exclamation from their aunt roused us up at once.

'Get to bed, you dreadful hussies.'

They fled without a moment's hesitation.

Mrs. Nichols then began to remonstrate with me on the infamy of my conduct. I approached the door apparently to get my shirt, for I was stark naked, but in fact to shut and lock my door, and then to turn on Mrs. Nichols, who apparently had quite forgotten she had only her short shift on, which not only allowed the full display of very fine, firm and ample bubbies, but not falling below the middle of her thighs, showed remarkably well made legs and small knees, with the swelling of immense thighs just indicated.

My stiff-standing prick in full vigour, and if anything still more stimulated by the unexpected beauties shown by Mrs. Nichols, I turned upon her and seizing her round the waist from behind, pushed her forward, and before she could recover herself I had hauled up her 'cutty sark,' seen a most magnificent arse, and into her cunt – not without somewhat painful violence, before she could recover from the surprise of the attack.

She screamed out murder, but there was no one who could hear but the girls, and they knew better than to interrupt me. I kept fucking away in spite of cries, and passing an arm round her body, with my finger I got to her clitoris, which sprang out into considerable proportions. My big prick and the frigging of her clitoris produced their natural result. In spite of herself she grew full of lust. I felt her cunt pressures, and knew how her passions were rising. Speedily, in place of resisting, she began to cry, 'Oh, oh,' and breathe hard, and then most gloriously wriggled her splendid arse, and as I spent she too was taken in the delicious ecstasy of the final crisis. She lay throbbing on my delighted prick until it stood as stiff as before. I began a slow movement, she made no resistance, except crying out, 'Oh! dear, oh! dear,' as if in spite of regrets, she could not help enjoying it; indeed, at last she said -

'Oh! what a man you are, Mr. Roberts; it is very wrong of you to do this, but I cannot resist enjoying it myself. It is years since I did such a thing, but as you have done it, it makes me wish you should do it again. Let us change position.'

'Very well, but you must throw off this tiresome chemise, or I won't withdraw.'

As her lust was so excited, she made no objection, so withdrawing we stood up; she drew her shift over her head, and displayed a far more splendid form, with an exquisitely fair and dimpled skin, than I could have thought possible.

'My dear Mrs. Nichols, what a fine perfect form you have got, let me embrace you in my arms.'

She was nothing loath, flattered by my praise. She laid hold of my cock with one hand, and closely clasped me with the other arm, while I threw an arm and hand round on her truly magnificent arse, and with my other hand pressed on a wonderful pair of bubbies as hard and firm as any maid of eighteen. Our mouths met in a loving kiss, our tongues exchanged endearments. She said -

'You have made me very wicked, let me have this enormous and dear fellow again.'

I said I must first gaze on all her beauties, especially on her gorgeous and enormous bottom. She turned herself round in every way, delighted to find that I so ardently admired her.

She then lay down on her back, and spread wide her legs, and called to me to mount and put it in.

'First I must kiss this beautiful cunt, and suck this superb clitoris.'

Her mount was covered with closely curled brown silky locks; her cunt was large with grand thick lips and well-haired sides. Her clitoris stood out quite three inches, red and stiff. I took it in my mouth, sucked it, and frigged her cunt with two fingers, which went in with the greatest ease, but were nipped tightly the moment the entrance was gained, and I frigged and sucked until she spent madly with absolute screams of delight. I continued to suck and excite her, which quickly made her cry out -

'Oh, darling boy, come and shove your glorious prick into my longing cunt.'

I sprang up and buried him until our two hairs were crushed between us. She held me tight for a minute without moving, then went off like a wild *Bacchante*, and uttered voluptuous bawdy expressions.

'Shove your delicious prick further and harder. Oh, you are killing me with delight.'

She was a perfect mistress of the art, gave me exquisite pleasure, and, I may add, proved afterwards a woman of infinite variety, and became one of my most devoted admirers. Our intrigue continued for years, while her age, as is the case with good wine, only appeared to improve her. Her husband was not a bad fucker, but having only a small prick, had never stimulated her lust as my big splitter had done.

We had on this first occasion three other good fucks, which she seemed to enjoy more and more.

As I had previously fucked the girls pretty well, my prick at last refused to perform. We had to stop fucking, but I gamahuched her once more after again posing her, and admiring her really wonderfully well made and well-preserved body. She had a good suck at my cock, without bringing him up again.

At last we separated, but not before she made a promise that she would sleep with me that night, and a glorious night we had. I had the more difficult task of reconciling her to my having her nieces. I used to have them one night, and sleep with her the next.

Ann, as I have said, was one of the lewdest and most lascivious women I had ever known. I had told them of the beauty of their aunt's whole person, and of her wonderful clitoris, and how she liked me to gamahuche it. This awakened the tribadic passions of Ann to gamahuche her aunt.

I, at last, persuaded her to let Ann join us, and both were afterwards extremely glad I had done so, for both were thorough tribades, and lasciviously enjoyed each other, while being fucked by me in turns. Mrs. Nichols too, once she got used to arse-fucking, delighted in it, and we had the wildest orgies together.

SPORT AMONG THE SHE-NOODLES

The hearty tone of late-Victorian pornography to be found in The Romance of Lust *rang loud and clear in certain naughty periodicals of the time such as* The Pearl *and* The Boudoir. *This is the origin of the following piece which bears all the hallmarks of this particular style. The narrator, Walter, tells the tale of a visit to his cousins, three sisters and a brother, at his uncle's country residence in Sussex. Walter is a jolly fellow and his cousins sporting types. One thing you can be sure of in a sex romp of this nature – nobody is going to be left out . . .*

Next day being the last representation of a celebrated piece at the theatre of the County Town, by a first-rate London company, papa expressed a wish that we should all go in the evening, but Annie and Sophie, giving me a knowing look on the sly, declared they had already seen it once and did not care to go again. For my part, of course, I had seen it half-a-dozen times in town, so it was finally arranged that Frank, Rosa and Polly only would go with papa and mama; they had a drive of more than an hour before them so started at 6 P.M., and as soon as they were out of sight we three started for the bathing place at the lake. It was such a deliciously warm evening, and it would be just the place for our anticipated pleasures, as I had suggested to Annie and Sophie during the day.

Bolting the summer-house door on the inside as soon as we got in, I suggested first of all to stimulate our mutually ardent desires by a bottle of champagne; this so exhilarated the two lovely girls that we indulged in

a second bottle before stripping for a romp. Seven
o'clock found us bathed in a flood of golden light from
the declining sun, which now shone directly in upon
us, this warned us to make haste and improve the
opportunity, so each one assisting the others and at
the same time indulging in many loving tricks and
liberties, we were soon in Adam and Eve costume.

'Now,' I exclaimed, 'Annie dear, you won't be jealous
if I make a woman of your sister, as we promised the
other day,' taking the youngest one up in my arms
with my rampant cock throbbing against her belly, as
I carried her to the lounge.

'What a naughty boy you are, Walter, anything or
anybody for a change is what fickle men like, but I
won't be jealous of Sophie, although I am of Mrs.
Leslie. I know you had her yesterday; that sheepish
tell-tale look, sir, when you met me on your return,
was enough to confirm my suspicions of what would
happen when you were *tête-a-tête* with that killing
lady,' she replied.

'For shame, Annie darling, you told me yourself the
other day love ought to be free everywhere; I don't
deny my guilt, but will do my best to earn forgiveness
now,' I said, pushing Sophie back upon the soft yielding
lounge, 'help me to ease this darling of her troublesome
virginity, and I will then repay your own longing
cunny for all your love and forebearance; I am sure
Mrs. Leslie would like to make you one of our party
without any feelings of jealousy; there are so many
ways of voluptuous enjoyment that if only one man to
three beautiful girls it can be so varied as to give
everyone the most intense delight.'

At this both the girls gave me rapturous kisses,
with every possible assurance that they would never be
selfish, and would be only to happy to extend the circle
of those they could be free and loving with, adding
with special emphasis, 'We are such noodles, dear
Walter, we knew nothing till you introduced us to the

arts of love, and as long as you can stay with us shall look up to you to guide us in everything; we know it's wrong, but what heavenly pleasure there is in the loving mixture of the sexes.'

ANNIE, taking my prick in her hand. – 'Now, sir I will show this gentleman the way into Sophie's cabinet of love; be firm, dear, he won't hurt you more than can be helped, and the after joy will soon drown all recollection of the first short suffering.'

SOPHIE, opening her legs as wide as possible. – 'I'm all on fire to taste the real tree of love, don't spare me, Walter, dear, I'd rather die than not have it now!'

The red head of 'Cupid's Battering Ram' was now brought to the charge; Annie opened the rosy lips of her sister's cunt and placed my cock in the exact position, but her touches, together with the thoughts of the delicious titbit I was about to enjoy, caused me to spend in a moment all over her fingers and into the virgin passage in front. 'Push on, push on; now's the time to gain your victory,' she whispered; 'that will make it easier to get him in,' at the same time lifting up Sophie's buttocks with her disengaged hand, so as to make her meet my attack in a more favourable manner. My first lunge lodged the head of Mr. Priapus fairly within the tight folds of the victim's vagina, and I had already won the first outworks of the virgin's defences.

Poor Sophie moaned under the sharp pain of my assault, but biting her lips to repress any cries of pain she courageously placed one hand on the shaft of my prick, as if jealous of her sister's loving help, and anxious to have the honour of herself showing me the way to achieve love's dearest triumph, or perhaps it was for fear of my withdrawing before completely accomplishing my task.

'You love!' I exclaimed, enraptured by this exhibition of pluck, 'I will soon make a real woman of you,' then pushing fiercely on, on, I gradually forced the tight sheath to dilate. Every obstruction gave way to my determined energy, and with a final plunge, I was buried to the roots of my affair, and shooting at the same moment my warm spendings into her inmost vitals. This exhausted me for a few moments, and I lay supine upon the heaving bosom of the lovely Sophie, till I could feel Annie's fingers busy tickling my balls and feeling the shaft of my cock. Just at the same moment Sophie, who had almost fainted under the painful ordeal, opened her eyes, and with a loving smile pouted her lips as an invitation for a kiss, which I instantly responded to, almost sucking her breath away in my ardour. My excitement was now raised to the highest possible pitch by her sister's titillations, and the loving challenge of Sophie herself to renew my motions with her, by heaving up her bottom and nipping my prick in her cunny in the most delightful way imaginable.

This time I prolonged the pleasure as much as possible, beginning slowly, and often stopping to feel the delicious throbbing of cock and cunny in their delightful conjunction. 'Ach! this is indeed love; it repays for all the pain I felt at first. Oh! oh! dear Walter, it feels as if my very soul was flowing from me in ecstasy!' she almost screamed out, kissing, biting, squeezing me with all her might at the moment of emission, which I again responded to with a flow of my own sperm.

I now declared we must refresh ourselves a little before going further, so she reluctantly allowed me to withdraw. A short plunge in the lake had a most invigorating effect. I felt as strong as a giant again, then another bottle of fizz renewed our loving ardour; the girls were handling my prick, which stood again as hard as ivory. So slipping on my shirt, as I intended to be the uppermost of the trio, I laid Sophie on her back, and the telling the obedient Annie to kneel over her sister and gamahuche her in return for Sophie's doing the same to her, I mounted up behind her, saying, 'I've made a woman of your dear sister, and will now treat you, my darling, to a new sensation.' But just at the moment Sophie, who had no idea of my intentions, seized hold of my cock, saying, 'She must kiss the dear sweet thing, which had afforded her such exquisite bliss.' Holding it tight in her hand, she took the head between her pearly teeth and kissed and treated him to such love bites that I soon spent in her mouth, which she greedily swallowed, with all the abandon of voluptuous enjoyment. Meanwhile, I had been frigging Annie's bottom with my two fingers, which I had managed to insert together, and that dear girl was sucking her sister's quim, and wriggling herself in the most excitable way possible.

Sophie was now going to insert my prick in her sister's cunt, but Annie, almost beside herself with excitement, exclaimed, 'No, no, my dear, put him where Walter has got his fingers; I should like to try that, it is so exciting; the very thought of it makes me mad with desire to know what it is like. His fingers have given me such pleasures that I am sure the dear thing in your hand will greatly improve the sensation!'

No sooner said than done; the obedient girl directed my cock to the beautifully wrinkled tight little brown hole of her sister's bottom at the very moment I withdrew my fingers. When I found they so thoroughly appreciated the idea I had resolved to initiate them into, being well lubricated and as stiff as possible, it soon passed the portals of Annie's second virginity. But, Heavens, what a delicious bout we had, she bounded about so with delight, that I had to hold tight round her neck to prevent being thrown out, whilst Sophie, below, gamahuched her delighted sister, and with her right hand continued to press my balls and prick, keeping time to every insertion in her sister's bottom. We spent together, almost screaming with delight, and then lay in a confused heap, enjoying the sensations of our delicious exhaustion.

As soon as they could kiss and persuade my rather enervated tool into renewed stiffness, Sophie declared I must oblige her with a taste of the new-found joy, and ravish her bottom as well as her sister's.

This was another delicious love engagement; the sisters gamahuching each other with the utmost erotic ardour, whilst my delighted prick revelled in the tight-fitting fundamental of the sweet girl, who wriggled and plunged about so excitedly that I had to hold fast to keep my place.

After this, we returned to the house, and passed the time very pleasantly till the return of the party from the theatre. I was anxious to hear Frank's account of how he had got on with Rosa during the evening, and especially as they drove home.

'Walter,' he said, as we were once more alone in his room after all had gone to rest, 'I've had a most enjoyable time of it since we started. Of course, as we went, it was daylight, so Rosa and I maintained a proper decorum, but at the theatre, papa and mama were separated from us by Polly, and we all five sat in the front row of the dress circle. How the sight of Rosa's swelling bosom (which her low-necked dress allowed me fully to see) made my prick stand at once; so I took her gloved hand and made her feel how hard and excited I was. As no one could see, she indulged me with quite a gentle frigging outside my trousers, till I spent profusely, to the great delight of the roguish beauty, as I could tell by the smile on her face and the excited looks with which she met my ardent gaze.

'What a shame,' she whispered in my ear. 'I know what you have done, you naughty boy. You should have reserved it for a more favourable opportunity.'

'Look out, darling, as we drive home; see if I don't repay your kind attentions,' I whispered in return.

'Both papa and mama were rather sleepy before the conclusion of the last piece, and to make them go off, as soon as we were seated in the carriage, I offered them my flask of brandy to keep out the effects of the night air. It had a pretty good strong dose of narcotic in it, and they were soon sound asleep in their corners. Polly also pretended to be dozing.

'Rosa was on my lap directly, and my hands were at once groping their way to the seat of pleasure whilst she was equally busy unbuttoning my trousers and handling the staff of life.

'Our lips met in long-drawn rapturous kisses, which fired every drop of blood in our veins, and both were too impatient for the real business to prolong our toyings with each other's privates; besides, I felt she was already spending over my busy fingers. She had my cock in a glorious state of erection; so opening her delicious thighs as she raised her clothes, she was at once impaled on the spike she so burned to have thrust into her. It was quite equal to the first time I fucked her. The long evening passed in expectation of what I might be able to do on our return journey; so it added to the piquancy of my arduous longings that I seemed in Heaven itself, and swimming in a very ocean of love, we spent over and over again; our melting kisses and tongue-sucking continually stimulating us to renewed exertions, till the near approach to home warned us of the necessity of bringing our pleasures to an end for a time. Even now, I tell you, Walter, my cock keeps throbbing and standing at the very thoughts of the delightful pressures she treated me to; her cunt bites so deliciously.'

In the morning, papa and mama had scarcely slept off the effects of the sleeping dose they had imbibed from the brandy flask of their dutiful son, and lay abed very late, in fact, almost to luncheon time; meanwhile, we, the younger members of the family, had privately agreed upon a plan of amusement for the afternoon and evening.

Finding that two pretty girls of sixteen and seventeen were living close by, with an invalid mother, whilst their brother was away, being a Midshipman in the Royal Navy, I proposed that Annie should spend the afternoon with us, en famille, without the least ceremony, and join us in any alfresco tea party at a little hut in the woods, which formed part of my uncle's estate.

At luncheon we informed the governor of what we had done and hoped that both he and mama would join in our outdoor party in the woods.

'No thank you, my dears, we are too afraid of the damp grass and rheumatics. Besides, we have not yet gotten over the fatigue of yesterday. We will stay quietly at home and hope you may enjoy yourselves thoroughly, as we should do if we were younger,' replied the jolly, kind-hearted old gentleman.

This was exactly what we had wished for and expected; so Frank and Annie at once sent off the servants with every requisite for our open-air tea party.

About three o'clock, the two young ladies arrived, and as all were ready, we at once set off for the scene of our anticipated fun, which was a rough bower covered with flowering honeysuckle and clematis, at the end of a long, shady, private walk, more than half-a-mile from the house.

Frank and myself particularly attached ourselves to the two fresh young ladies as being the greatest strangers, and therefore justly expectant of the most attention.

Emily Bruce, the eldest, was a charming dark-eyed brunette, her rather large mouth having a fascinating effect as you regarded her. In fact, such a display of pearly white teeth, I never saw before, and the very thought that they might perhaps be soon employed in love bites on my tender-headed prick filled me with maddening lust to possess myself of their owner.

Nor was her sister, Louisa, a bit less prepossessing, she being almost the counterpart of Emily, except that

166

one could easily see there was a slight difference in age.

Arrived at the bower, the servants were at once sent home, being told that they could clear away the things next morning, as it would be late for them to return in the evening, and at the same time, without asking the consent of her young friends, dear Annie scribbled a pencil note to their mama, to say that if they at all were late, she would insist upon them staying with her all night, and not to make herself at all anxious on their behalf – this was quietly sent off by one of the servants.

As soon as we were alone, Frank and I, uncorking the champagne, lighted our cigars, and saying that the sun was still too warm for outdoor romping, pressed the girls to try some very mild cigarettes of Turkish tobacco.

At last Annie and Rosa set the example by lighting up, and were at once laughingly followed by the others. Our two young friends protested they never took wine. Still, they evidently sipped it with great delight, and we bantered them upon being so tied to their mother's apron strings, etc., till they began to be quite free as my cousins and Rosa.

We had a good stock of fizz, besides sandwiches and cake, so that no one seemed at all anxious to take the trouble of tea-making.

Still we were careful that only enough should be taken to warm our friends up to a slightly excitable state, in fact, just to induce that state of all-overishness, which tingles through a young girl's sensitive frame when she feels the first vibrations of amorous desires, which she can as yet hardly understand.

Their sparking eyes, slightly flushed faces and above all, the dazzling beauties of their teeth, as they indulged in gay laughter at our badinage, set all of us aflame. I could see that Rosa and my cousins were longing to help in enjoying these innocent and ravishing young girls.

Now a game of hunt the slipper was proposed, and we at once joined to the soft, mossy green sward, outside the bower. This was a most delicious and excitable romp.

Whenever it came our turns, Frank and myself indulged in all kinds of quick and startling touches, which made the two little dears blush up to their eyes at first, and when we managed to catch one of them with the slipper we claimed a hearty kiss as penalty, which they submitted to with tolerable grace, yet evidently in a state of great excitement, it was all so new to them. We finished the game, had a little more champagne, then proposed a game of hide and seek in the wood, with the reservation that no one was to go too far off.

We were to be in pairs, I chose Emily, and Frank took Louisa. Polly and Sophie went together, whilst Annie and Rosa had to search for us when we called out.

It so happened that there was an old sand pit close by, in which several years before Master Frank had amused himself by making a Robinson Crusoe's cave, and planted bushes in front of it, so that the entrance was perfectly out of sight, and no one would fancy anyone could be screened by the small amount of cover which seemed to grow on the side of the pit; this was just the place for our purpose, and it had been beforehand arranged that we were not to be found for a long time. Gliding into the cave Frank let fall the old curtain that hung at the entrance, and we were at once in the dark, the place was large enough for us to sit together on a heap of fine soft sand at the further end.

'What a dear girl you are!' I whispered in Emily's ear, as I took a kiss in the dark, and drew her trembling body quite close by an arm around her waist.

'Pray don't,' she whispered in return, 'if you do not keep quiet I won't stop in this dark place.'

'Don't say so, it would be cruel, especially if you knew all I feel towards you, Emily dear. I must call you Emily, yes, and kiss you again and again, I love you so, your breath is so fragrant, what are you afraid of, there's nothing to fear among friends, darling,' I whispered, kissing my partner rapturously.

'Oh, ah, you take my breath away Walter, I'm so unused to such goings on. Oh, fie, sir, for shame, you make me feel all of a tremble, you take such liberties!' as I was working one hand inside the bosom of her dress, and getting possession of two hard round bubbies which throbbed with emotion under my loving caresses.

'It's all love, darling, and no one can see, can't you hear how Frank and Louisa are kissing; is it not delicious to think they are doing the same, and will be sure to keep our secret?'

A deep sigh was my only answer, and again our lips met in a long luscious kiss. My tongue was thrust into her mouth, and tickled the tip of her own velvety organ of speech. I could feel the nipples of her virgin bosom stick out as stiff as little cocks and whispered to her to allow me to kiss them.

'I can refuse you nothing,' she whispered; 'you are such a bold lover. I'm all in flame from head to foot at the numberless liberties you are taking with me. Ah, if mam only knew,' she sighed, as I was now sucking her titties, and running my disengaged hand up her thighs; they were nipped tightly together, but gradually relaxed under the gentle pressure of my hand, till I actually got possession of her cunny, which I could feel was slightly covered with soft downy hair, and soon began to frig her gently with my forefinger. How the dear girl wriggled under the double excitement, and I could feel one of her hands groping outside my trousers over my bursting prick, to return the pleasure

169

I was giving her. One by one she unfastened the buttons, then her soft delicate hand soon had possession of my stiff affair, naked and palpitating with unsatisfied desire.

'Ah,' she whispered, 'I am satisfied at last! we had a servant at home, a few months ago, who slept in our room, and used to tickle and play with us. She told us that men had a long thing as hard as iron, which they pleased the ladies by shoving up their bellies, and that was how the babies were made. Do you believe it? She was always shoving her fingers into us as you are doing to me now, and – and – and,' here she hesitated and seemed to shudder with delight, just as I spent all over her hand, and I could also feel her spendings come in a warm gush over my fingers. It was delicious. Her hand first held tight the top of my throbbing prick, then gently worked up and down the shaft, lubricated by my spendings. It was indeed a voluptuous treat; I begged her to thrust her tongue into my mouth, and we continued the mutual frigging till she almost fainted away in her ecstasy.

Slightly recovering, I asked her what it was she was going to tell me about the maid servant, when she hesitated.

'Do, dearest, tell me everything,' I implored, in a loving whisper, 'We are now without reserve to each other; you can have no secrets from your loving Walter.'

'It was so funny, I don't know how she could do it, but Mary was so fond of sucking and kissing us where you have your hand, dearest,' she replied, 'but it was so nice you can't imagine how we enjoyed having her do it to us.'

'My love, my Emily, let me kiss you now, and it would be sublime if you would kiss me. I long to feel the love bites of your beautiful teeth in my *Cupid's Dart*. Frank and Louisa are too busy to notice what we do,' I whispered in her ear, as I inclined the willing girl backwards on the soft pillow of sand, and reversing my position, we laid at full length, side by side, both of us eager as possible for the game; my head was buried between her loving thighs, with which she pressed me most amorously, as my tongue was inserted in her loving slit; this was a fine gamahuche, I stirred up all the lasciviousness of her ardent temperament till she screamed with delight, and caused Frank and Louisa to enquire what we were doing, but we made no reply. She sucked my delighted prick, handled and kissed my balls, till I spent in her mouth, as her teeth were lovingly biting the head of my penis. She sucked it all down, whilst I repaid her loving attentions to the best of my ability with my own active tongue.

As soon as it was over, I took Emily by the hand, and we groped towards our companions, who, I found, were equally busy as we had been. Frank thoroughly understood my intention; we all got together, and joined in a grope of cocks and cunnies without the least restrained, till suddenly the curtain was pulled down, and we heard the laughing voices of Rosa and Annie, as they exclaimed, 'See, here they are. What are these rude boys doing to you young ladies?'

Emily and Louisa were covered with confusion, but the girls lovingly assured them they would keep the secret, and introduce them to more fun after they had retired to bed, as it was now getting late, and we must all return to the house.

As I have before observed, the wing of the mansion in which we all slept was quite apart from the other wing in which papa, mama, and the servants were located, so as soon as we had retired, Frank and myself joined the girls in their room, or rather rooms, for they occupied two. The Miss Bruces blushed crimson at seeing us only in our shirts, especially as one was seated on the *pot de chambre*, whilst the other was exhibiting her charms to my inquisitive cousins before a cheval glass.

'All right,' exclaimed Annie, 'my dears, everything is free between us and the boys, but we mean to punish you for allowing the impudent fellows to presume upon such liberties with you in the cave. Your bottoms shall smart, young ladies, I can assure you,' as she produced a couple of light birch rods from a drawer; in fact I had provided them for her, the idea having been suggested to me by reading a book called *The Romance of Lust.*

A fine large bed stood by the wall, facing another at the end of the room, but our programme only required one couch. Annie and Rosa were determined to have their enjoyment now; everyone was ordered to strip off shirt or chemise, then I horsed Emily on my back whilst Frank did the same by her sister.

Sophie and Polly were entrusted with the rods, and gaily switched us and our riders' bottoms as we trotted round the room, the sisters hardly knowing whether to laugh or cry, when a more stinging cut than usual made them cry for mercy; our pricks were as rampant as possible, and we were not in need of any stimulation; still the girls were very hard on our rumps, although not quite so severe with the sisters. The darling Emily had so entwined her legs round me as I held them close under my armpits that her pretty feet in their bewitching slippers were frigging my cock between them most deliciously.

The sight of our red smarting bottoms and bursting pricks was too much for Annie and Rosa, and they were inflamed with lust, so throwing themselves backward on the bed, with their legs wide open and feet resting on the floor, the two dear girls presented their quims to our charge, as with both hands they held open the lips of their delicious cunts, inviting our eager cocks to come on. We charged them at once, under the impulsive urging of the rods, gave a few delightful fucking motions, then withdrew and trotted round the room again, this we constantly repeated to prolong our

172

enjoyment, till at last the dear girls could stand it no longer, their arms clasped us firmly, whilst the rods cut away with extra force to make us complete their pleasure; it was a most luxurious finish, we all spent with screams of delight, and lay for a few moments in a delicious state of lethargic exhaustion till we awoke to find Sophie, Polly, Emily, and Louisa all rolling on the floor in the delights of gamahuching.

After this the two dear girls begged, with tears in their eyes, that Frank and Walter would make women of them, so that they might really taste the wildest delights of love.

'Then, dears,' said Rosa, with a sly laugh, 'you must kiss them, and make their exhausted cocks stiff again, and then we will lend the boys to you.'

We sat on the bed by the side of our late fucking partners, who we kissed, fondled and frigged, whilst Emily and Louisa, kneeling between our knees, sucked our pricks up to standing point, as their hands drew back our foreskins or played with our balls.

Stiff and rampant as we were we entreated them to go on for a little longer, till feeling ourselves almost at spending point, Polly and Sophie arranged two bolsters and some pillows on the floor in the most advantageous manner, the sisters were each placed with two pillows under their bottoms, whilst their heads rested on the bolsters. Annie and Rosa then conducted the victims, who impatiently awaited their immolation to the god of love with open legs and longing cunts. The two mistresses of the ceremonies took our pricks in hand, and directed them to the path of bliss. Emily was my partner again; she threw her legs over my back and heaved up to meet the fatal thrust, which was to be the death of her troublesome virginity. I had no time to see how the others progressed, but heard a smothered shriek of agony from Louisa, as no doubt Frank achieved her fate for her; my partner was more courageous, she glued her lips to mine, sucking in my tongue in the most ardent manner imaginable, even whilst my prick was tearing through her hymen; my spending deluged her wounded quim, and we soon lost all thoughts of pain when we recommenced a lovely fuck, moving slowly at first, till her rapid motions spurred me on to faster plunges, her delicious tight cunt holding me like a hand, in fact so tight that I could feel my foreskin drawn backwards and forwards at every shove.

'Ah! you dear fellow, push on, kill me with delight!' she screamed in ecstasy, as we came again together, and I was equally profuse in my words of endearment.

As we lay still after it was over her tight-fitting cunt seemed to hold and continually squeeze my delighted prick so by its contractions and throbbings I was ready again directly, and we ran another thrilling course before she would let me try to withdraw.

Frank and Louisa had been equally delighted with each other, and thus the two sisters each lost her maidenhead almost at the same moment.

Not a day passed but we had some voluptuous games, whilst as to Rosa and Frank, they were openly engaged to be married, which was an especial gratification to the old people.

Time flew so rapidly that my visit drew to its close, and we were all thinking of devising some signal display of love, to be enacted as a parting scene ere I took my departure from my uncle's hospitable and happy domicile, when one fine morning in June, who should favour us with a call, but my lovely brunette Mrs. Leslie. She had driven over to invite myself and my cousins to spend an early day before the Colonel's return. 'You know,' she said, turning to my uncle, 'how stiff and starch all his ideas are, and I must have one day of real fun before he comes home from Paris. Will you let them come tomorrow and stop till the next day?'

My uncle being too kind to refuse, the arrangement

was made at once, Mrs. Leslie stayed to luncheon, and we took an afternoon stroll in the park afterwards. From time to time her intelligent glances assured me she was anxious for a *tête-a-tête* with me, so asking her to take my arm, we soon managed to give the others the slip, and lost ourselves in a dense copse. Sitting down on the soft mossy turf, under a shady little yew tree, we were quite hidden from observation.

'How I longed to kiss your sweet lips once more,' I exclaimed, clasping her in my eager embrace, and sucking her breath almost away in a luscious osculation.

'If that is all you thought of sir, you have been vastly unfaithful to your protestations of love, and I should really feel awfully jealous of your pretty cousins and Miss Redquim did I not see the unruly state of the jewel in your trousers,' she laughingly replied, as she took speedy steps to release and secure the impatient prisoner in her grasp, continuing, 'I wonder how he has amused himself since that ever memorable day when I first had the pleasure of both seeing and feeling the noble fellow. Now tell me true Sir Walter, have you seduced your cousins and their friend?'

I at once made a full confession of all our amours, and begged she would indulge us in every possible way on the morrow, as it would be the last grand chance I should have before returning to town.

'Most delightful state of things I am sure, but what a shame not to have run over and invited me to join in your amorous festivities. Surely you knew it was just what I should have delighted in. I have a great mind to disappoint you now, only I should also be punishing myself, so come on, you naughty young fellow, and I will consider between this and to-morrow what your penance will be,' she said, reclining herself backwards, her fine dark eyes full of humid languishing fire, which too truly indicated her voluptuous requirements.

Lifting her skirts quickly, I paid my devotions at the shrine of love by a kiss and playful bite of her clitoris, then, unable to dally any longer, placed myself between her readily yielding thighs, and was soon revelling within the soft juicy folds of her divine organ of bliss, delighted beyond expression by the throbbing compressions to which it treated me as I lay quietly enjoying the sense of complete possession, which is so delicious to contemplate, before commencing more vigorous action; our lips met again and our billing and cooing would have lasted some time had we not heard Frank declaring to Rosa and his sisters, 'What a damned shame it was of Walter and Mrs. Leslie to give them the slip, but he would find us and spoil our fun.'

This caused my charming inamorata to heave up her buttocks as a challenge to me, not to waste more time, so I put spurs to my steed, but none too soon, for just as we died away in a mutual spend, Frank, Sisters, and Co. burst upon the scene with a triumphant exclamation of 'here's Walter and his grass widow,' and before we could recover ourselves, the laughing party inflicted an awful slapping on our bottoms, till a truce was made and we all agreed to wait patiently for the morrow's party at Mrs. Leslie's.

Next day, favoured by splendid weather, we were early at the Colonel's residence, and the handsome swarthy Vishnu ushered us into the luxurious boudoir of his voluptuous mistress. 'You have arrived early, it is scarcely one o'clock, my toilette's not yet made, but how very welcome you all are to my house, I need not trouble to say, after the frank understanding we came to yesterday, as to our amusements now you are here. The chocolate is just ready, and I have infused in it an imperceptible something (a secret, my dear, which the Colonel brought from India), which will soon set all your young amorous blood in such a glow of desire that you will not know how to satisfy your intense cravings for the delight of love, and then naughty Walter shall be served out for his unfaithfulness to me.'

This speech made us all smile as we took up the small cups of delicious chocolate which Vishnu handed round, and as he disappeared our hostess, who had nothing on but her dressing-gown, having drawn Frank to her side on the lounge, asked us, as the day was so warm, to throw aside as much as possible of our superfluous clothing, which was speedily done.

'We must have a romp before luncheon, then repose or stroll about during the afternoon, and in the evening we shall, I hope, enjoy some novel ideas I have quite set my mind upon,' she continued during the short time we took to disrobe. 'That's right, only keep on the *chemiserie* now, at night we will discard the last rag; I have no chemise to take off, so will keep this convenient *robe de chambre*, but you may look Frank, if you don't think Rosa will be jealous,' as she opened the front, and displayed to his ardent gaze all the beauties of her person.

'If it makes her jealous, I can't help admiring such charms!' said Frank, 'but Rosa is far too sensible for that, and thoroughly enters into all our fun, in fact I am sure she loves Walter as well as she does me, only she can't marry both of us.'

'Ha! Ha! that accounts for Walter forgetting me, so to be revenged on them both you must have me now,' she replied, lifting up his shirt to see if he was ready, 'why your lovedart is almost exactly the size of his,' and without more ado she was on his lap, and spitted herself on Frank's cock, throwing off entirely the *robe de chambre* that she might enjoy him without impediment.

This instantly excited the girls, who lay down in pairs for a mutual gamahuche and bottom-frig, Rosa playfully telling me to let Mrs. Leslie have the double pleasure by fucking her bottom as she was riding Frank.

'Hold her tight, my boy,' I said, 'and I will let her beautiful little fundamental know what it is to keep a stiff prick waiting for his turn,' as I took a little cold cream from the dressing-table, and putting some on the head of my prick as well as the delightful wrinkled hole exposed to my attack, the head began to slip in at once, despite her struggles and screams, 'that we should injure her between us.' Further and further I gradually worked in, till I could feel my cock rubbing against Frank's with only the thin divisional membrane between them, our joint spendings deluging both cunt and bum, spurting the warm, frothy sperm over our balls at every thrust. This was not enough to satisfy her, but she kept us at our work until we repeated our emissions with screams of delight, and rolled on the floor in a confused heap amongst the dear girls, who were so excited by the sight of our ecstasies that they were revelling in every species of tribadism to allay their lustful yearnings.

After this Mrs. Leslie opened a side door, conducted us into her bathroom, where we refreshed ourselves and indulged in a variety of kissing, frigging, &c., but by her advice the girls refrained from exhausting us too much, and accepted cigarettes of Turkish tobacco to join us in a smoke, as we lighted some of the Colonel's fine cigars. It was a picture worthy of Apelles, as we could see the reflection of all our naked charms on the bathroom walls, which constituted one vast mirror of the very finest silvered glass, two rather good-looking fellows with big pricks, as rampant as could be wished, and five lovely ladies all smoking and puffing pretty curls or rings of vapoury nicotine, alternating that sober enjoyment for more active fun, by trying to burn the tip of their cunts with the fiery ends of cigarette or cigar.

About half-past two, we dressed, and then took luncheon, then strolled in the grounds or on the bank of a small stream, where some of us passed the time trying our piscatorial luck, till the bell rang for dinner, which passed pleasantly enough, and about 9 P.M., we assembled in the drawing-room, for a grand erotic séance.

Mrs. Leslie dismissed all her servants for the night, except Vishnu, who she said would be quite sufficient to attend to our little requirements.

The room was large and lofty, the windows closed and artistically draped with gorgeous black and gold curtains, the spaces between filled up with mirrors and branching candelabra, the opposite side of the apartment being also quite a tableau of flowers, mirrors, and lighted wax candles, which shed a brilliant and yet soft luxurious effulgence over the whole scene; two doors at one end gave access to retiring rooms, where we undressed, and in a very few minutes the whole party, in a state of ravishing nudity, were grouped round Mrs. Leslie as she sat on an ottoman, awaiting her decision as to the programme.

She first persuaded us to sip a little of her chocolate, then went on to say, 'As we are five to two you will find I have a stock of fine, soft, firmly made dildoes to make up the deficiency in males, which alternated with the real article will enable us to thoroughly enjoy ourselves. First, I believe Miss is a virgin, notwithstanding all she knows and has seen; her delicate little pussey must be itching to be emancipated from the thraldom of virginity. Walter must do the service for her at once, on Rosa's lap, so now to business, as I see our gentlemen are in a beautiful state of readiness.'

Polly blushed deeply, but readily seated herself on her friend's lap with her legs wide open, presented to my staff of life, whilst Rosa, passing her hands round the dear girl's waist, held open the lips of her cunny, and guided the head of my affair in the proper direction. Much as she had been frigged and gamahuched, it was a hard task; her cunt was so deliciously small and tight that in spite of her favourable position, I

179

could only just get the head of Mr. Priapus within the nymphae before she started with the intense pain, and gave a supressed scream of anguish, the tears starting to her eyes and trickling over her blushing face.

'Courage, darling, it will soon be over,' I whispered, kissing her excitedly, while Mrs. Leslie encouraged me by saying, 'Sharp and quick, Walter, a good thrust will force better than those gentle pushes; gentleness is not real kindness when taking a maidenhead;' at the same moment I felt she was attacking my virgin bottom-hole behind with a well-lubricated dildoe, its head being well in before I knew exactly what she was doing; this and the desire to possess Polly so stimulated me that I thrust furiously at the opposing obstacle, her heartrending cries adding to my pleasure, and making me mad with desire. At last I was halfway in, then a fierce lunge seemed to break quite through as I, at the same time, deluged the tight passage with a copious emmision.

The poor little victim had swooned, but Mrs. Leslie, working her dildoe behind, ordered me to let my cock throb inside Polly's tight sheath, as it would tend to bring her round, and excite her amorous sensibility to the utmost.

What delightful sensations I experienced, my prick feeling all the spasmodic contractions of her vagina, and having my bottom well dildoe-fucked at the same time, I spent again under the influence of this accumu-lated excitement just as my partner was coming round under the influence of some cordial which had been poured down her gasping throat, whilst strong smell-ing salts had been applied to her nostrils. She opened her eyes, giving a violent sneeze at the same time, which vibrated on my delightful prick, who instantly began gently to bestir himself in her tight scabbard; this roused her little by little, till throwing her arms round my neck, and returning my hot kisses with all the ardour of her nature, she cried and laughed by turns, as she begged me to make haste and complete her happiness.

By a side glance I could see Frank was in Mrs. Leslie's bottom, Annie in him with a dildoe, and Sophie doing the same to her sister, a perfect string of pederastic branchings from my own violated bum. It was such a scene as I had never seen before, and added additional fury to my already maddened lust. I came again and again before we finished, each spend more ecstatic than the last. The chocolate had so invigorated us, that we went through an almost interminable series of spendings, till at last the nature could stand it no longer, we rolled on the floor in a confused heap, and wound up in a mutual gamahuche; Mrs. Leslie secured the bloodstained quim of Polly, which she sucked till she had enjoyed the last drop of ensanguined spunk she could extract from the wounded slit of her young friend, who writhed in delight under the soothing touches of such a lascivious tongue.

It was between eleven and twelve o'clock, when just as we were recovering from a state of lethargic oblivion, and thinking of some re-invigorating refreshment, the sound of carriage wheels on the gravel drive up to the house, and then, rat-a-tat-tat on the loud knocker made us all start to our feet and rush for our clothes.

'The Colonel, by all that's unfortunate,' exclaimed Mrs. Leslie, 'make haste or he will catch us; who would have thought of his arriving at this time of night.'

The prudent Vishnu, pretending to be awakening out of his first sleep, so bungled and delayed opening the front door, that we were tolerably presentable by the time the Colonel made his appearance, and whatever his suspicions may have been, he went through the formality of introduction in the most friendly way possible, the presence of so many young ladies evidently quite disconcerting him for the moment.

I afterwards learnt from his wife that under promise

of secrecy she had confessed all to him, and vastly amused her husband by an account of our doings; but, at any rate, it stopped our fun at the time, and next day I was obliged to return to town, and thus brought to conclusion 'My Sport amongst the She-Noodles,' anything but 'Noodles' after I had so enlightened them, in fact quite as knowing as Adam and Eve after they found out they were 'Naked' having tasted the *'Tree of Knowledge'*, which, in my humble opinion, meant found out *'L'Arte de faire l'amour.'*

THERESE

Caught in the pursuit of certain solitary pleasures and in consequence confined to a convent, young Therese embraces religion with a great fervour. Such is her piety that her health begins to suffer – Therese is not a girl to do things by halves – and on medical advice she is sent home to her mother. It is then that she meets the two people who are to become the most important influences in her life – the venerable Father Dirrag and his devoted disciple Eradice. This lady is blessed with the same passionate temperament as Therese and the two become confidants, drawn to one another by their religious devotions. However there is one blemish on their friendship – the jealousy that Therese cannot suppress whenever Eradice speaks of her father confessor. Therese refuses to believe the stories of Dirrag's particular attentions to her friend, the frequent meetings at his home, his promise that under his ministrations Eradice will soon be capable of great miracles. It is only natural therefore that Therese should require some proof of this very special relationship . . .

Eradice must have noticed that I was envious, begrudged her her happiness and, worst of all, did not seem to believe her! I must admit that I was very surprised about her tales of his confidential talks with her at his home, especially since the good father had always carefully avoided talking to me, one of his most ardent penitents, about anything else but mortification of the flesh. And I knew another penitent, also a good friend of mine, who, like Eradice, also carried the stigmata of our Lord. He had never been as confidential to her as he had been to Eradice, and this girl friend, too, had all the requirements of becoming a saint. No doubt, my sad face, my yellowish complexion, my utter lack of any sign of stigmata were enough reasons for the venerable Father Dirrag not to have any confidential talks with me at his home. The possibility existed that he saw no reason to take on the extra burden of spiritual works in my behalf. But to me it was a bone of contention. I became very sad and I pretended not to believe any of Eradice's stories.

This irritated Eradice no end. She offered to let me become an eyewitness to her happiness that next morning. 'You will see for yourself,' she contended heatedly, 'how strong my spiritual exercises are, how the good father guides me from one degree of mortification to the next with the purpose of making a saint out of me. You will be a witness to the delight and ecstasy which are a direct result of these exercises and you will never doubt again how marvelous these exercises are. Oh, how I wish, my dearest Therese, that my example would work its first miracle upon you. That you might be spiritually strengthened to totally deny the flesh and follow the only path which will lead you to God!'

We agreed that I would visit her the next morning at five o'clock. I found her in prayer, a book in her hand. She said to me, 'The holy man will arrive soon, and God shall be with him. Hide yourself in that little alcove, and from there you can see and hear for yourself the miracles of Divine Love wrought upon me by the venerable father confessor. Even to such a lowly creature as I.'

Somebody knocked quietly on the door. I fled into the alcove; Eradice turned the key and put it in her skirt pocket. There was, fortunately, a hole in the alcove door, covered with a piece of tapestry. This made it possible for me to see the entire room, without, however, running the risk of being seen myself.

The good father entered the room and said to Eradice, 'Good morning, my dearest sister in the Lord, may the Holy Spirit of Saint Francis protect you forever.'

She wanted to throw herself at his feet, but he lifted her off the floor and ordered her to sit down next to him upon the sofa. Then the holy man said, 'I cannot repeat too often the principles which are going to become the guidelines for your future way of life, my dear child. But, before I start my instructions, tell me, dear child, are the stigmata, those miraculous signs of God's everlasting favour, still with you? Have they changed any? Show them to me.'

Eradice immediately bared her left breast, under which she bore the stigma.

'Oh, oh, please dear sister! Cover your bosom with this handkerchief! (He handed her one). These things were not created for a member of our society; it is enough for me to view the wound with which the holy Saint Francis has made you, with God's infinite mercy, His favourite. Ah! it is still there. Thank the Lord, I am satisfied. Saint Francis still loves you; the wound is rosy and clean. This time I have with me a part of our dear Saint's sacred rope; we shall need it for our mortification exercises. I have told you already, my dear sister, that I love you above all my other penitents, your girl friends, because God has so clearly marked you as one of the beloved sheep in His flock. You stand out like the sun and the moon among the other planets and stars. Therefore I have not spared any trouble to instruct you in the deepest secrets of our Holy Mother Church. I have repeatedly told you, dearest sister, "Forget yourself, and let it happen." God desires from Mankind only spirit and heart. Only if you can succeed in forgetting the existence of your body will you be able to experience Him and achieve sainthood. And only as a saint will you ever be able to work miracles. I cannot help, my little angel, but to scold you, since I noticed during our last exercises that your spirit is still enslaved by your body. How can that be? Couldn't you at least be a little bit like our saintly martyrs? They were pinched with red-hot irons, their nails were torn off their feet and fingers, they were roasted over slow fires and yet . . . they did not experience pain. And why not? Because their mind was filled with pure thoughts of God's infinite glory! The most minute particle of their spirit and mind was occupied with thoughts of His immense glory. Our senses, my dear daughter, are mere tools. But, they are tools that do not lie. Only through them can we feel, only through them can we understand the evil and the good. They influence our bodies as well as our souls. They enable us to perceive what is morally right and what is morally wrong. As soon as we touch something, or feel, or hear, minute particles of our spirit flow through the tiny holes in our nerves. They report the sensations back to our soul. However, when they are filled completely with the love they owe their God and Creator, when YOU are so full of love and devotion that none of these minute particles can do anything else but concentrate on the Divine Providence, when the entire spirit is given to the contemplation of our Lord, then, and only then is it impossible for any particle to tell our spirit that the body is being punished. You will no longer feel it. Look at the hunter. His entire being is filled with only one thought: his prey! He does not feel the thorns that rip at him when he stalks through the forest, nor does he notice cold or heat. True, these elements are considerably weaker than the mighty hunter, but . . . the object of his thoughts! Ah, that is a thousand times stronger than all his other feelings put together. Would you feel the feeble blows of the whip when your soul is full of the thoughts of happiness that is about to be yours? You must be able to pass this all-important test. We must know for sure, if we want to be able to work miracles, whether we can reach this degree of perfection, whether we can wholly immerse ourselves in God!

'And we shall win, dear daughter. Do your duty, and be assured that thanks to the rope of the holy Saint Francis, and thanks to your pious contemplations, this holy exercise will end for you with a shower of unspeakable delight. Down on your knees child! Reveal that part of your body which raises the fury of our Lord; the pain you will feel shall bring your soul in close contact with God. I must repeat again: "Forget yourself, and let it happen!" '

Eradice obeyed immediately without uttering a single word. Holding a book in her hands, she kneeled down in front of a little prayer stool. Then she lifted her skirts about the waist, showing her snow-white, perfectly rounded bums that tapered into two gorgeous alabaster, firm-fleshed thighs.

'Lift your skirts a little higher, my dear,' he said to her, 'it does not look proper yet. Fine, fine . . . that's a lot better. Put the prayer book down, fold your hands and lift up your soul to God. Fill your mind with thoughts about the eternal happiness which has been promised you!'

The priest pulled up his footstool and kneeled next to her, bending slightly backward. He lifted his cowl and tied it to the rope around his waist. Then he took a large birch rod and held it in front of my penitent friend who kissed it devoutly.

Piously shuddering I followed the whole procedure with full attention. I felt a sort of horror which is very difficult to describe. Eradice did not say a word. The priest gazed upon her thighs with a fixed stare, his eyes sparkling. He did not let his gaze wander for a single moment. And I heard him whisper softly, full of admiration, 'Oh, God, what a marvelous bosom. My Lord, those gorgeous tits!'

Now he bent over and then he straightened up again, murmuring biblical language. Nothing escaped his vile curiosity. After a few minutes he asked the penitent if her soul was prepared.

'Oh yes, venerable Father! I can feel my soul separate itself from my unworthy flesh. I pray you, begin your holy work!'

'It is enough. Your soul will be happy!'

He said a few prayers and the ceremony started with three fairly light blows of the rod, straight across her firm buttocks. This was followed by a recitation from

189

the Bible. Thereupon another three blows, slightly stronger than the first ones.

After he had recited five or six verses, and interrupted each of them the same way as before, I suddenly noticed to my utter surprise that the venerable Father Dirrag opened his fly. A throbbing arrow shot out of his trousers which looked exactly like that fateful snake about which my former father confessor had warned me so vehemently.

The monster was as long and as thick and as heavy as the one about which the Capuchine monk had made all those dire predictions. I shuddered with delightful horror. The red head of this snake seemed to threaten Eradice's behind which had taken on a deep pink colouration because of the blows it had received during the Bible recitation. The face of Father Dirrag perspired and was flushed a deep red.

'And now,' he said, 'you have to transport yourself into total meditation. You must separate your soul from the senses. And if my dear daughter has not disappointed my pious hopes, she shall neither feel, nor hear, nor see anything.'

And at that very moment this horrible man loosened a hail of blows, letting them whistle down upon Eradice's naked buttocks. However, she did not say a word; it seemed as if she were totally insensitive to this horrendous whipping. I noticed only an occasional twitching of her bum, a sort of spasming and relaxing at the rhythm of the priest's blows.

'I am very satisfied with you,' he told her after he had punished for for about five minutes in this manner. 'The time has come when you are going to reap the fruits of your holy labours. Don't question me, my dear daughter, but be guided by God's will which is working through me. Throw yourself, face down, upon the floor; I will now expel the last traces of impurity with a sacred relic. It is a part of the venerable rope which girded the waist of the holy Saint Francis himself.'

The good priest put Eradice in a position which was rather uncomfortable for her, but extremely fitting for what he had in mind. I had never seen my girl friend in such a beautiful position. Her buttocks were half-opened and the double path to satisfaction was wide-open.

After the old lecher had admired her for a while, he moistened his so-called rope of Saint Francis with spittle, murmured some of the priestly mumbo-jumbo which these gentlemen generally use to exorcise the devil, and proceeded to shove the rope into my friend.

I could watch the entire operation from my little hideout. The windows of the room were opposite the door of the alcove in which Eradice had locked me up. She was kneeling on the floor, her arms were crossed over the footstool and her head rested upon her folded arms. Her skirts, which had been carefully folded almost up to her shoulders, revealed her marvellous buttocks and the beautiful curve of her back. This exciting view did not escape the attention of the venerable Father Dirrag. His gaze feasted upon the view for quite some time. He had clamped the legs of his penitent between his own legs, and he dropped his trousers, and his hands held the monstrous rope. Sitting in this position he murmured some words which I could not understand.

He lingered for some time in this devotional position and inspected the altar with glowing eyes. He seemed to be undecided how to effect his sacrifice, since there were two inviting openings, His eyes devoured both and it seemed as if he were unable to make up his mind. The top one was a well-known delight for a priest, but, after all, he had also promised a taste of Heaven to his penitent. What was he to do? Several times he knocked with the tip of his tool at the gate he desired most, but finally he was smart enough to let wisdom triumph over desire. I must do him justice: I clearly saw his monstrous prick disappear the natural

191

way, after his priestly fingers had carefully parted the rosy lips of Eradice's lovepit.

The labour started with three forceful shoves which made him enter about halfway. And suddenly the seeming calmness of the priest changed into some sort of fury. My God, what a change! Imagine a satyr. Mouth half-open, lips foam-flecked, teeth gnashing and snorting like a bull who is about to attack a cud-chewing cow. His hands were only half an inch away from Eradice's full behind. I could see that he did not dare to lean upon them. His spread fingers were spasming; they looked like the feet of a fried capon. His head was bowed and his eyes stared at the so-called relic. He measured his shoving very carefully, seeing to it that he never left her lovepit and also that his belly never touched her arse. He did not want his penitent to find out to whom the holy relic of Saint Francis was connected! What an incredible presence of mind!

I could clearly see that about an inch of the holy tool constantly remained on the outside and never took part in the festivities. I could see that with every back-ward movement of the priest the red lips of Eradice's love-nest opened and I remember clearly that the vivid pink colour was a most charming sight. However, whenever the good priest shoved forward, the lips closed and I could only see the finely curled hairs which covered them. They clamped around the priestly tool so firmly that it seemed as if they had devoured the holy arrow. It looked for all the world like both of them were connected to Saint Francis' relic and it was hard to guess which one of the two persons was the true possessor of this holy tool.

What a sight, especially for a young girl who knew nothing about these secrets. The most amazing thoughts ran through my head, but they all were rather vague and I could not find proper words for them. I only remember that I wanted to throw myself at least twenty times at the feet of this famous father confessor and beg him to exorcise me the same way he was blessing my dear friend. Was this piety? Or carnal desire? Even today I could not tell you for sure.

But, let's go back to our devout couple! The movements of the priest quickened; he was barely able to keep his balance. His body formed an 'S' from head to toe whose frontal bulge moved rapidly back and forth in a horizontal line.

'Is your spirit receiving any satisfaction, my dear little saint?' he asked with a deep sigh. 'I, myself, can see Heaven open up. God's infinite mercy is about to remove me from this vale of tears, I . . .'

'Oh, venerable Father,' exclaimed Eradice, 'I cannot describe the delights that are flowing through me! Oh, yes, yes, I experience Heavenly bliss. I can feel how my spirit is being liberated from all earthly desires. Please, please, dearest Father, exorcise every last impurity remaining upon my tainted soul. I can see . . . the angels of God . . . push stronger . . . ooh . . . shove the holy relic deeper . . . deeper. Please, dearest Father, shove it as hard as you can . . . Ooooh! . . . ooh!!! dearest holy Saint Francis . . . Ooh, good saint . . . please, don't leave me in the hour of my greatest need . . . I feel your relic . . . it is sooo good . . . your . . . holy . . . relic . . . I can't hold it any longer . . . I am . . . dying!'

The priest also felt his climax approach. He shoved, slammed, snorted and groaned. Eradice's last remark was for him the signal to stop and pull out. I saw the proud snake. It had become very meek and small. It crawled out of its hole, foam-covered, with hanging head.

Everything disappeared back into the trousers; the priest dropped his cowl over it all and wavered back to his prayer stool. he kneeled down, pretended to be in deep communication with his Lord, and ordered his penitent to stand up, cover herself and sit down next to him to thank God for His infinite mercy which she had just received from Him.

What else shall I tell you? Dirrag left, Eradice opened the door to the alcove and embraced me, crying out, 'Oh, my dearest Therese. Partake of my joy and delight. Yes, yes, today I have seen paradise. I have shared the delights of the angels. The incredible joy, my dearest friend, the incomparable price for but one moment of pain! Thanks to the holy rope of Saint Francis my soul almost left its earthly vessel. You have seen how my good father confessor introduced the relic into me. I swear that I could feel it touch my heart. Just a little bit deeper and I would have joined the saints in paradise!'

Eradice told me a thousand other things, and her tone of voice, her enthusiasm about the incredible delights she had enjoyed left no doubt in my mind about their reality. I was so excited that I was barely able to answer her. I did not congratulate her, because I was unable to talk. My heart pounded in wild excitement. I embraced her, and left.

So many thought are racing through my mind right now that I hardly know where to begin. It is terrifying to realise how the most honourable convictions of our society are being misused. How positively fiendish was the way in which this cowl-bearer perverted the piety of his penitent to his own lecherous desires. He needled her imagination, artfully using her desire to become a saint; he convinced her that she would be able to succeed, if she separated her mind from her body. This, however, could only be achieved by means of flagellation. Most likely it was the hypocrite himself who needed this stimulation to repair the weakened elasticity of his flagging member. And then he tells her, 'If your devotion is perfect, you shall not be able to feel, hear, or see anything!'

That way he made sure that she would not turn around and see his shameless desire. The blows of the rod upon her buttocks not only increased the feeling in that part which he intended to attack, but they also served to make him more horny than he already was. And the relic of Saint Francis which he shoved into the body of his innocent penitent to chase away impurities which were still clinging to her soul, enabled him to enjoy his desires without any danger to himself. His newly-initiated penitent mistook her most voluptuous outburst of carnal climax for a divinely inspired, purely spiritual ecstasy.

THE LOINS OF
AMON

The Loins of Amon *is an erotic entertainment on an epic scale, a grand costume drama set in a mythical Ancient Egypt where mighty armies clash and priests sacrifice virgins in arcane and bestial rituals. Centre stage in this robust play stands Prince Ineni, an Egyptian noble with a claim to the throne and an outspoken opponent of the cruel and powerful priesthood. Manoeuvred by his enemies into leading a small army on a suicidal mission into Palestine and Syria, Ineni does not expect to return alive. Surprisingly his army is triumphant and he returns a hero, only to be arrested by the priests and sentenced to death. With the help of his favourite harem girl he succeeds in escaping to Nubia and from there he leads a revolt which places him on the throne as Pharaoh. Within a few weeks, however, he orders the virgin sacrifices to be resumed and himself begins plotting against a bold new pretender to the throne . . .*

As can be deduced from this bald account, here is an erotic book whose plot is not primarily sexual – though the narrative flesh that cloaks this skeletal scenario contains incidents that are as brazen and seductive as any other featured in this volume. Here, for example, is the initiation of a Syrian girl into the mysteries of the harem . . .

Riding amongst the last signs of life, touring the city on horse for any sign of trouble, Ineni was suddenly aware of two shadowy figures walking along the foot of the great wall of a noble's house, far from the poor quarter of the city. He galloped his horse towards the faint movement in the shadow and saw two women stepping quickly along towards the entrance of the house.

In the moonlight, he could see that one was well advanced into middle age, the other – taller and slimmer – a mere girl. The older woman appeared not to hear as he approached, but the girl turned while still walking and looked back. Her robe, close around her, tautened into long, suggestive folds, bulging over her breasts, falling away in slim lines to her hips, tightening around her shoulders and buttocks in a twisted clasp.

Ineni drew up his horse alongside them and the old woman drew back in fear. The younger had a sweet, almost child-like face, with a small nose, a pouting lower lip and large soulful eyes, which looked, now, at the Egyptian with nothing but curiosity.

'Where are you going?' Ineni demanded of the elder woman.

She looked pale and frightened as she answered, her voice little more than a whisper.

'We have been watching your glorious troops in action,' she said. 'Now we are retiring in thankfulness that the battle was short and saved us from the northern invader.'

'You have worked your fawning subservience to a nicety,' Ineni said, scornfully. 'Had I been the king of the Hittites you would have been licking my feet here. As it is I suspect you would be glad to thrust a knife between my shoulders.'

'No my lord, that is not true.' The woman was almost in tears in her fear. 'Both I and my daughter here abhor the barbarity of the Hittites.'

It was clear the woman was one of the noble's harem – probably the daughter, too, Ineni decided, as he looked them over. The woman continued to shift uneasily as if she were likely to dart away through the gates at any moment. Her daughter – large undulation of her breasts under the robe, clearer now – continued to gaze at Ineni with a curiosity which amounted almost to boldness. She was a very pretty creature.

'Your lies do not become you, woman,' Ineni said sternly. 'But although I could have you slaughtered, I shall bid you quietly goodnight if you will tell your daughter that she is to come with me.'

The woman clutched the girl's hand, seeming to grow suddenly bolder in protection of her young. The girl's slim fingers twined around her mother's but she didn't take her eyes from the Egyptian prince.

'Oh my lord, she is yet a virgin,' she whispered.

Ineni raised his eyebrows in surprise.

'Indeed the harems must be well filled if a place

200

could not be found for such a dainty morsel,' he said. 'She has, indeed, the face of a child, but her body, I would say, is that of a woman. Tonight she shall behave as befits a woman.'

'My lord, I beg you. I will bring you other more beautiful women if only you will not harm my daughter,' the woman pleaded.

'Why this concern?' Ineni asked with a laugh. 'Your daughter will not be harmed, woman. She will learn what all daughters must learn – how to take a man's weight on her hips, his spear between her legs.'

As he said this, Ineni looked straight at the girl, but her eyes showed no trace of her feelings. The older woman was clutching her arm now. Tears shone in her eyes.

'My lord, I will give you anything within my power if you will not take her. She is my only daughter and she is but sixteen.' A tear flowed gently down the woman's face as Ineni regarded the girl again with surprise.

'A woman, indeed for sixteen years,' he said. 'But how do you feel, my daughter at the thought of making love to the leader of the Pharoah's army?'

The girl spoke, for the first time, quietly, in a voice which made her seem suddenly more mature.

'My fate is in my lord's hands,' she said.

'Words of wisdom, my child. I am sorry for your mother's fears, but they are groundless and I cannot deprive myself of such a pleasant hour or two on their account.'

So saying, Ineni leaned suddenly from his horse, caught the girl around her slender waist, feeling the warm, living flesh against his arm, and whisked her onto the horse in front of him. Her mother, almost pulled off her feet as her daughter was dragged away from her, gazed at them in mute horror, tears coursing down her cheeks, unmoving, as if she knew the futility of movement.

Beginning to trot gently away, Ineni called back softly to the woman. 'Don't worry, I will bring her back, safe and happy in a few hours time.'

Jogging back through the city – deserted and quiet now except of the Egyptian guards on the walls – Ineni pulled the girls' dark head back against his lips, feeling its almost liquid texture. He kissed the back of her neck and she moved it against him, completely acquiescent. His free hand, held her against him, moving strongly over the outline of her breasts and ribs, tracing with a fierce tense hand, their firm, springy contours.

Her body, under the robe was wonderful to the touch. It sent a thrill through his fingertips so that his body gave an involuntary shudder of anticipation.

'Such a virgin,' he whispered to her as they rode. 'Your mother must be mad to withhold you from your destiny.'

'It was not my wish, my lord,' the girl said, softly. 'I have longed for the moment although now I am half afraid.'

'Don't be afraid,' Ineni whispered gently. 'You could have no better tutor.'

The girl nestled contentedly against him, breathing slightly, aloud, through parted lips as his lips caressed her hair and his hand her body outside the robe.

Soon they had reached the Egyptian tents and with the bright rays of light splintering the eastern horizon, Ineni pushed the girl gently ahead of him into his nightly shelter.

His heart was thumping fiercely and his hand found an echoing tremble in the girl's quivering flesh. Now that the moment was upon her, she was very frightened.

Ineni turned her and pulled her to him. Her soulful eyes were deep and giving, her body trembling slightly like a felt but unseen ripple on a pool. His hands moved over her, intently feeling her body with its warm vibrations, sensing the roundnesses, the fleshy weight of breasts and buttocks through every pore. He kissed her, thrusting his tongue into her mouth, forcing apart her unwary lips, penetrating her for the first time. In his arms she was like a soft shifting of desert sand, light, slipping and moving in little eddies.

He pressed his hips in against her, clamping them to hers and through hers in a strong, relentless movement. Her loins, for a moment, seemed hesitant and unsure and then his pressure was answered. The soft, hot flesh of thighs and hips pushed against his so that he could feel their tubular imprint, could feel it flattened and spread by his own strong force. And in the centre of this pressure where their central cores seemed soldered together was his pulsing, hot pyramid, which crushed and bent against her triangle of junction; crushed until it was so painful that he had to ease back for a moment to relieve it.

The girl's hands were tentatively pressed on his arms now, moving slowly like searching, timid animals, feeling the long, hard lines of muscles which tensed and relaxed as he moved her against him. Her tongue was answering his, learning readily, flickering softly over his lips and in with a swift determination.

Gently, with hands which she could hardly feel, Ineni eased off her robe. She made no effort to help him, seeming, now, overcome with a stomach-clutching tension which allowed her only to breathe with difficulty. Her body when it rested, nude, in his arms, was shivering.

Again he brushed his hands over her, heat seeming to leap from flesh to flesh at every spot his hand touched. Her buttocks were full – quite fleshy for one so slim – and as his hands explored them, fingers probing gently against the sensitive flesh between them, she tensed them, swaying them involuntarily away from his hand, so that her hips pressed in against his.

He slipped his hands lightly over her back and shoulders, drawing it over her flesh to the front of her body where her breasts, large and fragile-feeling, like enormous rain-drops, also trembled at his touch. The nipples were small and hard and as he moved his lips from her neck to kiss them, she gasped, made to push his head away with her hands, but then clasped it closer, wriggling her breast against his mouth as he nipped her gently with his teeth.

Ineni piloted the girl across the room to his bed of hides, leaning her gently backward so that she collapsed on her back on them, soft arms moving automatically around his shoulders as he sank down beside her. Lying on his side against her, he stroked the whole of her body with his hand, running his fingertips down from her shoulders out over the breasts, in again to her waist and then across the slight, smooth bulge of her lower belly.

As his finger explored the outer fringes of the soft hair which dwindled down to a point at the junction of her closed legs she began to wriggle her bottom uneasily. Slight, strangled whimpers choked in her throat.

At her leg junction, Ineni pressed his hand along the flesh of her thighs which felt like the skin of a grape. As he forced his fingers through between her thighs, she involuntarily pressed them closer together so that his hand was caught in a vice of flesh, unable to move up to its goal. But then her legs relaxed and he moved up a little before, involuntarily again, they tightened. Thus his hand continued its interrupted progression until, with the girl straining in thrilled fear, his fingers were brushing the warm, wet flesh of the lips of her vagina. She pushed a hand down at his arm, holding it away, reluctantly, not really wanting to hold it away, but afraid. And then he bent his face down on hers and kissed her passionately, losing his tongue in the depths of her mouth. She gave a little groan, there was a tremor of relaxation – and then his fingers had pushed up and into the hot, moist aperture as the girl gave a gasp of pain.

In the first moments, she jerked his hips away from him, afraid of being hurt, afraid of unknown mysteries. But as, moaning quietly, she became used to the intruding pressure, she allowed her legs to be opened so that his hand no longer brushed against the inside surface of her thighs as he dug into her farther.

For some time, Ineni coaxed her, getting her used to the feeling of a strange flesh inside her passage and then, face and body flaming, he released her for a moment and slipped out of his tunic.

His body compared with hers was huge and rugged and his over-strained penis soared out from his loins like a temple obelisk.

He had risen to climb out of his clothes and he stood above the girl, looking down on her so that she would see the secret body of a man in all its splendour for the first time.

The girl, slim body rising and falling slightly with her disturbed breathing, looked through half-frightened, half-desiring eyes at the rugged nakedness before her. Her gaze swept down his body to the all-important source at his leg junction and there rested in wonder and fear on the great, thick, rigid rod which jutted out at her and over her.

Exploring, timidly, her eyes ranged over the large, dangling testicles, half lost in the shaggy covering of black hair and then her eyes moved up again to meet Ineni's with a look which plainly showed her mixture of willingness and fear.

Quickly he lay down against her once more, running his hand in fluid movements over her body so that she began to tremble. Then her caught her hand and pulled it against his penis, closing her fingers around the stiff, bursting flesh. For a second or two her hand remained limply where he had placed it, making a hot fusion between them and then she began gently to slip her fingers up and down and round the organ, feeling it, squeezing it, wondering at it. Bolder she moved on to his testicles, drawing her finger tips over them in an intuitive recognition.

Ineni, lying taut against her, felt his great projection raging as if it were water boiling and sizzling over a fire. His whole body was alive with thrills and skewers. He could wait for her no longer.

Raising himself, he moved one leg over her, lowering it between hers and then he moved his body onto hers drawing over his other leg in the same movement so that his hips were between the girl's thighs.

Her hands pressed against his chest for a fraction of a second as if she would try to push him away, but then they relaxed again and moved around his neck, pulling his face down to hers so that, she in turn, could dart her moist little tongue into his mouth.

With that indication of her readiness, Ineni raised his hips onto hers, feeling her hot and waiting beneath him. With her smooth, little face pressed against his, cheek to cheek, looking over his shoulder into the gloomy shadows of the tent roof, tensely waiting, he reached down to her leg junction. A soft movement spread her legs a little more so that she was completely exposed and then he had guided his pulsing spear at the moistened cavity. For a moment, in which life seemed to stand still for the girl, he hesitated – and then he thrust into her, holding her tightly in his arms so that she could not wriggle away as he did so.

The girl screamed and squirmed as the mountain of flesh burst into her, but she was firmly caught against his body and he drove into her again.

'Oh, oh, you're hurting me,' she screamed, trying to sway her hips from under the anchoring weight of his. But Ineni's body was now a great yearning, down at his penis the hot, moist relief for the yearning – a hot, jellied feeling – so that he began to grunt and his breath grated in his throat. He held the girl with all his force, crushing her, rendering her body helpless. Her upper body was unable to move, only her legs could writhe and struggle and her central opening slip and jerk against the rigid pain.

Ineni ignored completely her whispered gasps for mercy, her tears. And in a short time the gasps had changed, mellowed into gasps of pure yielding and joining and enjoying as the pain, too, changed and mellowed.

He reached down, grasping a slim, smooth thigh with each hand and drew her legs apart and up around him, plunging deeper into her abdomen. There was to be nothing timid and too-gentle about this union. The girl would remember the first time in a sharp, clear image for the rest of her life.

Her hips wriggled and swayed under him, crinkling the flesh of her belly in little, momentary ridges. Her thighs clasped him as if she would hold him in her for ever. Her moans became the fuller, deeper moans of accepted challenge. Her eyes were closed as her fingers stroked down over his cheeks and drew his face onto hers for his mouth to make an outlet for her searching, giving tongue.

With quick, furious movements of his hips, Ineni thrust into her and into her again, regulating the speed to ensure her satisfaction.

His penis seemed to be burning as if it were on fire and in the tight, tender grasping of her channel he was pushing always against a slight force which agonisingly forced back his skin, contracted around the knob in a painful embrace.

The girl's whimpers became, suddenly, a greater, more prolonged consistent moaning and she caught at his thighs where they pressed against the underside of hers, pulling them at her while her mouth opened as if she were gasping for air. Her whole tender frame began to writhe and twist in an agony and in the rushes of air which burst from her throat, Ineni sensed rather than heard whispered pleadings for speed as she felt the enormity of sweet pain building up, inevitably, in the soft, marshy regions of her genitals.

In turn he felt the pain, as if he were trying, agonisingly, to urinate and couldn't. His breath exploded from his stomach in fierce, coughing gasps and he slowly swept his penis in a great, bulging crush in and in with a painful grinding, forcing it more and more slowly into the depths which felt strangely solid as if he were reaching the flesh of other openings.

And with a sudden, continuous, high-pitched moaning, the girl found words: 'Quick, quick, quick, quick, ooooh!' in a cascade of incoherent emotion. Her hands clutched him with the force of a madman, digging into his shoulders, her knees stretched back, so that her buttocks were wriggling under his thighs, her face contorted and then her whole body was wracked and tormented in a series of convulsions and her mouth opened in a great 'Aaaaaaaaah . . .' and her soft passage reached the extreme of sensation and the liquid juices exploded as the breath was drawn from her body in a furious, aching sigh.

As he had felt the channel grow big around his penis, Ineni forced himself into the girl, holding her, pressing and grinding against her for seconds without jerking his hips, his head swaying in ecstasy on his shoulders and then he withdrew, thrust slowly in again – and again – and with a last deep surge, his entrails seemed to break through his penis and spatter in swift floods high up in the girl's body. He rammed in and into her, gasping, with her pulling his thighs to her, until the very last of his emotion had been dragged from him and then he settled slowly down on her hot, soft body and lay, crushing her breasts and belly with his weight until the immediate exhaustion had dissipated.

He rolled off the girl and stroked her belly gently. There was blood on the hides.

The girl smiled at him through deep, grateful eyes

which knew, now, all of the world that she had not known before.

'You were very cruel to me at first,' she whispered with a smile. 'But I am glad you were. It was a sweet pain.'

Ineni kissed her, stroking her full breasts and she looked down at his penis with a curiosity which contained now, little embarrassment. It was thick and heavy even now and she traced a vein with her finger tip, glancing up at his eyes with a quick, child-like smile.

'Now I am fit for the best harem,' she said with an air of satisfaction.

'There are many things you have yet to learn,' Ineni replied with amusement. 'You must be ready to obey your lord's every whim, his every perversion, to give him the fullest enjoyment no matter what he demands.'

'Is there more he might demand?' the girl asked, raising dark eyebrows, while her hand moved gently, possessively almost, around the thickening penis.

'You sweet innocent. He might demand of you three score positions, or your mouth, perhaps, or your tender behind.'

'What would he want with my behind?' the girl asked in surprise.

'If you like I will teach you,' Ineni said.

The girl looked at him uncertainly, large brown eyes troubled.

'I am a little afraid,' she said. 'But I want to be taught.'

Her slender fingers had continued to caress Ineni's penis, which had swung in gentle stages to a fully rampant position. As he kissed the girl, his organ was crushed, vertically, against the soft flesh of her belly, indenting it with the pressure. He slid his hand down her back, brushing lightly the firm, stretched skin until his hand soared out over the twin smooth mounds of her buttocks. They were full and voluptuously bulbous to the touch and he cupped his hands around them, stroking them, kneading them. He rubbed his hand in little circular motions over the deep inturned join and the girl began to wriggle a little so that her buttocks moved and tautened under his hand, brushing against his palm.

'Turn over onto your belly,' he whispered. And after a moment's hesitation, she rolled gently away from him and over, face flat on the hides, turned to one side watching him, waiting.

Her bottom rounded out below him like a full water bottle and he continued to stroke it, his penis beginning to throb in its heat. His fingers moved gently into the hot ravine and the girl involuntarily tightened her buttocks into taut melons, trapping his fingers between them.

He dug the softer, inside flesh with his finger tips and waited for her to relax. When he felt her muscles loosen again, he brushed his fingers into the depth of the crease, while the girl squirmed with tiny, rippling movements of her hips which creased her buttocks in sinuous hollows and rounded them out again into full moons of flesh.

She began to breathe heavily and Ineni felt with his finger tip for the tight little pucker of flesh. He found it and began to press. The girl seemed to hold her breath for a moment, but then relaxed again and he insinuated his finger carefully and slowly into the loosening bud which was gradually becoming an aperture. His finger moved in and the firm, gristly flesh clasped him like a strong elastic band. As he thrust in, and girl's body flexed rigidly and he eased the pressure for a moment, but continued relentlessly as she slumped again. Soon his finger up to the first joint was warmly enclosed in the tight, rubbery core of her squirming rump, pressing, digging, enlarging in preparation for the greater intrusion.

The girl's face was hot and flushed, pressed tightly into the hides. Her eyes were closed and she breathed heavily and unevenly through open lips.

Ineni's eyes feasted on the creasing flesh of the slim, writhing body as his finger plunged unmercifully into the depths of the girl's bottom. Her breasts were crushed and half flattened against the hides and her hands slowly clutched and unclutched the material as he entered her.

With his penis rigid and pulsing at the very feel of the soft, springy texture of her behind, Ineni felt a surge of power sweep through him. With a sharp movement, he forced another finger into the girl's anus, crushing it in with the first so suddenly that she gave a little squeal and jerked away. But his fierce insistence allowed her no escape and soon she was moaning quietly at the thick ravaging so close to her aching vagina.

Judging the time right and, in fact, unable to restrain himself any longer, Ineni withdrew his fingers and slithered onto the warm skin of the girl's back. His penis rode up vertically between the spheres of her buttocks and he pressed against her for a moment, revelling sensually in the squeezing pressure as she flexed them containing his penis in the deep crease.

'Spread your legs,' he said fiercely.

The girl obeyed after a little hesitation. Her thighs slithered out below his hips until they made an obtuse angle with each other, extended on either side of him in quivering anticipation.

Quietly, Ineni guided his penis down to her anus, raising his hips so that his body pivoted against her on the arm of flesh. He moved her buttocks apart with his hands and prodded gently against the spot.

For some time he lay on her, jerking up and down in little movements while the knob searched, vaguely and without penetration, against a surround of flesh. And then he began to feel a give in the fleshy resistance, a sharp feeling of containment.

The girl gave a gasp, tautened her buttocks and pulled away from him slightly.

He kissed the back of her neck, stroking her hot face with his fingers.

'It will not hurt in a moment,' he whispered.

The girl relaxed again and he resumed the gentle pressure.

This time as he felt the tight containment, the sudden, defined solidity of feeling at the very extreme of his penis, the girl uttered an 'Oooooh!' but did not pull away. Her buttocks went rigid, but relaxed in a moment and he continued prodding gently at the bridgehead. The tiny entrance was clasping at his organ in an agonising grip and he longed to plunge straight into the depths; but he bore the slowness with patience, consolidating gradually for the sake of the girl.

Her anus was broadening, loosening slightly as she became used to the intrusion and although she uttered agonised gasps from time to time, she relaxed almost immediately and Ineni was soon acutely aware of a small section of his penis rubbing in a tight friction well inside the opening.

He pulled her thighs towards a right angle from under his body so that she was stretched away from him in three directions at the latter end of which he was joined to her through the small posterior aperture, leaning more and more heavily onto her bottom with his hips.

The girl began to breathe heavily, lips apart, eyes closed as he explored the outer cavern of her rectum. Her buttocks began to wriggle, apart from her, it seemed, in small intense movements, alive under him, excited by the intimate thickness of him on her and in her.

'Kneel up,' he said in a voice broken with the fierce carnal emotion of the sucking of his organ.

The girl complied, pulling her thighs in a slithering

movement under her, arching her back in a concave and then a convex as she thrust her buttocks up for him.

Now she sloped away before him, from where his great, throbbing rod surged roughly into her back channel, rounding in from her taut, stretched buttocks to her slim, firm waist on which the top part of her body swayed in an agony of half-pain and pleasure, from side to side on the bed of hides.

Her face was crushed in hot helplessness of unseeing, her breasts brushed against the surface below her as she swayed.

Ineni had also moved up between her legs as she knelt and was now firmly pressed against her doubled over buttocks, watching his penis slipping in and out of her anus.

The outer skin slipped like some, thin, sensitive peel on the inner piston as he jerked in and out and the knob, when he occasionally withdrew it completely, or when the girl jerked forward involuntarily at a sudden further pressure, was a furious, outraged red.

Grasping her firmly on either side of her waist, where the flesh creased in thin superfluous folds from her bending, Ineni was overcome with the sheer physical necessity of plunging into her completely, of losing his penis in her so that his whole body, the whole weight of his hips could ram against her, the full length of his rod be clasped to its base in the slim, tight passage.

Squirming her anus on the end of his organ, the girl writhed unaware of the length yet to go. Her breath was issuing in what was almost a continuous thin, low croon at the new experience.

Ineni's grip on her waist tightened. His mouth twisted with the passionate anticipation of his thrust – and then he rammed into her, splitting, like a knife through canvas into the depths of her behind, his penis surging forward like a great, inevitable wave, slower as the thicker base reached the opening, but inexorable and unable to be denied.

The girl screamed at the sharp, painful entry.

Her bottom writhed like an animal trying but unable to reach the spear in its back.

'Oh – oh, it's too much – oh, oh!' The words could hardly form themselves as she tried to escape the pain.

But Ineni held her in a grip against which she flailed in vain. His face, strained back on his neck, was furrowed in passion, his thighs rigidly tensed with his hips as he thrust into her again and again.

The narrowness was agonisingly sensual, seeming to crush his penis, to be tearing the skin from it, leaving it doubly naked and sensitive. His hips pistoned backwards and forwards with increasing rapidity, his penis drawing out and then rushing forward the whole length of her back passage so that she cried out with each hot, furious in-thrust.

Deep in his belly, Ineni was half-conscious of the fierce, unbearable sucking of his entrails. His penis seemed heavy, fully-laden, its very fibre whirling in sharp painful spirals. He rammed his hips against the buttocks of the girl and held them there, crushing against her, wriggling from side to side, while his penis moved in different angles in the depths of her rectum so that she seemed to be almost swooning.

Her anus was larger, easier, now, and between her gasps she was breathing words, indistinct and half-formed.

'Yes, yes . . . hurts . . . wonder . . . oh . . . oh!' They came to him like a far echo in a temple as his head felt tight and crawling.

His hands moved fiercely along the girl's body, grasped her breasts cruelly, clutched them in handfuls, pinched the nipples, returned again to her hips, where they dug deeply into the firm flesh as his hips danced a passionate dance against her behind.

The sucking in his belly had spread like a growing

fire until it seemed that his whole body below his waist was being drawn into the girl, as if the whole of him would disappear into the soft, dark regions of her black passage.

At his penis was the extreme heat of the fire, a painful, burning furnace against which he was helpless, a furnace impossible, now to extinguish, a furnace which he could only go on stoking and stoking in abandoned, willing slavery.

In, in, in he jerked, with his penis expanding and expanding, his mouth opening and closing, eyes fixedly on the face of the girl. Her face, too, was a mask of passion; her buttocks swayed in fury on the end of him; her anus had become a gaping hole into which he had no difficulty of access. He was lost in it to the hilt as his hip movements reached a peak of rapidity, his penis bursting in quick explosions into the waiting sheath, each explosion coming more quickly on the last until they were almost a continuous stream, so that it must have seemed to the girl she was filled with respite with a great thing which was splitting her bottom in two.

His breath was an explosion of gasps. His penis was poised on the brink. The girl was ramming her buttocks back at him. Her mouth was saying 'Go on, go on!' His belly was flooding down to his extreme projection. There was a pause of agony in which the world stood still. And then his organ was undulating in great squeezing jerks which drew sperm in quick jets as when a water-bottle was squeezed.

Ineni went on ramming into her for some time with his penis so concentrated in sensation that it hurt. A gasp accompanied each fresh sucked out release of liquid into her.

As his thrusts dwindled and the dregs of his passion spurted weakly into her bottom, the girl was almost weeping with passion, still thrusting back her hips as if she wanted more.

Ineni withdrew from her at last and rolled over, exhausted, onto his back. His penis slumped, deflated, against his thigh. For some time the girl lay, buttocks crushed together, moving slightly on the hides and then she wriggled towards him, lay her head on his chest and gave a great sigh.

Half an hour later, Ineni, as good as his word, was riding back to the city, with the girl sitting in front of him. She was quiet and thoughtful.

'You have learned well,' Ineni told her with a smile. 'You gave me more pleasure than many an experienced woman of the harem.'

'My lord it was wonderful to me,' the girl whispered. She looked at him sadly. Her hands and lips were trembling.

'What is the matter my sweet little flower?' Ineni asked.

A tear flowed down the girl's cheek and when she answered, the words were a mere, frightened whisper.

'My lord I cannot bear the thought that you are going. I want to stay with you.'

Ineni smiled in surprise, touched by the girl's concern.

'But I promised your mother I would bring you back,' he said gently.

'I don't care. I don't care.' There was a desperation in the girl's voice which troubled him. 'I want to stay with you. Oh, please take me into your harem. Take me with you to Egypt.'

Ineni stroked his chin. This was an unexpected result of his passion. Of course, the girl had been a virgin. She had just endured feelings she had never dreamt of before . . .

ROMAN ORGY

The scene is Imperial Rome and a banquet is taking place at the house of the ambitious senator Lucius Crispus. Crispus is a social climber, a vulgarian who uses his wife's money to buy himself into a the good graces of the aristocracy. His wife, Clodia, is a cool and elegant beauty who watched the antics of Lucius and his slaves with disgust. To please his guests Lucius has squandered a fortune on two erotic dancers from Spain — slim, supple girls with large breasts and no shame. Intoxicated by their sensuous skills, inspired by the plaudits of his guests and egged on by those he wishes to impress, Lucius turns his lascivious attention to his shy new Egyptian slave girl . . .

Like its companion piece The Loins of Amon, Roman Orgy *is a rumbustious sex novel set against the backdrop of history. A creation of the pseudonymous Marcus Van Heller, a stalwart of the Olympia Press stable of erotic writers, it paints a picture of the slaves' revolt in Imperial Rome that is not to be found in any school textbook!*

Among the many pairs of eyes which had witnessed the using of the Egyptian slave girl by Lucius Crispus, was a pair of cool grey. At the moment they were hard eyes, very hard eyes.

They belonged in a face which any Emperor would have been proud of: a broad, strong face with a square jutting chin, a straight fine mouth and a broad forehead from which the eyes looked deeply out, hard and unafraid. A face which could have made a kingdom into an Empire, a face which was going to lead ten thousand men to their doom. The face of a slave.

It was during the lecherous performance of Lucius Crispus that the slave became aware of Clodia's eyes upon him – as they had so often been upon him of late. As Crispus was urged to greater efforts by the licentious crew of Rome's aristocracy, she finally called his name.

'Spartacus!'

He turned his grey eyes toward her and walked over to her side.

As he walked, the muscles in his calves below the tunic bulged; long lengths of muscle stirred in his arms. In spite of his height – he was slightly taller than any other man present – his body radiated a potential dynamism. It seemed unlikely that he could be taken off his guard.

He bent towards his mistress and the cloth of his tunic stretched in wrinkles across his shoulders.

Clodia's eyes held his with a look he could not understand as she said quietly:

'I'm tired of this. I'm going to bathe. I shall need you to stand guard over the door.'

She bade goodnight to her women guests who watched her sympathetically as she left. It was very hard on her, her husband acting like this in public, and Clodia such a beautiful woman and not one man noticing her leave. It was a wonder she didn't divorce him – or get herself a lover.

Spartacus strode silently after her, leaving the noise of the banquet behind, through the portico flanking the huge quadrilateral, which in turn enclosed the gardens with their walks and abours and the baths which Crispus had had specially built to the pattern and proportions of the huge public thermae.

It was not unusual for Spartacus to be asked to accompany his mistress. He was the head of the several hundred slaves which Crispus boasted as his entourage and he occupied a comparatively privileged position. Descended from the Thracian princes, he could boast at least as much culture as his master – which he had to admit was not saying an awful lot – and he knew himself to be more of a man.

But lately, it seemed, Clodia had been singling him out to be with her in nearly everything she did, everywhere she went. He had become virtually her personal bodyguard.

Watching her walk before him through the torchlit porticos, Spartacus wondered why she stayed in Crispus' house. It was well known – even among the slaves – the he treated her badly. There was nothing to stop her leaving.

Spartacus' lips tightened as his mind dwelt on Crispus. His master treated nobody well, in fact, except those he considered of superior rank and birth on whom he fawned his attentions or whom he tried desperately to impress – not without success.

Spartacus was aware that Crispus regarded him with a certain reluctant respect, which he felt sometimes bordered on hatred. For a long time he had been at a loss to understand this, but eventually it had dawned on him that, to his master, he represented the threat of enslaved but superior classes who in different circumstances would have thought him nothing but an ignorant upstart. There were many such slaves; cultured Greeks and Egyptians, many of them.

He wondered why Crispus did not put him in the slave market at times, to be rid of him, but then again it had dawned on him that he represented a challenge. If Crispus got rid of him, he would have admitted his inability to dominate, admitted defeat.

Following Clodia into the bath buildings, Spartacus wondered why she should require him to accompany her. Was she afraid one of her guests might wander away from the banquet and try to take liberties with her? – nobody would dare. Was she afraid of her slaves? They wouldn't dare – besides he was a slave. Spartacus became suddenly aware of the intimacy of leaving the bright, noisy company and disappearing through the grounds with his mistress to guard her while she bathed.

'Wait here.'

Clodia left him with this command and disappeared into one of the dressing rooms just inside the building.

Spartacus stared around him in the flickering torchlight. Beyond was a large vaulted hall, its walls of blue and white stone mosaic. The centre of the roof was taken up by a large space in the vaulting through which the sun poured at noon and the stars glittered at night. In the middle of the floor was the great bronze basin of water, water which steamed now from the heat of the hypocausta beneath.

The slaves were never allowed to use these baths, which had separate hours – like the public baths – for men and women. It was still permissible in the public baths for mixed bathing, but it was never seen. No woman cared to sully her reputation. There had been so many scandals in the past.

In the past ... How many years had Spartacus been here in Rome, in the great town house of Lucius Crispus? How many years had he listened to the suffering and indignities of the slaves? How many years since he had seen this Thracian hills, those beautiful, free, Thracian hills? How long would it go on? ...

His thoughts were suddenly stopped dead by the appearance of his mistress. Without a glance at him she ran across the marble floor and disappeared down the stone steps into the warm water of the sunken bronze basin. Spartacus was dumbstruck, a hundred times more so than when he had seen the Spanish maidens dance in the banquet room. Clodia had been quite naked!

He gazed incredulously through the ill-lit gloom of the bathing room. It was so. Through the gloom and the rising vapours he could see her white body floating lazily on the surface of the greenish water. Even now he could make out – how anguishingly vague – the lines of her pale breasts breaking the surface.

Spartacus' mind wouldn't function for some seconds. This had never been known. A Roman patrician woman undressing before a male slave! He turned and peered back through the gloom of the grounds, half afraid that he might be struck down for the sacrilege of having seen what had been paraded before him.

In the fleeting glimpse he had seen the body of one of the most beautiful women of Rome; a body which he knew many noble Romans would have given a fortune to see. Cold virtue in a beautiful woman always increased desire for her.

How could she have been so indiscreet? Why? She could have slipped on her stola and then bathed in one of the smaller baths out of sight. It was as if she had paraded herself intentionally.

Spartacus stood, undecided, at the entrance to the building. He felt he should withdraw to the grounds just outside, but hesitated to disobey his mistress' explicit command. It seemed further sacrilege to remain where he was, particularly as Clodia was making no effort to escape his view, seemed, in fact, to be parading herself quite unconcernedly.

As he watched her misty outline, she turned on her stomach and floated, face down in the water, her long, unloosened hair streaming over her wet shoulders, rounded tips of buttocks showing like some ghostly half-submerged fish.

Spartacus folded his arms. Under his hands he felt the smooth, tight bulging of his biceps and the feeling reassured him. This was Clodia's fault. He would stay where he was.

From time to time, he watched her leisurely lolling in the warm water, he saw her raise her head, or simply turn it, towards where he stood in the shadow of the entrance. Perhaps she was afraid he would go and leave her unprotected. Although why he would was unthinkable. To disobey an order!

Reflecting, with the image of her nudity in his head, Spartacus began to remember little incidents of the past few weeks: the way her eyes were so often upon him, the fact she had asked his advice upon some Thracian vase she had considered buying, that once her hand had rested on his arm, as if absently, when she gave him an order. Spartacus reflected on these things and gazed with his cool, grey eyes through the steam at the bronze basin.

Time passed. To Spartacus it seemed an eternity, at any moment of which he expected some guest to stray away from the noise of the banquet which he could no longer hear, and find him standing his lonely guard over the senator's naked wife.

But when at last the silent worry of his thoughts was interrupted, it was such an interruption as to fill his head with an even darker cloud of anxiety.

From the bronze basin, Clodia's cultured voice reached him. There was a trace of nervousness in the usually firm, imperious tones.

'Spartacus. A cloth and my robe are in the dressing room.'

He hesitated a second or two for her to add something, but she lay back in the water, waiting.

His heart was beating a little faster than normal as he went into the dressing room. There on a wooden seat were strewn her clothes. His face flushed as his eyes passed, in the gloom, from her stola to the under tunic, the brassiere which clasped those proud breasts, the loincloth which contained those virtuous hips.

He picked up the woollen napkin and the blue robe made of the still rare silk from the mysterious Orient.

As he strode toward the pool, muscles flexing and unflexing in his powerful legs, he was filled with the foreboding of strange things. This was no ordinary night. This was no ordinary duty he was performing.

He reached the pool's edge and stood looking down into the opaque green waters where Clodia, still unconcernedly, floated. She seemed to ignore him as he gazed down at the parts of her body which showed through the steam.

Spartacus waited, while Clodia paddled. He could

224

see the smooth slope of her white shoulders, the deep cleft of the upper part of her breast. Half lying in the water, she turned her eyes towards him.

Her face was radiant with the pale beauty, the clear-cut lines of a Roman aristocrat. Her hazel eyes were bright with a peculiar fire.

'You dislike your master, Spartacus,' she said. Her voice had regained its old, firm tones.

Spartacus said nothing.

Clodia laughed. One of the few times he'd ever heard her laugh.

'Your silence condemns you. He dislikes you too.'

She hesitated and still Spartacus said nothing.

'Today he finally admitted defeat. He decided to get rid of you, sell you in the slave market.'

Spartacus stared at her. So at last it had happened. But her next words astonished him.

'He wanted to sell you, but I put my foot down. Because I want to keep you.'

'My lady is kind,' Spartacus said softly.

'No, not kind,' she said, 'just self-indulgent.'

Giving Spartacus no time to ponder her words, she began to raise herself to the marble floor of the baths.

He stared at her, unable to avert his eyes as she came, like a nymph, out of the water. First her breasts stunned his eyes, large, firm and white with the red smudge of nipples a startling contrast to the colour of the skin. And then her belly, flat, smooth, white; and then her abdomen, with the two pink creases in the soft flesh and the black down of hair reaching to a point between her legs; and the long thighs, themselves like marble, supple, cold and beautiful.

She stood dripping in front if him. Her eyes were those of the sphinx. His lips opened slightly.

'Rub me down,' she said quietly. 'Have you forgotten yourself?'

The whole of Spartacus' skin all over his body seemed to be pulsating as he bent to his task. Clodia stood quietly watching the bunching of his powerful arm muscles as he wiped the moisture from her arms, her breasts, her belly, her back, her buttocks. Spartacus hesitated. Her buttocks were full, contained firmly in long sweeping lines. His hands trembled as he felt their shape and texture through the woollen napkin.

'Go on,' Clodia's voice commanded from above as he knelt. Her voice sounded firm but there was a hollow undertone as if she were steeling herself. He realised suddenly that she was trembling.

His big hands moved down the backs of her thighs, shaping the almost imperceptible down into a slim arrow. His hand contained the rounded calves in the napkin and he swivelled round and rubbed up her legs in the front.

He was more aware of the trembling. Clodia shifted her legs apart, moving on the balls of her small, bare feet. Spartacus looked up at her. Her lips were parted as she looked down on him. Her eyes pierced his with a look which was command and desire and not without a tremulous undercurrent of fear.

'Go on,' she said softly. There was a tremble in her voice as well as her limbs.

Spartacus hollowed his hands around the napkin and moved them up her leg. Astonishment had now given place to a masculine certainty and strength. There was no doubt in his mind, only a deep, luxurious wonder.

His hands moved up over the knee, soaking the moisture from the skin into the napkin. Through it he could feel the solidity of the thigh. He wanted to touch the thigh without the napkin, but he continued pulling the napkin, like a broken glove, up the leg to where it broadened into its fullness and his eyes were on a level with the crease of flesh between her thighs.

Once more he hesitated.

'Go on.' The voice above him was a controlled Vesuvius.

Spartacus held the napkin in the flat of his right hand. With the other he boldly grasped Clodia's thigh, his finger denting the buttery flesh and with a long, slow movement, he wiped the napkin between her legs, dabbing in into the intimate places of her crotch.

As he felt the soft yielding flesh under the napkin flatten out against the inside of the thighs, Clodia's hand moved uncontrollably down to his head and her fingers grasped his long, fair hair and pressed his face to her lower belly.

Spartacus rose slowly up her body, his lips tracing a path up over her navel, the taut flesh of her ribs, resting on the beautiful pearl hills of her breasts, brushing the rich, hard protrusion of nipples, sucking in the hollow of her shoulder, on up the white slender neck, until they found her lips and fastened there, his lips on those of Clodia, famed in Rome for her beauty, Clodia whose slim, smooth tongue now forced its way between his lips, between his teeth and snaked in his mouth, the mouth of her slave.

After a moment she drew away from him, trembling violently.

'Give me my robe,' she said. 'We must not be seen here.'

Spartacus put her robe over her trembling shoulders, she pulled it tightly around her and, bidding him follow her, walked quickly away from the baths.

Walking behind her once again, Spartacus was filled with the joy of incredible discovery, an emotional power which was overwhelming. Here he was following her as he had so often followed her before – but now what a difference! Now he knew those breasts which had vaguely excited him before as they pressed through her stola. Breasts which had excited so many men in Rome; breasts so inaccessible and far away. Now he knew that slender back which shaped into the

227

girdle of the robe as she hurried before him, knew those buttocks which were outlined by the clinging silk, those thighs over which the sulk hung loosely from its swelling over the rump. Now he understood the looks which Clodia had cast toward him. Now he understood the touch on his arm. Soon she would be his, unbelievably his.

Hurrying before Spartacus, Clodia was aware that his eyes were on the tension of her buttocks under the robe. She pulled the robe tightly around her to give him a more exciting spectacle.

Now they were going to her room and she would seduce him. It was no sudden decision Clodia had made. It had been developing in her mind for months.

She was well aware of Lucius' lack of interest in her. She was no longer terribly interested in him. She had in fact made up her mind at one time to divorce him.

But then she had become suddenly aware of the slave, Spartacus. There was some magnetism in him, some superior strength of character which made her, even now, half afraid of her fascination for him.

She had seen Lucius' recognition of the same quality, had watched the battle Lucius, who could not bear to find himself in competition with a stronger man, had fought with himself. She had watched the indifference of the slave to the attempts of an inferior being to degrade him.

It was a fascination, a very physical fascination, which had kept her in Lucius' house. She would sit and watch Spartacus, his big muscles tensing in his big body as he performed his tasks; she would watch the calm, handsome face and if the cool, grey eyes alighted on her she would look quickly away lest he should notice her interest.

The desire had grown in her to touch that athletic muscular body. A desire which had finally found its outlet a few days before when she had allowed her fingers to rest lightly on his arm while directing him in some duty.

And then she had wanted that touch, that physical communion returned. Had wanted to give, to yield under the superior power which she sensed in the man.

Even now it was a desire completely physical which drove her on. The unheard of, forbidden liaison with a slave. That taboo which gave such an emotional desperation and glory to the act.

Although, it was true, a slave could eventually become a freed man – and perhaps rise to office – there was no denying the fact that a slave, as a slave, was the scum of the Empire. Such a liaison would have the whole of Rome howling for the blood of both parties; such a liaison would resound beyond the boundaries of the peninsula to the very outposts of the Empire.

It was partly the knowledge of this that had driven Clodia on in her desire rather than deterred her. She had a will the equal of most in the city and Spartacus, all unwittingly, had driven her towards the inevitable with every movement of his body, every look in his eyes, every one of the few words he ever uttered.

The noise of the banquet, still in progress, reached them as they walked in the shadow of the portico and mounted the steps to the upper story. Without a word, Clodia led the way through Crispus' room to her own. Starlight shone in through the window which looked out onto the quadrilateral. Spartacus moved uncertainly in the poor light and stood silent and still, while Clodia pulled a heavy shutter into place across the window. She lit torches in their brackets on the walls, and while she moved quietly to the door to close it, Spartacus looked with quick curiosity around her room, which he was seeing for the first time.

The room was dominated by Clodia's bed, the bed in which she must have spent so many lonely nights, listening perhaps to the breathing of her husband in the next room. It was a huge bed of oak. The woodwork was inlaid with tortoise-shell, the feet were made of ivory. All three materials shone with a lustre which bespoke much labour from Clodia's female slaves. There were two divans also, strewn with exotically coloured cushions, and in a corner near the window space was a tripod table on which lay Clodia's mirrors of silver and few adornments.

The furniture, as was customary in the grand houses, was sparse but superb.

After Clodia had shut the door she and Spartacus stood looking at each other for a few moments. Her beautiful face was slightly flushed; there was a tint of fear in her eyes which she tried vainly to conceal.

The interval of walking had made Spartacus wary. He was well aware of the penalty for this sort of thing and, although his length of rigidity had itched against his loincloth from the moment he'd seen Clodia run from her dressing room, he now remained where he was, making no move towards her.

Looking at him, Clodia too, felt the slight embarrassment that the interval had built. She had a sudden, fleeting fear that she might be scorned.

She brushed past Spartacus and stretched out on the counterpane and cushions of the bed.

'My bones ache with all that sitting in the banquet room,' she said, holding his eyes again with her own. 'I want to be massaged.'

Spartacus moved towards her, his sandaled feet rustling lightly on the floor. She saw in his eyes the deep unwavering purposefulness that so many were to see and it filled her with a shuddering anticipation.

'Have you seen the women wrestlers being massaged in the palaestrae?' she asked softly. And as he nodded, she added, slipping from her robe: 'Well I am just one of them waiting for the masseur. Clodia does not exist.'

As his fingers began to move over her body and her breath fluttered in her throat, she thought, 'Perhaps this is the *only* time that Clodia exists.'

Once again her full, beautiful body was exposed to her slave. But Spartacus, running his hands over the beautiful tapering arms, the slim shoulders, the glossy swelling of her breasts, knew that he was no longer the slave but the master.

His strong fingers kneaded the firm flesh of her belly, drawing it in little ridges, flattening it with his palms. He stroked the sinuous lengths of her thighs, his chest palpitating, an aching pressure under his loincloth.

His hands rifled her body, knowing the virtuous flesh, all the more sensual for its virtuousness. As his fingers moved between her legs she gave a muffled squeal and jerked over onto her stomach, burying her face in the cushion. Her back heaved as his hands caressed her bare bottom. The white skin of the firm mounds was so smooth it seemed glazed. The hips flowed out from her slim waist, full and receptive; her feet twitched and her thighs rubbed convulsively together has his hands made bold love to her.

Spartacus gazed down, from his ascendant and intimate proximity, on the beautiful rounded lines of her body and choked with a desire to flop his hips down on that filled-out cushion of a bottom and nuzzle his loaded cudgel between the warm, downy pressure of her thighs where they joined her buttocks.

He worked in fingers up between the tight challenge of her thighs, with the flesh giving before his hand, running in ripples up to the arch in which the moist lips nestled.

His hand trembled as he reached his goal, trembled as he was about to touch the intimate secret of Clodia, cold, unfathamable Clodia whose beauty was the talk of Rome. And then his hand, unrestricted now by any napkin, ran along the soft flanges of flesh, savouring their warmth, their heat, their moistness of gentle perspiration.

Clodia gave a sharp intake of breath as his fingers explored, and she slid up the bed overcome with desire.

His hand followed and this time she lay still, breathing wildly as his fingers parted the lips.

As he caressed the little clitoris she gave a squeal into the cushion and the squeal became a gasp as his fingers plunged up through the elastic brim of flesh into the warm depths of her passage.

'Spartacus . . . Spartacus!'

She uttered his name as if in delirium and rolled onto her back. Her hands seized his arms, digging fiercely into their strands of muscle and pulled him down on her. Her lips pressed onto his, working on them as if she was trying to eat them; her tongue jerked into his mouth, gliding like quicksilver.

Spartacus dropped onto her body, her body taking his weight as if she were some complementary part of him, giving in places, resisting in others.

'Spartacus, Spartacus,' her mouth breathed incessantly, as if she had been saying the name to herself for months and it was a relief to say it aloud at last.

He shifted on her, hips grinding on hers, feeling, even through his tunic, the flesh of her belly billowing and swelling under him. The rigidity of his penis hurt him in its confinement.

Her hands moved round his back, arms locking him to her, legs twining with his. Her eyes were closed, mouth open. She seemed more beautiful in her passion than he had ever thought her before.

'Spartacus,' she breathed. 'Don't torment me. You are the master.'

Feverishly, yet with the same sure glint in his eyes, Spartacus raised his hips off her and slithered out of his loincloth. He didn't bother to remove his tunic; it pulled up to his waist. From the foot of the bed his sandals dropped with a thud to the floor.

Her long fingers came down between his thighs and grasped him, making it throb. Then she was stroking his small tight buttocks, urging them at her and her thighs had opened wide.

232

Spartacus slithered down her. He wrapped his strong arms around her body – and with a swift, full stroke, he shot into her like a Roman legion cutting through the tangled brushwood of a forest in Gaul.

Clodia gave a strangled gasp as she felt the dull pain of his entry. He seemed to split her in all directions. He was bigger by far than Crispus.

He thrust into, splitting her farther and farther as his thickening organ coursed up into the core of her body. She wanted him to fill her; she wanted him to make her ache, make her sore, make her cry with the sweet tears of exquisite pain. At last this man, this silent, magnetic man, was hers, was alone with her in the world, his mind focused only on her and the superb satisfaction of her body.

Spartacus, soaring into her with an unleashed ferocity, felt a tingling in every pore of his body where it touched her. His chest against her sleek, bolstering breasts, his belly against hers, his hairy thighs brushing her columns of marble-smoothness – above all his great, uncovered tool, hot and bursting with sensation, moving tightly, excruciatingly into her lower mouth.

He gasped out his breath, crushing his lips over her face, over all those beautiful features.

Writhing under him, moaning her ecstasy, the cold, virtuous Clodia was in a bitch-heat of passion, pulling her thighs back to her breasts, almost to her shoulders even, wriggling her buttocks so that the counterpane crinkled and dampened under the sweating movement. Spartacus exulted in his raging lust.

His hand roamed over her skin, holding the flesh which belonged to him, doing what he liked with the beautiful body which all Rome would have given its eyes to see.

Gripping her shoulders, squeezing until the white skin turned red, grasping the breasts as they overflowed from under him, holding the waist, cradling the buttocks in his big palms, feeling them overflow from his fingers, so that his fingers dug into them as if they were soft, silken cushions.

Clodia groaned and panted as his hands reached under her buttocks, carressing the soft, sensitive skin, moving down to the source of their liaison.

She spread her thighs to the limit, forcing herself to endure the pain which accompanied the ecstasy, moaning with a masochisitic pleasure under his rough impalement of her. His crushing, aggressive weight seemed to be forcing her through the bed, which creaked under the furious rhythm of their intercourse. She felt inside her belly, as in her throat, a sort of growing restriction of breath, a bubble of sensation which seemed to grow and grow until she knew she could contain it little longer.

The heavy staff which surged in the wetness of Clodia's channel was the only part of himself that Spartacus could now feel. His knees slipped on the silken counterpane as he moved up to try to shove more of its length into the passage.

Her chin was on his shoulder. He could feel the heat of her normally cold cheek on his own hot flesh. Her mouth was fluttering over his face. His own name Spartacus, seemed to mix with the animal noises of her moans. She strained toward him as he felt a heat in his belly move down to his loins. She panted and the gasps became a continuous low-pitched moan which suddenly choked off into a staccato spluttering and screaming as she pushed her belly up at him.

She was still groaning as the tide of life-giving fluid swept through Spartacus making him cry out with the unbelievable ecstasy of it, making him want to destroy this beautiful creature whose body he was wildly ravaging, whose hips still squirmed slightly under his, whose cheek was still against his, whose arms clasped his shoulders tightly, whose buttocks still tensed in his hands.

He wanted to destroy, to make this woman completely his. Passion made his head swim, his eyes glaze. But to his astonishment, Clodia suddenly began to struggle under him, scratching at him with her nails so that thin weals of pain stung his arms.

'Beast, beast!' she cried. Tears were suddenly in her eyes. Spartacus fought down her arms, held them at her sides as her body writhed to escape. Bewildered he recoiled.

It was as he stumbled from the bed, confused and distracted that he heard a gasp from behind him. He whirled around in horror.

In the doorway, a look of shocked disbelief on his face, stood Lucius Crispus.

JACQUELINE

The relationship between teacher and pupil sometimes spills over into life outside the class room and extra-curricular links are forged to the satisfaction of both parties. So it is in the case of the young student Jacqueline, an orphan of noble parentage, now living with her aunt in the family castle. For her niece's teacher, the lady has engaged a young philosopher who is himself an aristocrat, though estranged from his family. It will come as no surprise to the reader to learn that Countess Jacqueline and Baron Francois are soon forsaking the rigours of the intellect for the pleasures of the flesh. A fast learner, Jacqueline is as much a giver as a taker in this interchange of knowledge; and Francois's labours are so appreciated that Jacqueline invents a nickname for his main study aid — she christens his male member 'Francinet'. Thus the two of them (or should it be three?) are happily engaged when Jacqueline's cousin joins the class . . .

As usual, we took our daily afternoon stroll in the park.

After we had said hello to the statue of Leda, who, also as usual, was dying under the caresses of her swan, we wandered into the lane with the nymphs. We always like to look at those marble nymphs who laughingly and playfully surrender themselves to the lustful fauns.

Looking at them gives us a thousand voluptuous ideas, and soon we leave them to their eternal games and go into the bushes to play a few games ourselves, always trying to outdo those marble statues.

This particular day, Francois began his game by putting me down upon the grass without giving me time to take off my panties. His feverish hands groped under my dress and his nimble fingers loosened my garters and began to take off my silken stockings. He loved to hide his head under my petticoat, kissing my thighs impatiently, working his way slowly toward my

239

curly fleece, where his tongue would be lapping the juices and his teeth put tiny marks in the rosy lips. This game usually drives me wild. I put my legs over his shoulders to make it easier for him to get his mouth deeper into my love nest and my feet tap the rhythm upon his back. Francois gets wilder and wilder and finally I reach a climax, giving a loud scream and collapsing into a delicious numbness.

Just as I fainted away I thought I heard something rustle in the bushes. I pushed Francois' head away, and though I thought it might have been a bird or a squirrel, I did not want to take any chances. I pulled up my stockings, smoothed my dress and left the bushes, motioning Francois to follow me.

I was utterly surprised. A charming young girl stood before me. Her blue eyes were wide open and expressed confusion, and the wind had disarranged her hair, which was as golden blond as mine.

When she saw us, she began to blush. But I opened my arms with a wide smile. She embraced me, kissing me upon the forehead. I kissed her ardently, meanwhile looking around if there was someone else present. As soon as I was satisfied that she was alone, I introduced her to Francois.

It was my cousin Amaranthe.

After we had strolled through the park some more we went back to the castle together. Amaranthe told us that she had just arrived, and after she had taken her second breakfast with my aunt, the latter had told her that she would find us somewhere in the park.

My cousin was very vivacious and on occasion her remarks sounded like a pun about what I was afraid she might have witnessed in the bushes. The way she looked at us, I was almost sure that she knew what we had been doing.

Francois did not say a word; he just looked at my lovely cousin who had taken my arm. We must have been a charming couple. Amaranthe was a stunningly beautiful girl, about a year younger than I, vivacious, witty and with a little bit of devil in her.

Despite what had happened, I was very glad to see her again, and I liked the idea that she was going to stay with us for a month. The idea that she would be a stumbling block to our love games did not occur to me. On the contrary! And, since she had not yet indicated what, if anything, she had seen us do in the bushes, I decided to question her about it that evening and make her my confidante.

. . . Yes! I could even give her a couple of lessons myself! This silly idea flitted across my mind when I felt her warm hand and smooth arm pressed against mine.

This idea made me so happy that I began to laugh, kissing Amaranthe on both cheeks, brushing her lips as if by mistake, but in reality I had planned it that way.

When I turned around to look at Francois, I saw that a curious smile played around his lips.

Amaranthe's room is next to mine. After dinner I decided to pay my cousin a visit. We have a lot to talk about since the last time we saw each other.

Amaranthe told me about her voyage. She vivaciously described the changes of coaches and horses, her staying at the various inns, and all the thousands of little things that happen during a long trip. She told me that she was happy as a child having escaped from her home for a while, and she also mentioned that I had changed so much, that I had become so much of a woman . . .

The one question I want to ask her burns upon my lips, but I recognise from Amaranthe's slight innuendos, her behaviour, and especially from the tone of her voice when she tells me that she went out in the park to look for us, that she is fully familiar with our secret and that she has watched us in the bushes from beginning to end.

There is no longer any doubt left in my mind when she begins to ask impish questions about my tutor.

It is no longer necessary to pretend that there is a secret. Smiling, while trying not to blush, I admit the truth to my dear cousin.

Amaranthe laughs, and says, 'Oh, yes, my dear. I have seen the two of you playing around in the bushes. And I must admit that I have seen a lot of things which were very interesting and also ... a little bit shocking.'

'Tell me, my dearest Amaranthe, what did you see?'

'But, darling, why should I tell you! You know much better what you have been doing in those bushes than I. After all, you were a participant, and I was only an onlooker.'

'Please! Tell me ...'

'All right! As you know, I was looking for the two of you somewhere in the park. It seemed to me that those marble nymphs were pointing at the bushes, so I went in to look for you there. When I came closer I heard someone groan and moan; obviously I came even closer so that I could see what was going on. Can you imagine my surprise, darling cousin, when I saw you down on the grass, your legs sticking up in the air, and your dear tutor using his head for a purpose which I had always heard was the task of another part of a man's anatomy. It sure looked funny to see his slobbering face between your thighs ...

'But I also realised that you were enjoying it tremendously because your sighing and groaning became stronger, expressing the greatest joy. Your fists were balled, your feet drummed upon his back, and spasms seemed to jolt your body and jerk your hips.

'I stood there, not moving, frankly shocked, but against my will. My eyes were forced to stare upon the spectacle in the grass. Suddenly you uttered a loud scream.

'I suddenly came to my senses and ran away, very scared. But then, you came out of the bushes, smiling and happy, and I understood immediately . . . I must admit that I am a little bit jealous of you for having such a fabulous teacher . . .'

During those last words my cousin's eyes were filled with lust and desire, betraying far more clearly than words her true thoughts. I knew that she was burning up inside, and could not wait to be initiated into the joys and pleasures of the game of love.

The memory of that afternoon, plus Amaranthe's vivid description of it, had made me very excited, and I embraced my cousin passionately kissing her upon the lips. At first Amaranthe was a little taken aback, but I kissed her so passionately, and held my lips so firmly upon her mouth, that her lips parted and allowed my tongue to explore her mouth. She was soon panting under my feverish kisses and let herself fall back limply upon the couch.

She began to kiss me in return, which gave me another idea! I suddenly wanted to give her the same caresses with which Francois always brought me to a climax. I pulled her legs slowly apart, pulled down her panties and lifted her skirts. For the sake of appearances, Amaranthe put up a very mild struggle which was not too convincing. Her struggle stopped the instant my lips approached her blonde fleece and my tongue went into her little rosy slit.

She shuddered under my caresses and began to moan slightly when I went on to explore her little secret spot which was so much like my own. I did my best to imitate Francois with hands, tongue and lips, and I must admit that I was doing it rather well, because Amaranthe began to groan and buck. I recognised her pleasure, because of the little cries of joy were similar to the ones I had so often uttered when Francois was sucking and licking my love spot.

I was very pleased to be able to give my cousin so much pleasure with my caresses. My tongue was very busy in that little triangle, the warm moist flower which I sprinkled with my spittle, mixing it with the warm juices exuding from her love nest.

Suddenly Amaranthe, who had been trembling like an aspen leaf, cried out loudly. She lifted her buttocks high off the couch, her legs and arms spasmed, her entire body shuddered, and I realised that she had tasted a true climax for the first time in her life. She remained motionless upon the couch, and I pulled my head slowly back, covering her marble-white thighs with ardent kisses.

I was suddenly very tired. It had greatly pleased me to initiate my dear cousin in the pleasures of love. I had passionately made love to her with my tongue and lips. It made me happy, though a curious pain was mixed with my joy; I had not had any real satisfaction. I was about to dampen my glowing desire with my own fingers when I suddenly uttered a sharp cry of surprise which awakened Amaranthe from her slumber.

Francois came from behind the Chinese screen.

I did not even have the chance to ask him how he got into the room, and whether he had seen what Amaranthe and I had been doing. He suddenly jumped towards me and mounted me as if I were a dog.

Looking at the throbbing Francinet, I realised that Francois had seen everything and that it had brought him to an extreme state of excitement. He did not waste time on preliminaries, but shoved Francinet deep inside me and began to push with such vehemence that I could feel his balls slam against my buttocks.

Ooh! It was marvelous. I was roughly taken before

the very eyes of my dear Amaranthe. Soon the passionate glow inside me was extinguished.

I was no longer able to take it, and I pushed Francois away from me. My sweet Francinet left its moist sheath, but it seemed that his excitement was too great because he immediately stretched out and became erect again, as thick and stiff as he had been before entering me.

He went directly toward my cousin; Francois mounted her and Francinet found the way to his satisfaction without any trouble at all. Amaranthe was more than prepared. First, I had whetted her appetite with my moist caresses, and secondly, she was practically under me when I was mounted and taken by Francois. The scene she had watched had more than excited her and her desire was at its peak.

At first I did not enjoy the idea at all. I was aware that my cousin was about to enjoy what I considered the ultimate climax of the game of love, and that she did not have to suffer the long months of preparation which I have had to endure. In short, I felt a tinge of jealousy.

But then I realised that it was, after all, my own fault, and that I had no right to object because of a silly little jealousy. It did not take me long to push those unpleasant ideas out of my mind, because the scene I was about to witness was extremely interesting and I became fully absorbed in it.

I looked at my dear Francois from behind and could see the muscles of his firm buttocks harden, when he pushed Francinet deep into my dear cousin and began to work her over with tremendous jolts. Amaranthe's charming legs were trampling, sticking high up in the air.

And I heard her moan and groan her little screams of joy, her Oohs! and Aahs! and finally, 'Ooh, darling . . . I'm dying . . . oooh, darling, darling . . . it . . . is . . . too much!'

A scream, louder than all the other ones, announced that the thunderstorm of love was over. I got up from my seat and walked over to the couple, who were now relaxing upon the large couch.

Francinet looked just plain terrible after this double attack. And my dear Amaranthe was in about the same condition I had been in only a month earlier. She silently looked down upon the large spot of blood which announced louder than words what she had just irreparably lost.

For a long time the three of us rested in silence upon the huge couch, and then we began to laugh. Our tiredness had passed. The curious situation which had developed was truly amusing!

My dear teacher complimented me upon the effectiveness with which I had demonstrated that his lessons had not fallen upon deaf ears, and he thought it magnanimous of me that I had wanted my cousin to share my happiness. Then he began a long lecture about love between women, pointing out the things that were missing, though he had to admit grudgingly that their mutual caresses could be infinitely more tender.

To round out his lesson for the day, Francois showed us that three people can act out more love fantasies than two.

The day after this memorable evening Amaranthe insisted upon reciprocating my little service of love and showing her gratitude for having been initiated into those precious caresses which had culminated in her receiving the ultimate delight of making love.

Francois had taken his horse and was riding in the fields to get lots of fresh air and to recuperate from his exhausting labours. He wanted to restore his powers quickly.

Amaranthe and I were alone in my room.

As a matter of fact, I was still in bed when my

charming cousin knocked on my door. She was wearing a charming night gown of lace and silk, and her clear blue eyes still showed the strain from the previous night. But they looked happy and content nevertheless, and a certain glint betrayed that she was already in a certain state of excitement.

She slipped under the covers next to me, cuddled up, and began with the youthful impatience of a beginner to caress me copiously. She imitated as well as she could everything I had done to her that previous night; instinctively she invented the most refined caresses and I quickly reached a point where I felt an intensive lust.

Even though her rather inexperienced caresses and kisses did not have the expertness of my dear Francois, who was a connoisseur in that area, I did reach a very intensified climax.

As soon as I had come to my senses again, I patiently explained to Amaranthe how much her quick approach had spoiled part of the intimacy of my excitement.

And since, by now, we were both naked in the large bed, I could demonstrate my teachings upon her own charming body. I proceeded very carefully and slowly, thereby intensifying her voluptuous yearnings and putting off the climax which she so greatly desired. I carefully went over every part of her exposed body.

I covered every corner with my kisses, the little breasts with the rosy tips, her narrow waist, her flaring hips, the insides of her slender thighs, her flat belly, the blonde curls of her armpits and the delicious fleece which was hiding her moist warm flower.

I stroked with my hands the soft skin of her belly and legs. I turned her over on her stomach and kneaded and squeezed her firm buttocks. Then I let my tongue slowly penetrate her love nest till it had found the little tickler. I rolled it around till it was quite erect, my nimble hands twitching the hardened rosy nipples of her breasts.

Amaranthe was surprised at the effects. She arched her back, her legs trampled in the air, and her fists drummed upon the mattress. I turned her around again, falling upon her and we rubbed our fleeces together. Amaranthe groaned and moaned, went into a jolting spasm and experienced a satisfying climax. When she had rested a while she noticed that the nipples of my breasts were standing proudly erect and that a hot flush covered my body. The dear girl understood immediately. She kissed them and nibbled on them, her hands searched for my fleece, caressing my thighs; in short, she did to me what I had done to her, and I, too, went into a tremendous climax. Our games went on and on till late in the afternoon and finally we fell asleep in each other's arms, completely exhausted, but happy.

The dinner bell woke us up with a start and we were rather late when we appeared for dinner. Francois stared at us with a knowing smirk, and he even used the absence of my aunt for making a few unseemly remarks which were designed to make us feel silly, also indicating that our teacher knew exactly how we had spent our day.

Poor Amaranthe blushed and was red as a peony, but I quickly changed the subject by kidding Francois about his sudden urge to be alone with his horse all day, asking him a thousand questions about his ride into the country.

Fortunately my aunt returned quickly and we sat down to dinner. Needless to say we honoured our sumptuous meal with great appetite, repairing our strength with delicious bits of meat, fowl and fish, not to speak of a reasonable quantity of burgundy wine.

The time during which my dear cousin Amaranthe stayed at the castle was one uninterrupted series of delicious joys. She participated in every respect in my lectures and became an equal partner in our daily strolls through the park.

The botanical excursions in the neighbourhood of the castle were continued and expanded, and Amaranthe was surely not the last who gave herself in full abandon to the wild caresses, kisses and other games of our beloved teacher.

My cousin showed, on the contrary, an ardent desire to learn during those games. But her stay here will soon come to an end, and it seems to me as if she is squirrelling away a great store of experiences before she has to go back to her dull parental home. I cannot blame her that she is trying to cram as much experience as she can into the few remaining days. It is understandable that she desires to know as much as she can about the game of love, because after her departure she will be on her own without the superb guidance of our teacher. She will have to pluck gallant flowers that will bloom upon her life's path without supervision, and taste the joys of lasciviousness guided by her own instincts. It is our holy task to prepare her for the future as well as it is in our power . . .

These are our last outings. The weather is beautiful. The sun's rays are burning the fields golden and bathing Nature in full splendour.

We are searching for the loneliest, most hidden spots to enable us to give ourselves completely and unhindered by curious onlookers to the most voluptuous games our combined fantasies can think of. We wander throughout the entire area; sure of the fact that friendly Nature somewhere has a place for us with a soft bed of grass, with walls and ceiling of thicket and tree leaves. And . . . we find it! The loneliness and the silence of the place are so great that it seems to us as if we are the only three people left on earth. We have no objections to Amaranthe's suggestion to undress completely. In no time Francois, my cousin and I are as naked as the day we were born. It seems as if we were transported back in time to Paradise!

Suddenly the feeling overpowers us and we play the wildest, most delicious games. Amaranthe and I embrace each other passionately, our lips firmly pressed against one another, our fleeces rubbing and our tongues playing a marvellous game.

Francois uses the opportunity to his own advantage. He climbs on top of me and sends Francinet on its natural way. Meanwhile his lips have reached the thighs and his tongue the fleece of Amaranthe; he reaches around till his tongue has discovered her most sensitive spot and Francois begins to buck and slurp at the same time, using both our bodies.

It is marvellous! Excited by the moist caresses, Amaranthe kisses me more devotedly and passionately than ever, and a double joy floods my entire being. I can feel Francinet penetrate me with doubled force. And Francois, too, is enjoying double passion; and glowing passion with which his lips explore the inner secrets of my dear Amaranthe makes itself felt by the double size of the throbbing Francinet who is pushing deep inside me.

We groan and pant, and tumble around and around in the soft grass. Arms, legs and bodies are wildly intertwined. Lips, tongues and hands caress every available part of soft flesh; our fleecy triangles are moist and twitching, Francinet grows harder and stiffer, throbbing wildly with every shove given by Francois. We stay in this passionate embrace, forming a perfect triangle, and each angle is the ultimate passion for the other. Amaranthe and I shudder in this delightful embrace while Francinet keeps pounding unmercifully into me, and Francois' tongue drives deeper and deeper into the fleece of Amaranthe.

Suddenly my cousin and I are in the grip of a long and shaking spasm. Our lips let go of one another to cry out our joy. Our happiness is complete because I realise that the tongue of Francois has given Amaranthe the same climax which I have just been given by Francinet.

The three of us continue our lessons and excursions till the very day that my dearest Amaranthe has to take her leave from us. My cousin's parents have completed their move to Bordeaux, and she must leave now to return into the fold of her own family.

Before she went to the coach she kissed both of us so intimately and passionately that it caused my dear aunt to raise her eyebrows in wonder. Her farewell kisses were obviously far more than convention demanded!

LASHED INTO LUST

Subtitled 'The Caprice of a Flagellator' and introduced by one 'Robert Lovebirch', this frivolous item is set in turn-of-the-century Paris. The great courtesan Diane de Blédor has summoned her female intimates to inaugurate her new home, a 'delicious little mansion', a gift from an English lord. The company comprises a selection of the most exotic (and most exotically named) whores in the city, including Dolores the Andalusian (who comes from Lille), the independently minded Folette Chanteclair, one Gilette Beausourire, and the aggressive Nini Taquin. Before the occasion degenerates into a (topless) duel between Diane and Nini (on discovering that they share the same lover), the ladies draw lots to determine the order in which they will each tell the story of how they lost their virginity. Here follows the story of the unpretentious Gilette . . .

With a shrug of her shoulders, Gilette began her story:

I wasn't bred at Court – I come from Montmartre . . .
I didn't begin with a clergyman, – only what I did
brought me in money! . . . It's not so many years ago
either – only eighteen months . . . I was still able to
call myself a virgin . . . But I didn't make so great a
fuss about it. . . . I was apprenticed to a milliner . . . I
used to be laughed at in the workshop because I had
not yet *jumped over the ditch*. Every morning when I
came to work the other girls used to shove their thumb
between the fore and middle fingers; they pushed it
under my nose, saying: 'Well, has it gone at last this
time? – what? . . . not yet?' And, when I got vexed,
they said to me, shrugging their shoulders out of pity:
'Poor child – You'll never come to anything . . . , what
a lot of time you want to get it cracked . . .' And that
used to make me so wild, to put me into such a rage
as you can't imagine . . . So, one morning, quite beside
myself, I said to them: 'Well now, yes, I've done it this

time – I've *jumped the ditch* at last – But after all, what can it matter to you?'

And the forewoman said to me in a jeering tone: 'Eh! but that's proper! I believe you . . . But how was it done? . . . tell us all about it, do! . . . Show us . . . ??' and so on, and so on . . . As for me I answered *'Merde!'* 'Eat it darling!' they replied all together . . . I had enough of it and, taking up my hand, quitted them and started off for a stroll.

As I was passing through the Passage Jouffroy, I stopped to look in at a jeweller's shop-front, when a gent, pretty well dressed, also stopped at the side of me. 'Mademoiselle' he said to me, 'listen to me, do!' 'Oh! of course, why not?' answered I. He looked at me, I looked at him, and we looked at each other; and then we burst out laughing together. All at once he said to me: 'Will you come and have some lunch with me?' 'What?' said I, 'who do you take me for, you raving idiot? You've forgotten to put your spy-glass up to your bull's-eye? . . . Can't you see that I've got none of that, for sale? . . . I've still got my . . . Godmother . . . Look here, old chap, you're out of the run altogether . . .' Didn't he just laugh!At any rate, he didn't get vexed and that calmed me down a bit . . .

He stood me a good lunch, after which he took me for a drive to the *Bois de Boulogne*. On the way he wanted to make free with his paws, but I stopped him, saying: 'Come now, none of that, hands off! Old buffer! . . . I'm going in for a virginity competition, that's what I'm about doing!' He didn't seem exactly to suck that in, the muff. But as after all he'd behaved very nicely to me, standing no end of flowers and sweets, I put on my most serious look and said to him: 'But you don't seem to believe me, that's not nice of you!' He smiled. But I told him all, and as he appeared still to have some doubts, I banged my fist on my knees, crying: 'Damn it all! It's not that I want to go to bed with you, you humbug! . . . I want to keep my maidenhead, but as you seem to want to make a fool of me, well, – deuce take it! – I'll go to a doctor's and get myself examined, and then – you may stand dinner!'

Damn me, if the cove didn't then and there order the coachman to turn round ... He had me driven to a doctor's, a friend of his; there, I was put upon a sort of machine called a spec – , spec ... let me see – spectrulum – .' 'Speculum!' interposed, rather drily, Nini Taquin.

'Just as you like,' continued Gilette. 'Well, they put me on to the speculum. The other one, the doctor, examines me, messes me about, I think that he even just scratched my button a little, the beast ... At all events, on leaving, I said triumphantly to my gentleman – I never knew his name, although later on I slept with his friend the doctor – I had his address, – I said: "Was I right, or not? – Am I, or am I not, like *Joan of Arc* ... ?"'

He began to laugh and said to me: 'My dear, you're as pretty and nice as can be. You've still got it, no doubt, – but you won't keep it for ever. If you like to come to bed with me tonight and stop a few days with me, seven or eight at the outside, I will give you one thousand francs. Will that suit you?'

I turned scarlet. The offer was brutally sudden. But, after all, a thousand francs! That sounded in my ears like the flourish of trumpets of a regiment of cuirassiers. Nevertheless I hesitated. He insisted. At last, I said to him: 'Does it hurt much?' 'Oh! no,' he replied, 'just a little pricking at first, and then afterwards it is so nice, so really nice!' 'I am ready to believe what you tell me,' I said, 'but if I sleep with you and that in the middle of the night you get up and hook it without giving me the money? ...'

He had a generous idea. He took a thousand francs note out of his pocket-book and handed it to me, saying: 'You see I am not as distrustful as you!'

I thanked him, but, as I was still suspicious, – could he not after all take his note back again when I was asleep? – I asked him to accompany me to the Savings Bank where I lodged 800 francs, for which I got a receipt-book. I kept 200 francs for myself.

My gent took me with him to dinner . . . He made me eat oysters, cray-fish soup, a lot of things that made me feel quite funny. He made me drink champagne only, but only sufficient to make me merry – no more; then he took me with him in a cab to where he resided. It was near the Parc Monceau. On the way he bought me a lot of elegant underclothing; muslin shifts and cambric handkerchiefs . . .

The first thing he did when we got to his home, was to offer me a small glassfull of fine old cognac. He took me on his knees, and kissed me. After which he began conversing with me for at least a quarter of an hour. I had imagined, that once at home, he would have shoved me on to a bed or a sofa and settled my business at once; so that I was somewhat afraid. For, there is no mistake, it *is* rather strange, and makes one feel queer, to go in for it for the first time, when one has no idea what it is. But my fears were soon dissipated . . . he talked to me nicely . . . fetched me some delightful little slippers, of red morocco leather embroidered in gold – he then took out of a wardrobe a lot of linen underclothing, a pretty corset, all perfectly new, which appeared to be quite my fit, besides some lace petticoats and pretty open-work silk stockings.

He gave me all this, saying: 'This was destined for my mistress, but she left for America, where she died. I make you a present of all that, my little dear . . . It is now barely eight o'clock. I will take a turn as far as my club, but by way of precaution, and so that you may not be disturbed, I shall close the door from the outside. Get yourself ready; I shall be back again in an hour. Put on the petticoats, the bodice, one of the new shifts, in one word, deck yourself out; we shall sup together at about eleven o'clock and after that – *Vive l'amour!* ... Should you find the time tedious, here are newspapers and books ...'

I did my best to make myself spruce and afterwards took up a book to read. My unknown friend did not return until ten o'clock. It was now four hours since we had quitted the dinner-table ... He kissed me, told me that I was lovely, and seating me again on his knees, said to me: 'If it is all the same to you, my *bijou*, will you do me a favour?' – 'I will gladly,' answered I 'if it is possible.' Then said he, 'We will take a bath together.' 'Why,?' I asked, 'and where?' 'In my bath-room ... a perfumed bath ... we shall be all the fresher and we shall smell nice!' This explanation convinced me. I consented.

He conducted me, one arm round my waist, into a room feebly lighted, but, pressing upon a knob, he at once lighted three electric lamps fixed to the ceiling and I found myself in the most charming bath-room imaginable. In the centre of the room was a large bath of black marble, and in one of the corners was a white marble toilet-table furnished with all sorts of scent-bottles and silver pots. All around, next to the wall, were arranged low divans and large Venice mirrors, two of which were pier-glasses ...

After closing the door, my lover led me to one of the divans where he lavished caresses on me and fondled me during some minutes ... For the first time he risked a little exploration underneath my petticoats, felt my calves, which he found to his taste, then mounted up to the thighs, stopping finally at my 'pussy-cat', where he played a little with the fur, after which he fairly attacked my 'tickle toby' ... It was thus that he made me *spend* for the first time and, to tell the truth, as he had not gone too far, it set me all on fire, for I found the sensation quite delicious to be thus provoked by the hand of a man ... I began to long for more.

I must tell you at once that he had not yet seen or touched me, for I had not allowed him to be present when the doctor had been examining me ...

'Permit me to undress you,' said he, and without awaiting my answer he begun to undo my bodice. Slowly, and on purpose, he undid button after button. I was always on his knees ... When he had come to the last button-hole, he kissed me several times on the throat, he then took off my bodice. For some minutes he amused himself by showering kisses on my shoulders, arms and hands ... Then he unlaced my stays and taking a full grip of my breasts with his hands he pressed them softly in a rhythmical movement, after which he carried the teats alternately to his mouth, sucking them and fondling them with his tongue ... This made me feel queer all over; my breasts swelled, the teats stood up rigid, and took on a more rosy hue ...

All at once he seized my head between his hands, and after letting my large masses of hair float on my shoulders, he thrust his tongue into my mouth. My tongue encountered his and I felt a sort of electric commotion: I seemed to be seated upon something round and hard, something like a cylindrical tube which almost lifted me up: it could be nothing else than his instrument. I thought as much, and for myself, all alone, I spent a second time, becoming wet all the way down my thighs ...

Little by little, my friend took off all my clothes. It took him nearly two hours to do it. When I had nothing more on me than my shift, he then once more pressed me to his breast and then led me before one of the pier-glasses. There he took off my chemise and began to examine and admire me from every side. To say that I did not blush, that I was not rather ashamed, would be to tell an untruth ... But I was so much excited by his manipulations, by his caresses and kisses; I had been so wound up; my desires had been brought to such a pitch, that I longed with impatience for the moment when I should taste the real thing itself, not the sham . . .

The bath was ready. He poured some lavender water into it which perfumed it. Then he made me get in: the water was just sufficiently tepid to be pleasant . . . In a moment he was undressed, and leapt into the bath, as naked as I was myself . . . His member was fearfully stiff. I have never since seen one better made. Oh, my dears! If you had seen how I looked at it with terror when I thought that he would thrust that big broom-handle into my belly . . .

He came into the bath and stretched himself along-side of me . . . For the first time I found myself in contact with the naked body of a man . . . it made me tremble . . . he played for some time with me in the water, tickling me, playing with my ahem! – and pawing me all over, then, making me stand up, and standing up himself, he took from a silver shell attached to the wall a cake of very fine scented soap . . . And, to my great astonishment, began to wash my bush, gentle and delicately, first of all the foliage which played round about it, then the outside, and lastly the inside . . . the soap frothed . . . and I felt quite agreeable sensations steal gradually over me.

'It is so that I may love you all the better,' said he, seeing me astonished, 'I want to plant my tenderest kisses upon it. But now, please do the same to me.'

I took the soap, and began with the hairs, then taking hold of his member in my left hand, I lathered it vigorously. It was as hot as fire, and swelled out well-nigh to bursting. During this time he was giving me kisses on the back of my neck, and nibbling the wanton hairs behind my ears, until he fell back exhausted with me into the water, where, in a passion-ate embrace he bit slightly the lobes of my ears, almost crushing me in his vigorous arms, and yet I found it nice ... Oh! it was delicious! ... But the critical moment was near. My friend soon got over his passionate fit: he left of the bath, wiped himself dry, then, making me get out in my turn; draped me in a warm bathing-gown and wiped me dry with care, at the same time giving me some little furtive caresses ... then he sprinkled a cloud of violet-scented *poudre-de-riz* over me, after having first of all, with a vapouriser transformed my terrified 'puss' into a perfumed tabernacle ... He now opened a door, which gave into the bed-room, where, in an instant, I found myself extended on a low Louis XV bed ... My chemise had remained in the bath room and the white bathing-gown he had thrown over my shoulders did not accompany me to the odorous couch, where his arms had gently deposited me ...

He had now attained to a state of frenzied excitement. The caresses, which I still remember today, were as passionate as they were lascivious. He began by kissing my mouth, then, going gradually down, he covered my throat, my breasts, my belly with kisses also, until he reached the sanctuary of Venus. Then his tongue became astonishingly agile, admirably skilful. It was hard and vigorous ... It seemed to forage out all the corners and recesses of my cunt, and he, most beautifully sucking my 'button', whilst I twisted on the couch writhing with voluptuous spasms ... We were both of us terribly excited, as can easily be imagined ...

Without uttering a word he threw himself into position on the top of me, opened out my thighs, which, docilely enough I let him do, then, putting his member into my hand, he begged me to show him the way ... I made no objection, I was mad with irresistible desire ... He delicately, opened out the way with his fingers, introduced therein the head of his instrument, first of all gently, then a little farther, and *then*, with

one sharp shove, he sent it in right to the bottom . . .
I gave out a cry of pain, but at the same time, experienced an intense feeling of heavenly enjoyment which
shook me to the very marrow of my bones . . . I don't
know why, but at that moment I began to cry . . . I
was deploring the loss of my virginity . . . Big tears
flowed down my cheeks . . . But he drank them up with
his eager lips, to shower new kisses and caresses upon
me; he came again in the charge two, three, five, as
many as seven times . . . and the more he tossed, handled, thrust, battered, rammed, rogered and rum-
maged me, the more I enjoyed it . . .

In this manner eight days of intoxicating physical
bliss rolled rapidly away. On the eve of his departure
for America, as he said, he quitted me, after having
kept me in bed with him for twenty-four hours and
having performed on me the exploits of a Hercules . . .
He got the full value of his money, and left me quite
smashed up and broken, with a last one hundred francs
note as a souvenir . . .

As I could not draw the 800 francs I had deposited
at the savings Bank until I was of age, when I had gone
through the little money I possessed, I was obliged to
walk the streets . . . On the second evening I chanced
upon a 'slap up' gent, upon whom I managed to play
the *virgin dodge*. He stumped up five hundred francs,
which helped me to carry on until I found my present
lover. – I have finished . . .

FLOSSIE –
A VENUS AT
SIXTEEN

'Towards the end of a bright sunny afternoon in June, I was walking in one of the quieter streets of Piccadilly, when my eye was caught by two figures coming in my direction.' So begins the story of Captain Jack Archer and his dalliance with the young Flossie Eversley – an example of late Victorian titillation remarkable for the precocious antics of its impossible heroine. The two figures whom Jack encounters in Piccadilly belong to the 'finely-made' Eva Letchford, a lady in her mid-twenties who by happy coincidence is a previous acquaintance of the Captain's, and of course Flossie herself. In Jack's eyes the girl is a beauty with waist-length brown hair, 'deep violet eyes and full red lips'. However, the attribute that makes the most forcible first impression on him is 'the extraordinary size and beauty of the girl's bust'. The Captain, it is evident, is something of a tit-man; he is also a very lucky fellow.

It transpires that La Letchford is only too keen to thrust her young charge in Jack's direction and Flossie herself is only too happy to be thrust. Within a few hours the debauch begins, though sometimes it is hard to decide who is debauching whom. Our Venus, Flossie, is a natural between the sheets and has already acquired some 'French tastes' from her Parisian school-days. She is also eager to share the Captain's favours with her mentor, Eva, and as Jack is not a man to turn down a freebie he takes on the arduous duty of keeping that lady happy as well. The following extract begins on the morning after the night before . . .

'Good morning, Captain Archer, I trust that you have slept well?' said Flossie on my presenting myself at the flat early the next day. 'My friend Miss Letchford,' she went on, in a prim middleaged tone of voice, 'has not yet left her apartment. She complains of having passed a somewhat disturbed night owing to – ahem!'

'Rats in the wainscot?' I suggested.

'No, my friend attributes her sleepless condition to severe irritation in the – forgive the immodesty of my words – lower part of her person, following by a prolonged pricking in the same region. She is still feeling the effects, and I found her violently clasping a pillow between her – ahem – legs, with which she was apparently endeavouring to soothe her feelings.'

'Dear me! Miss Eversley, do you think I could be of any assistance?' (*stepping towards Eva's door.*)

'You are *most* kind, Captain Archer, but I have already done what I could in the way of friction and – other little attentions, which left the poor sufferer somewhat

267

calmer. Now Jack, you wretch! you haven't kissed me yet . . . That's better! You will not be surprised to hear that Eva has given me a full and detailed description of her sleepless night, in her own language, which I have no doubt you have discovered, is just a bit *graphic* at times.'

'Well, my little darling, I did my best, as I knew you would wish me to do. It wasn't difficult with such a bed-fellow as Eva. But charming and amorous as she is, I couldn't help feeling all the time "if it were only my little Flossie lying under me now!" By the way how utterly lovely you are this morning, Floss.'

She was dressed in a short sprigged cotton frock, falling very little below her knees, shot pink and black stockings, and low patent leather shoes with silver buckles. Her long waving brown hair gleamed gold in the morning light, and the deep blue eyes glowed with health and love, and now and again flashed with merriment. I gazed upon her in rapture at her beauty.

'Do you like my frock, Jack? I'm glad. It's the first time I've had it on. It's part of my trousseau.'

'Your *what*, Flossie?' I shouted.

'I said my trousseau,' she repeated quietly, but with sparks of fun dancing in her sweet eyes. 'The fact is, Jack, Eva declared the other day that though I am not married to you, you and I are really on a sort of honeymoon. So, as I have just had a good lot of money from the lawyers, she made me go with her and buy everything new. Look here,' (*unfastening her bodice*) 'new stays, new chemise, new stockings and oh! Jack, *look!* such *lovely* new drawers – none of your horrid vulgar knickerbockers, trimmings and lovely little tucks all the way up, and quite wide open in front for . . . ventilation I suppose! Feel what soft stuff they are made of! Eva was awfully particular about these drawers. She is always so practical, you know.'

'Practical!' I interrupted.

'Yes. What she said was that you would often be

wanting to kiss me between my legs when there wasn't time to undress and be naked together, so that I must have drawers made of the finest and most delicate stuff to please you, and with the opening cut extra wide so as not to get in the way of your tongue! Now don't you call that practical?'

'I do indeed! Blessed Eva, that's another good turn I owe her!'

'Well, for instance, there isn't time to undress *now* Jack, and – '

She threw herself back in her chair and in an instant, I had plunged under the short rose-scented petticoats and had my mouth glued to the beloved cunt once more. In the midst of the delicious operation, I fancied I heard a slight sound from the direction of Eva's door and just then, Flossie locked her hands behind my head and pressed me to her with even more than her usual ardour; a moment later deluging my throat with the perfumed essence of her being.

'You darling old boy, how *did* make me spend that time! I really think your tongue is longer than it was. Perhaps the warmth of Eva's interior has made it grow! Now I must be off to the dressmaker's for an hour or so. By the way, she wants to make my frocks longer. She declares people can see my drawers when I run upstairs.'

'Don't you let her do it, Floss.'

'*Rather not!* What's the use of buying expensive drawers like mine if you can't show them to a pal! *Good* morning, Captain! Sorry I can't stop. While I'm gone you might just step in and see how my lady friend's gettin' on. Fust door on the right. *Good* morning!'

For a minute or two, I lay back in my chair and wondered whether I would not take my hat and go. But a moments' further reflection told me that I must do as Flossie directed me. To this decision, I must own, the memory of last night's pleasure and the present demands of a most surprising erection contributed in no small degree. Accordingly, I tapped at Eva's bedroom door.

She had just come from her bath and wore only a peignoir and her stockings. On seeing me, she at once let fall her garment and stood before me in radiant nakedness.

'Look at this,' she said, holding out a half-sheet of notepaper. 'I found it on my pillow when I woke an hour ago.

' "If Jack comes this morning I shall send him in to see you while I go to Virginie's. Let him – anything beginning with 'f' or 's' that rhymes with luck – you. 'A hair of the dog', etc., will do you both good. My time will come. Ha! Ha!

' "Floss."

'Now I ask you, Jack, was there ever such an adorable little darling?'

My answer need not be recorded.

Eva came close to me and thrust her hand inside my clothes.

'Ah! I see you are of the same way of thinking as myself,' she said taking hold of my fingers and carrying them to her cunt, which pouted hungrily. 'So let us have one good royal fuck and then you can stay here with me while I dress, and I'll tell you anything that Flossie may have left out about her school-life in Paris. Will that meet your views?'

'Exactly,' I replied.

'Very well then. As we are going to limit ourselves to *one*, would you mind fucking me *en levrette*?'

'Any way you like, most puissant and fuck-some of ladies!'

I stripped off my clothes in a twinkling and Eva placed herself in position, standing on the rug and bending forwards with her elbows on the bed. I reverently saluted the charms thus presented to my lips, omitting none, and then rising from my knees, advanced, weapon in hand, to storm the breach. As I approached, Eva opened her legs to their widest extent, and I drove my straining prick into the mellow cunt, fucking it with unprecedented vigour and delight, as the lips alternately parted and contracted, nipping me with an extraordinary force in response to the pressure of my right forefinger upon the clitoris and of my left upon the nipples of the heaving breasts. Keen as was the enjoyment we were both experiencing the fuck – as in invariably the case with a morning performance – was of very protacted duration, and several minutes had elapsed before I dropped my arms to Eva's thighs and, with my belly glued against her bottom and my face nestling between her shoulder blades, felt the rapturous throbbing of my prick as it discharged an avalanche into the innermost recesses of her womb.

'Don't move, Jack, for Heaven's sake,' she cried.

'Don't want to, Eva, I'm quite happy where I am, thank you!'

Moving an inch or two further out from the bed so as to give herself more 'play', she started an incredibly provoking motion of her bottom, so skilfully executed that it produced the impression of being almost *spiral*. The action is difficult to describe, but her bottom rose and fell, moved backward and forward, and from side to side in quick alternation, the result being that my member was constantly in contact with, as it were, some fresh portion of the embracing cunt, the soft folds of which seemed by their varied and tender caresses to be pleading to him to emerge from his present state of apathy and resume the proud condition he had displayed before.

'Will he come up this way, Jack, or shall I take the dear little man in my mouth and suck him into an erection?'

'I think he'll be all right as he is, dear. Just keep on

nipping him with your cunt and push your bottom a little closer to me so that I may feel your naked flesh against mine ... *that's* it!'

'Ah! the darling prick, he's beginning to swell! he's going to fuck me directly, I know he is! Your finger on my cunt in front, please Jack, and the other hand on my nipples. So! *that's* nice. Oh dear! how I *do* want your tongue in my mouth, but that can't be. Now begin and fuck me slowly at first. Your *second* finger on my clitoris, please, and frig me in time to the motion of your body. Now fuck faster a little, a deeper into me. Push, dear, push like a demon. Pinch my nipple; a little faster on the clitoris. I'm spending! I'm dying of delight! Fuck me, Jack, keep on fucking me. Don't be afraid. Strike against my bottom with all your strength, harder still, harder! Now put your hands down to my thighs and *drag* me on to you. Lovely! grip the flesh of my thighs with your fingers and fuck me to the very womb.'

'Eva, look out! I'm going to spend!'

'So am I, Jack. Ah! how your prick throbs against my cunt! Fuck me, Jack, to the last moment, spend your last drop, as I'm doing. One last push up to the hilt – there, keep him in like that and let me have a deluge from you. How exquisite! how adorable to spend together! *One* moment more before you take him out, and let me kiss him with my cunt before I say goodbye.'

'What a nip that was, Eva, it felt more like a hand on me than a – '

'Yes,' she interrupted me, turning round and facing me with her eyes languorous and velvety with lust, 'that is my only accomplishment, and I must say I think it's a valuable one! In Paris I had a friend – but no matter I'm not going to talk about myself, but about Flossie. Sit down in that chair, and have a cigarette while I talk to you. I'm going to stay naked if you don't mind. It's so hot. Now if you're quite comfy, I'll begin.'

She seated herself opposite to me, her splendid naked body full in the light from the window near her.

'There is a part of Flossie's school story,' began Eva, 'which she has rather shrunk from telling you, and so I propose to relate the incident, in which I am sure you will be sufficiently interested. For most of her school days in Paris, nothing very special occurred to her beyond the cementing of her friendship with Ylette Vespertin. Flossie was a tremendous favourite with the other girls on account of her sweet nature and her extraordinary beauty, and there is no doubt that a great many curly heads were popped under her petticoats at one time and another. All these heads, however, belonged to her own sex, and no great harm was done. But just after her sixteenth birthday there arrived at the convent a certain Camille de Losgrain, who, though by no means averse to the delights of gamahuche, nursed a strong preferences for male, as against female charms. Camille speedily struck up an alliance with a handsome boy of seventeen who lived in the house next door. This youth had often seen Flossie and greatly desired her acquaintance. It seems that his bedroom window was on the same level as that of the room occupied by Flossie, Camille and three other girls, all of whom knew him by sight and had severally expressed a desire to have him between their legs. So it was arranged one night that he was to climb on to a buttress below his room, and the girls would manage to haul him into theirs. All this had to be done in darkness, as of course no light could be shown. The young gentleman duly arrived on the scene in safety – the two eldest girls divested him of his clothes, and then, according to previous agreement, the five damsels sat naked on the edge of the bed in the pitch dark room, and Master Don Juan was to decide by passing his hands over their bodies, which of the five should be favoured with his attentions. No one was to speak, to touch his person or to make any sign of interest.

273

Twice the youth essayed this novel kind of ordeal by touch, and after a moment's profound silence he said, 'J'ai choisi, c'est la troisieme.' 'La troisieme' was no other than Flossie, the size of whose breasts had at once attracted him as well as given a clue to her identity. And now, Jack, I hope the sequel will not distress you. The other girls accepted the decision most loyally, having no doubt anticipated it. They laid Flossie tenderly on the bed and lavished every kind of caress upon her, gamahuching her with especial tenderness, so as to open the road as far as possible to the invader. It fortunately turned out to be the case that the boy's prick was not by any means of abnormal size, and as the dear little maidenhead had been already subjected to very considerable wear and tear of fingers and tongue the entrance was, as she told me herself, effected with a minimum of pain and discomfort, hardly felt indeed in the midst of the frantic kisses upon mouth, eyes, nipples, breasts and buttocks which the four excited girls rained upon her throughout the operation. As for the boy, his enjoyment knew no bounds, and when his alloted time was up could hardly be persuaded to make the return voyage to his room. This, however, was at last accomplished, and the four virgins hastened to hear from their ravished friend the full true and particular account of her sensations. For several nights after this, the boy made his appearance in the room, where he fucked all the other four in succession, and pined only for Flossie, who, however, regarded him as belonging to Camille and declined anything beyond the occasional service of his tongue which she greatly relished and which he, of course, as gladly put at her disposal.

'All this happened just before my time and was related to me afterwards by Flossie herself. It is only six months ago that I was engaged to teach English at the convent. Like everyone else who is brought in contact with her, I at once fell in love with Flossie and

274

we quickly became the greatest of friends. A month ago, came a change of fortune for me, an old bachelor uncle dying suddenly and leaving me a competence. By this time, the attachment between Flossie and myself had become so deep that she could not bear the thought of parting from me. I too was glad enough of the excuse thus given for writing to Flossie's guardian – who has never taken more than a casual interest in her – to propose her returning to England with me and the establishment of a joint menage. My 'references' being satisfactory, and Flossie having declared herself to be most anxious for the plan, the guardian made no objection and in sort – here we are!'

'Well, that's a very interesting story, Eva. Only – *confound* that French boy and his buttress!'

'Yes, you would naturally feel like that about it, and I don't blame you. Only you must remember that if it hadn't been for the size of Flossie's breasts, and its being done in the dark, and . . .'

'But Eva, you don't mean to tell me the young brute wouldn't have chosen her out of the five if there had been a *light*, do you!'

'No, of course not. What I *do* mean is that it was all a sort of fluke, and that Flossie is really, to all intents and purposes . . .'

'Yes, yes, I know what you would like to say, and I entirely and absolutely agree with you. I *love* Flossie with all my heart and soul and . . . well, that French boy can go to the devil!'

'Miss Eva! Miss Eva!' came a voice outside the door.

'Well, what is it?'

'Oh, if you please, Miss, there's a young man downstairs called for his little account. Says 'e's the coals, Miss. I *towld* him you was engaged, Miss?'

'Did you – and what did he say?'

' "Ow!" 'e sez, "engyged, is she", 'e sez – "well, you tell'er from me confidential-like, as it's 'igh time she was *married*", 'e sez!'

Our shouts of laughter brought Flossie scampering into the room, evidently in the wildest spirits.

'Horful scandal in 'igh life,' she shouted. 'A genl'man dish-covered in a lydy's aportments! 'arrowin' details. Speshul! Pyper! Speshul! – Now then, you two, what have you been doing while I've been gone? Suppose you tell me exactly what you've done and I'll tell you exactly what *I've* done!' – then in a tone of cheap melodrama – 'Aha! 'ave I surproised yer guilty secret? She winceth! likewise*e* winceth! in fact they both winceth! Thus h'am I avenged upon the pair!' And kneeling down between us, she pushed a dainty finger softly between the lips of Eva's cunt, and with her other hand took hold of my yard and tenderly frigged it, looking up into our faces all the time with inexpressible love and sweetness shining from her eyes.

'You *dears!*' she said. 'It *is* nice to have you two naked together like this!'

A single glance passed between Eva and me, and getting up from our seats we flung ourselves upon the darling and smothered her with kisses. Then Eva, with infinite gentleness and many loving touches, preceded to undress her, handing the dainty garments to me one by one to be laid on the bed near me. As the fair white breasts came forth from the corset, Eva gave a little cry of delight, and pushing the lace-edged chemise below the swelling globes, took one erect and rosy nipple into her mouth, and putting her hand behind my neck, motioned me to take the other. Shivers of delight coursed one another up and down the shapely body over which our fingers roamed in all directions. Flossie's remaining garments were soon allowed to fall by a deft touch from Eva, and the beautiful girl stood before us in all her radiant nakedness. We paused a moment to gaze upon the spectacle of loveliness. The fair face flushed with love and desire; the violet eyes shone; the full rounded breasts put forth their coral nipples as if craving to be kissed again; below the smooth satin belly appeared the silken tuft that shaded without concealing the red lips of the adorable cunt; the polished thighs gained added whiteness by contrast with the dark stockings which clung amorously to the finely moulded legs.

'Now, Jack, *both together*,' said Eva, suddenly.

I divined what she meant and arranging a couple of large cushions on the wide divan, I took Flossie in my arms and laid her upon them, her feet upon the floor, Her legs opened instinctively and thrusting my head between her thighs, I plunged my tongue into the lower part of the cunt, whilst Eva, kneeling over her, upon the divan, attacked the developed clitoris. Our mouths thus met upon the enchanted spot and our tongues filled every corner and crevice of it. My own, I must admit, occasionally wandered downwards to the adjacent regions, and explored the valley of delight in that direction. But wherever we went and whatever we did, the lithe young body continued to quiver from head to foot with excess of pleasure, shedding its treasures now in Eva's mouth, now in mine and sometimes in both at once! But vivid as were the delights she was experiencing, they were of a passive kind only, and Flossie was already artist enough to know that the keenest enjoyment is only obtained when giving and receiving are equally shared. Accordingly I was not surprised to hear her say:

'Jack, could you come up here to me now, please?'

Signing to me kneel astride of her face, she seized my yard, guided it to her lips and then locking her hands over my loins, she alternately tightened and relaxed her grasp, signifying that I was to use the delicious mouth freely as a substitute for the interdicted opening below. The peculiar sucking action of her lips, of which I have spoken before, bore a pleasant resemblance to the nipping of an accomplished cunt, whilst the never-resting tongue, against whose soft folds M. Jacques frigged himself luxuriously in his

277

passage between the lips and throat, added a provocation to the lascivious sport not to be enjoyed in the ordinary act of coition. Meanwhile Eva had taken my place between Flossie's legs and was gamahuching the beloved cunt with incredible ardour. A sloping mirror on the wall above enabled me to survey the charming scene at my leisure, and to observe the spasms of delight which, from time to time, shook both the lovely naked forms below me. At last my own time arrived, and Flossie, alert as usual for the signs of the approaching crisis, clutched my bottom with convulsive fingers and held me close pressed against her face, whilst I flooded her mouth with the stream of love that she adored. At the same moment the glass told me that Eva's lips were pushing far into the vulva to receive the result of their amorous labours, the passage of which from cunt to mouth was accompanied by every token of intense enjoyment from both the excited girls.

Rest and refreshment were needed by all three after the strain of our morning revels, and so the party broke up for the day after Flossie had mysteriously announced that she was designing something 'extra special', for the morrow.

MY SECRET LIFE

First published privately in eleven volumes between the years 1885 and 1895, My Secret Life *is undoubtedly the most extraordinary sexual autobiography ever to see the light of day. Unlike the other books whose excerpts feature in this volume, this is no work of imagination, it is a chronicle of one man's sexual life as complete in detail as the pseudonymous author, Walter, can make it. This monumental work provides a remarkable picture, not just of one sexually obsessed Victorian, but of a society at work and play fired by the ceaseless dynamo of sexual activity. Inevitably, given that Walter was not a poor man, many of his sexual partners – urchins, maids, street-walkers – were seduced as much by money as by lust, though, as he says, 'Women were the pleasure of my life. I loved cunt, but also who had it; I liked the woman I fucked and not simply the cunt I fucked, and therein is a great difference.'*

The consequence was that Walter forged lasting relationships with many of the prostitutes he favoured. Towards the end of his life Walter became particularly fond of 'Helen M.', a woman he met at the Argyle Rooms in London: 'Of full but not great height, with the loveliest shade of chestnut hair, she had eyes in which grey, green and hazel were indescribably blended with an expression of supreme voluptuousness in them, yet without bawdiness or salacity, and capable of any play of expression . . . I have had many splendid women in my time, but never a more perfect beauty in all respects' . . .

On returning to England I visited Helen and told her of my adventures abroad. She wished she'd been with me, always had longed to see a brothel there, would have gone with me there. She seemed excited about the lubricious cunts, yet calling me a beast all the time. I fucked H within five minutes after I'd entered her house, then laying, telling her these things, she began to frig herself, and almost instantly spent crying out – 'spunk', and grasping my prick. – She'd finished so quickly that I believed her emotion a sham, but on feeling her cunt – washed not long before – it satisfied me she'd spent. She then told me that several times when she'd a great letch come on her, and thought about, that she'd spent involuntarily without touching her cunt. It's not impossible, for in my youth I have spent involuntarily, at the sight of a female whom I wanted – when I was very randy.

One day the following week she'd be alone and would get her 'poor friend to come'. He was usually smuggled in. 'Then you can see him fuck me." – She didn't say what after. 'He'll want me, for Mr Blank has been staying with me, but is going on Thursday, – you mustn't come to the house till you telegraph to *** (a female relative). – If Blank's not left town she'll meet you at the end of the street, and you mustn't come.' – Such arrangements in fact had existed for some time. – I didn't like it, but would have risked anything to have her.

'You want me to fuck you *after* him' – said I. 'I don't, you beast, you shan't do it any more.' – 'You like me to see his prick and to see you fucked.' – She laughed – 'I like to know you're looking at us, and that he don't know.' – 'We men are easily cheated.' – 'It would take a clever woman to cheat *you*,' she replied.

The day came, the coast was clear. In my shirt I stood waiting for my treat, had kissed and gamahuched her, and with difficulty restrained myself from fucking her. Her friend was an hour behind time. H was fidgety and feared her letter hadn't reached him. A ring, followed by a peculiar knock at the street door was heard. – 'It's he,' said she smiling bawdily. Before that, talking about him she said as if she enjoyed the idea, 'Won't he have his cock full, he hasn't fucked for a fortnight.' – 'Perhaps he has.' – 'I'll swear he hasn't, he loves me, he'd wait a month for me and would marry me tomorrow, but what's the good, he can't keep himself, his family only allow him a pound a week – he'd wait to have me any length of time, and he cannot afford a woman.'

She had thrown a gown over her chemise, so as not to seem too ready – and ran down stairs to open the door to him herself. One of her servants had been sent out, and she had let *me* in herself – much maneuvering was now needed in her domicile. Fear of being caught out in intrigues is one of the miseries of ladies who play these pranks. – Leaning over the banisters I overheard much, he explained his delay, they kissed then. 'My

282

friend has just come.' – He was in her secrets and knew some one visited her. – 'He is in my bedroom – don't make a noise.' – 'I'll take my boots off.' – He did. – 'There,' said she, 'wait till I beckon you, I'll go up and see if his door is closed, he is fearful of Blank coming back.'

Upstairs she came, saw me on the landing and nodded. – In I went, closing my door and soon he was in the back bedroom. A few minutes after I was at their door as before. She was exciting him, feeling his prick, both sitting on the bed, his back to the door. Then they nearly stripped. – She said – 'Stand up there, let me see it stiff.' – He complied like a child, obeyed her always I'd found – lifted his shirt, and I saw his powerful machine standing like a prop. – 'You have fucked since you did me last.' – 'I declare to God I haven't.' Then – 'Oh let me do it, dear.' He went towards her, when a powerful gust of wind (it was a very windy day) blew up the staircase, their door slightly moved, and caught his eye, he came and shut it, I retreated in fear seeing him advance, for had he opened the door he must have caught me. – I had I thought lost the spectacle of his fucking her.

But nothing exceeds the cunning of a Paphian. – Soon I heard her loudly calling out, 'Mary, Mary.' – Up came the servant, who was told something and went down stairs. It was a dodge to open the door without his noticing it. Cautiously I'd opened mine and peeped. H was just retiring and winked at me. Her door was now left ajar. – Again and almost directly after, I heard 'Ahem,' as if clearing her throat – her signal; the next instant, I was at the door. He was laying on his back, his big prick stiff as a poker shadowing his navel, his left hand feeling her quim as she stood by the bedside and looking up at her affectionately. He thought not of the door, or of any thing else but her cunt.

She handled his prick, then his balls for a minute.

'Let's fuck naked' and she threw off her chemise, then he his shirt. She laid down beside him for a second, the next he mounted her, and I heard his sigh of pleasure as his prick went up her sex. Then on he went thrusting. – 'Don't hurry,' said she – but he fucked hard. – 'I must,' he sobbed in a gentle voice. – I was mindful of what H had often said in our conversation, and what I now knew from experience, that a man in the full tide of sexual pleasure thinks of nothing else. – I opened the door slightly, then more, and entered the room as his thrusts grew quicker, saw in H's beautiful face that she was spending, heard, – 'Aha – my darling – love – aha' – from him then both were quiet. – I stood there till H opened her eyes. Then closing the door ajar and standing with my prick nearly bursting, listened.

'I must go to him [me], he doesn't like to be left long – I'll tell him some excuse and come back soon – put on your shirt, stay here, don't make a noise.' – Out she came, shutting the door, smiling at me, holding her cunt as French harlots do – and I suppose all do under similar circumstances – and the next instant was lying on the bedside with thighs wide apart. Her quim overflowing with thick sperm delighted me, the sight made me wild to enter the lubricated sheath, my prick bursting, yet I restrained myself, had sufficient control to do that which whilst waiting I'd resolved. I pulled open the lips, frigged her spermy clitoris, whilst talking bawdily. 'Did you see his prick?' – 'Yes.' – 'Isn't it a fine one?' – 'Yes.' – 'He never fucked for a fortnight, look what he's spent, how thick it is.' – 'Wash it and I'll fuck you,' said I, not wishing anything of the sort. I'd caught her. She'd before often said she let me fuck her thus solely for *my* pleasure. – 'No – fuck me – put it in.' – 'No. – I'm frightened.' – 'What of? what nonsense – put it up – he's a gentleman.' – (He was) – 'No, wash – you don't like it so.' 'Yes I do, fuck me, I like it so, fuck me,' said she impatiently. 'Get

284

lengthwise on the bed then.' She did, I mounted her, my prick plunged up and revelled in the grateful lubricity of her sheath. 'Ain't we beasts? – Oh – I'm coming – fuck.' – Our tongues joining, stopped further utterance, till my sperm gushed out into cunt. I was as quick as he in spending, certainly his prick hadn't left her cunt seven minutes, before my prick had done its work and quitted her also, tho I lay long up her after my spend.

'Pull it *out* dear, I must go back to him, I told him I would.' – 'He'll fuck you again.' 'That's certain.' – 'Let him fuck in my sperm.' – 'All right, he'll think it's his own, but I must go downstairs first, don't you come out till your hear me cough.' – She went downstairs, and soon returned to his room again. – My door was ajar, again I heard the cough, and looked thro the aperture of the door.

She was just placing herself beside him, he was on his back handling his tool which was half stiff. At once she manipulated it, they kissed and talked. – 'What did he say?' – 'I told him that my dressmaker was downstairs, etc.' – 'He's easily humbugged.' – Both laughed. – 'You must be quick, I mustn't keep him longer. Your prick's quite stiff.' – He felt her cunt. – 'You've not washed.' – She said that she'd not had time 'but must do so before she went to me.' – 'Will he do you?' – asked he in his quiet gentlemanly voice – so they talked for five minutes, kissing and dallying. Then her legs were in the air, thighs clasping his, and the rhythmical oscillation of their buttocks began. He was leisurely enjoying a longer job now. Soon as I heard him sigh and saw his thrusts were quicker, I opened the door, knelt at the bed foot, saw his prick moving and balls as they shook with his thrusts. Had I stood upright he'd not have noticed me in his paroxysm of pleasure – Helen did – I heard soft murmurs, saw his buttocks quiver, her eyes close, knew the spends had come, and went back to my room, closing their door ajar.

This back room was only partially furnished – no water was left there with intent, so that he might go to the bedroom below, next the drawing room. She told me this before. Shortly they both went down there – then to the kitchen where she gave him food – tho well dressed he was glad of a meal. Then up she came to me and stood looking at me with voluptuous eyes. – She hadn't washed, shammed that she didn't want it again, but at the sight of her glistening vulva, my prick stood, and with a deliciously slow fuck we spent together again. Four male libations were in her cunt, and she'd spent at each fucking. – Soon after I left.

The conversations I heard and had with her are nearly word for word. – I wrote them down the same evening.

A few days after, I was there then with pleasure in confessing, for – 'I have no one to tell anything to but you, and him now,' said she. – She told me he had slept with her. 'God knows how often I spent, we were both done up. Come on dear, fuck me – I haven't had it since – he's ill. – I'm making him beef tea.'

At intervals of a week or two this was repeated – I saw him fuck her, and fucked her directly afterwards. Sometimes only once, sometimes twice, and the fun and room were a little varied at times to avoid surprise. She never afterwards denied her liking for the double libation. – 'What beasts we are.' – 'Not beasts at all dear, and if we are, we like it' – this was said regularly whenever the double fucking came off, but I had her at other times when he was not there.

A little before this H's protector was as I'd guessed in money difficulties. She told him that an old kind friend wanted to visit her, that money must be got somehow or they must part, and he consented to me – and only me – visiting her. – She had told him I was too old to

286

poke, and only gamahuched her. Of course I've only her word for that. I never saw him or he me. He was very unhappy about it, but sooner than let her again be gay he would consent to almost anything. – Money and other circumstances, however, prevented my seeing her more frequently, tho I went with greater ease of mind. She also was not under such anxiety, and we had our frolics with increased pleasure – for her lascivious delights with me were greater than ever.

Later on she told me her protector was getting as erotic as I was, tho he was a very much younger man. My impression is that she taught him. – Sometimes it was: – 'What do you think? Phil wanted me to do so and so with him?' – or: 'We poked in this attitude the other day.' – Or: 'He likes hearing how formerly I've been poked,' and so on. – Then she and I had great pleasure in doing the same things together.

One day I wished we had a looking glass to see ourselves in when fucking. I had told her of the glasses at French houses – she excepting in a cheval glass, had never seen herself reflected in copulation, and wished she could. – I offered to buy one, but what would Philip say? 'He'd be delighted, we often wish for one when I tell him I've heard such things, but he's hard up just now – he knows you are the only man who visits me.' – He didn't know of her lovers. – Then I paid for a looking glass which she got. It was nearly as long as her bed, was placed against the wall, the bed nearly close to it, and henceforth we could see our every movement.

I shall never forget the day the glass came. We put it up together at the right level, directly we'd done so we rapidly stripped start naked, mounted the bed, and fucked contemplating ourselves, and that afternoon not a drop of sperm was left in my balls. I gamahuched her, and she frigged herself as well, looking in the glass. At my next visit I heard that Phil had done the same, that night after night they couldn't sleep for the rutting state the glass put them in, so hung a curtain over the glass when they wished to excite themselves no more. To see H frigging herself then was indeed a great treat. Her delight was to make me kneel on the bed naked facing the glass, with my stiff one which she held in one hand, whilst she frigged herself with the other, looking in the glass all the time. It was to me a delight – for her form and face were lovely, – to see her in the venereal spasm – an exquisite sight. – Unfortunately however the bed was so placed in the room then, that I could not see either bed or the reflection from the only door available for peeping, hence the fucking exhibitions were always given in other rooms.

Soon after we had the looking glass, a harlot temporarily out of business was often there. She had been a servant, then seduced, then well kept, then general practitioner in copulation, then lodging-house keeper, and was now impecunious. She h&d been good looking but was to me plain, yet was plumpish and her breast and leg were not uninviting. She had been a sort of go-between, scape goat and so on to Helen when gay, and of whom she was fond. – H seemed glad of her, for she was the only Paphian who now visited her, and with whom she could discourse of big pricks, etc., etc.

She (I shall call her Miss Def) was a thorough bawdy talker, nothing seemed to please her so much as narrating some meretricious experience, the tricks that she and others had played with men. There was no disguise now before me or between the two women, for that intimacy and confidence which it seems I have the art (unintentionally) of inspiring in gay ladies, had been given me by Helen, as far as a woman who has been gay can. But Paphians whether in or out of the calling never tell *all* to *anyone*, not even to their lovers. – Does a married woman? These narratives were not inventions got up for my edification, there was no object in doing that. – I never gave Def a farthing –

they came out quite naturally in our conversations when sitting together, which naturally turned on fucking.

In that and in amorous reminisceces H was as much pleased as I was. The Priestesses of Venus, I am convinced, all like their occupation, and to talk over past frolics when they have quitted the life, whatever they may aver to the contrary. – When they are sick and plain in face or form, and unsuccessful, they are repentant and virtuous, are 'Magdalenes'. Repentance usually pays better *then* than fucking.

I've seen lots of Magdelenes, but never one in good health or who was good looking. – They were failures in their occupation, they wanted face, form, skill, and go, and I guess had ill-fitting cunts, or certainly something wrong in cuntal quarters. So they repented, turned virtuous, were 'reclaimed', became Magdalenes and got shelter and money – I dare say when better, or at home in the colonies, they didn't forget they'd got cunts, useful for other things besides pissing.

One afternoon after luncheon, we three had champagne which I had taken there, our talk got smutty. Miss Def showed her legs which were good, and then her breasts. 'Show him your cunt,' said H. She did and we talked ourselves into a lewed state, which indeed I always was in directly I set sight on H's charms. What led to it was a tale told by Def, about a man in bed between two women all naked, and there not being room, one woman laid across the foot of the bed the feet of the two touching her, and she frigging herself whilst they were fucking. 'Let's get on to the bed and do the same,' – I suggested.

We all stripped and got on the bed (it was hot weather), Def's cunt was an unusually hair one, a regular well-fucked, and forty-years-old cunt. – She kissed my prick and H's cunt as well, before we laid down. Then our lewedness, and the delicious contact of soft skins, voluptuously suggested all sorts of letches. – Laying on my back feeling Helen's cunt, 'I'll frig you with my foot,' said I to Def. She delighted, let me, and placing my heel against her cunt after she had turned to a convenient position, I pressed and rubbed it there, she clutched my foot round the ankle and guided it, accommodating her cunt so as to get the friction as pleased her. H half sat up still feeling my prick, and watching this foot frigging. – 'Give a poor body a fuck, I haven't had a bit of cock for months,' said Def after awhile. 'Fuck *me*,' said H impetuously and lying down, for she was hot, and desire sometimes seems to seize her impatiently. Taking my heel from Def's cunt, I mounted my beauty's soft belly and began the exercise with my prick, my toes now downwards naturally.

After a few thrusts. – 'Def's frigging herself,' said H – She could see, I laying face downwards could not till I turned my face to the looking glass which I'd bought. – 'Go on fucking, I'm looking at Def frigging.' – Helen's feet and mine were both against the woman's naked body – we could feel the jog of her body as she frigged. 'Put my toe in your cunt and frig with it,' said I, wanting to feel a cunt with my toe, which I'd never well done before. 'Yes, frig with it,' said H with a baudy laugh. – Miss Def caught at my foot quickly without reply, the erotic desire seized her, and I felt my great toe was against the soft slippery surface, could feel distinctly her large clitoris and thick nymphœ, as well as if feeling them with my fingers. H, without letting my prick out of her cunt, managed to twist herself so that she could see that the toe of my right foot was there. 'The hair of her cunt's all round your toes – fuck me, – fuck' – said she with delight and energy, getting straight with a sigh of pleasure, moving her backside voluptuously. – I reciprocated, lunged my prick well into her hot avenue, in which it had got a little displaced in her moving to see where my toe was.

Then we fucked on whilst Def frigged, we thought

of her whilst our pleasure increased. – 'Is your toe on her cunt? – Ahaa' – sighed H – 'Yes, I can feel her frigging her cunt with it.' – 'Ahaa – I'm spending – ahaa – frig *me* – with your toe – some day. – Ahar – won't you? – Ahaa – Aha fuck – bash it up me. – Aharr.' – 'Spend darling, my spunk's coming. – She's frigging – Ahaa' – and in a bawdy delirium our pleasures ended in the ecstacy of the crisis, the woman at the bottom of the bed forgotten. As we ceased fucking Def continued her frig – did what she liked with my foot which she moved on her cunt. – With my other foot I felt her thighs agitated, she sighed, she moaned, my toe and her cunt moved rapidly, and just as we recovered from our pleasures, she gave a sob, a sort of gulp almost as if choking – a most extraordinary noise – and was quiet – my toe still resting on her clitoris, she still holding my foot.

I jumped up as soon as my prick had left H's inundated quim, finding my toe moist with Def's effusion. The devil had spent copiously. My getting up roused her, and she felt H's overflowing quim. 'He's spent a lot, how I'd like a fuck, I haven't had one for an age,' quoth she. All three washed, and after a rest I fucked H again whilst the other handled my balls, delighted with the opportunity of pulling about the testicles, whose juices she so longed to have in her. Then after a glass or two more wine, she asked me to fuck her and H incited me, – begged me – to 'give her a treat' – but I didn't, having no taste for her, and the condition of my toe which I had washed came to my mind and stopped all passion – I have rarely refused a cunt which was new to me; but I did hers.

H's poor lover was still absent. – She and her protector had been in the country and *he* was still. – Donkey Prick then frequently had Helen, then *he* having also been away, she ran short of her delight. I hadn't been in the house five minutes before she said, 'Come upstairs' and began undoing her clothes before she reached the room. Afterwards she named many times for me to be there, when she could have Priapus also, but with difficulty arrangements could be made to suit all. 'I like to know you're looking at us.' – 'Yes and you like me to fuck after him.' – 'Yes I do – ain't we beasts?'

The man was cunning and often shut the door. He was whimsical – wouldn't often undress – and she loving his prick let him have his way. – One day I was there, he as usual in the kitchen – for she cooked for him there and from that place he could more easily escape by the back way. – But the fellow wouldn't come upstairs, and fucked her on the kitchen table – she was so long away that I wondered. – When she came up, she had just got him out of the house, and the sperm was abundant in her quim, tho a quarter of an hour since she'd fucked. She was dressed, and I fucked her from behind against the bed, the only time I think I had then done so on these double fucking occasions – tho I've tailed her in every possible attitude – I delighted usually to see her face as I fucked her whilst we talked. – 'Ah! – isn't his prick a big one?' – 'Yes I should like to feel it.' – 'I should like to feel both pricks at once. – Aha – beast – fuck harder – Ahar.' – 'His sperm's thick today.' – 'Yes isn't it lovely, smooth? – ahaa – don't stop – fuck – I'm coming.' The angelic smile came over her face, her cunt gripping and we spent together. This is typical. We never fucked without talking about pricks and sperm and making all sorts of lewed suggestions to each other, till pleasure stopped utterances.

There was a garret where sometimes the little servant – when she had one – slept. It contained scarcely any furniture but a bed. One day when there was no fear of surprise, she said she'd make him to up there and get him naked. It was in the afternoon of a warm autumn day, he'd had a feast of rumpsteak and had tippled enough whiskey and water, when I heard him going up the stairs, and in time out I stepped and listened. He was jovial and incautious, yet I was fearful of going up until I heard, 'Ahem' – for the carpetless stairs creaked. Then I heard every word as plainly as if I'd been in the room. – He wanted to go to sleep first. – 'Fuck and sleep afterwards. – Piss first.' – 'I don't want' – but I heard the water rattle, and laughter as they got on to the bed, and then, 'Ahem.'

As I peeped thro the door left ajar – the bed had been cunningly placed so as to prevent his looking at the door – he was lying on his back with shirt on only, she frigging his cock, which was thick but pendant. – 'You've fucked before today.' – he denied it – was tired. – She was angry, was sure he'd been fucking hard the night before, and came used up – she'd had enough of him, he'd been like that often lately, she wasn't going to have his lasts – and so on. – 'Suck me.' – She wouldn't – he'd better dress and go off to do it, – get another woman. – 'Show me your cunt.' – Then he frigged himself and got a glorious erection. – 'Lie down.' – She wouldn't now. 'No, stand up naked and let me see it, stand up or you shan't have me.' – He drew of his shirt and stood naked with a donkey sized doodle. It was worth seeing, a noble, well proportioned shaft standing out seven or eight inches from the belly, and perhaps nine from his balls, and looking an inch and a half in diameter. It was white skinned, and had a full plum shaped tip of a bright red, it was circled at his belly with a well defined thicket of lightish brown hair, (he was fairish with blue eyes) which didn't creep towards thighs and navel. His ballocks was ponderous. Altogether, it was the biggest prick but one I've ever seen, and the handsomest. The sight of it made my own stiffen voluptuously, and at the same time desire to handle his – I don't wonder at the ladies who are connoisseurs in Priapean tools, admiring his and wishing to enjoy it once, tho certain it is that a pego of average size gives as much sexual

293

pleasure to a woman as the greatest cunt whacker. –
A huge stiff prick when a man is standing naked
always looks a little ridiculous, so it's strange that my
prick should have stood sympathetically at the sight
of his.

H sat looking at it silently. – Once for an instant
she turned her eyes to the door where I was peeping.
There was admiration, pride, and lust in her eyes. –
The expression of, – 'Isn't it a beauty, and it's going
up me?' – looking back at it again, her thighs spas-
modically closed, then opened, as if a spasm of pleasure
was passing through her, and putting her fingers on
her cunt she kept them there.

But the prick began to droop. She gave it a violent
frig, it then stood stiff, then rapidly fell, and she bull-
ied him – I was pleased to see a man not thirty with
his prick not quite ready, as mine has been on one or
two occasions, tho I can still fuck her twice in the hour.
– After some more angry remarks from her, she threw
off her chemise and mounted him, her rump was
within six feet of my eyes, and I saw her introduce the
prick into her cunt and do the fucking. – His tool kept
shrinking – she called him a 'used-up beast' told him to
go, but wanted the spend, kept reinserting his machine
when needful, and fucking energetically. I had a glorious sight of this grand propagator, which she often
brought out to the tip and then plunged up her. Then
her bum oscillated quickly, her cunt nestled down till
his balls were close up to it – she cried out loudly. –
'Fuck – spend, Arthur. – ahaa' – and was quiet.

In a minute. – 'You've not spent.' – 'I was just
coming.' – 'You haven't any spunk in you,' and moving
her buttocks, out came his prick shining with her
spending and stiff enough. – I saw H's face, which was
lewed. Without a word turning on to him again, up
went the long thick gristle into her, and she oscillated
her splendid buttocks till she'd spent twice more without his spending once; she after each crisis ballyrag-

294

ging him, he making all sorts of excuses. More than half an hour had she been at the work, and yet went on till at length she got a spend out of him – I never saw her so hot before, her face was moist and scarlet, her eyes humid, with her spending, yet fierce, and as she rolled off she gave his prick a slap. 'You've been fucking before today, you liar, get off as fast as you can, you don't bring your fucked out balls into my house again – you won't fuck me again, you mean beast.' – All his sins came out, she'd already told me of his meanness.

He made all sorts of excuses but she wasn't pacified. She put on her chemise, came down to my bedroom landing and called out, 'Arthur's going, let him out – don't let him go into the kitchen.' – He heard this, came down dressed and still excusing himself – she replying to all, – 'It's a lie. – It's a lie' – till he was out of the house. Then she came to me and smiled. – 'Isn't it a splendid prick?' Then she told me she'd heard the stairs creak, but he'd not noticed it. – 'I'm quite wet, I spent three times, he spent at last, the black-guard is fucked out, yet he knew three days ago he was coming – my cunt's wet – won't you have me?' I said no, but was wrought up to the highest pitch of lust, and in half an hour had fucked her twice. She declared donkey prick should never have her again, but I was sure he would. – 'He has a noble prick hasn't he?' said she admiringly. – 'Yes, but he's a coarse brute, not even handsome, not a gentleman.' – 'Certainly not a gentleman, but he's a noble prick, all the women want him, he pays none, I'm told.' – I fancy Miss Def – now with a house of her own again – was the informant.

I never yet saw a woman fucking a man so plainly, as on that bright afternoon. The beams of the sun at last struck right across her backside, her arsehole, cunt, his prick and balls I saw as plainly as if I had been within a foot of them, and had held a candle to look. – How I longed to feel his tool as she fucked him, and how delighted she would have been. But she was annoyed when afterwards I said, 'Your bum furrow is getting brown, H.' – 'You beast – what if it is, so is yours.' – 'I know it.' – She never could bear to be told about her furrow browning, or later on that hairs were beginning to show round her bum hole, as they do in most women after five and twenty and in southern nations earlier. It detracts from the beauty of the region.

On both occasions, *she* had covered *him*, to prevent him going quickly to the door and his chance of catching me. The next time for some rason of her own – who fathoms a woman's dodges? – she had him in her own bedroom which had now been changed. I waited in the backroom. He was still enough and full, laid on her, half fucked her, and then she made him finish with her rump towards him. H laughed as he got off his bed with his great tool sticking out. Then it disappeared up her, and I thought must have hurt her. The fucking was soon over. How beautiful it was, how exciting it looked! They remained coupled for a minute, then she uncunted him saying, 'You lie down, I must go to my sister and will be back in a minute.' He threw himself on the bed, giving her rump a slap as they parted and the next second she was with me on my bed. 'Don't talk loud, he thinks my sister's here, he's never seen her.'

Her eyes shone with voluptuous light and softness. 'Hasn't he spent? my cunt's full, hasn't he a lovely prick?' said she sighing and laying down. I looked at it, pulled open the lips, pushed one finger up, then my balls could wait no longer, I had been stiff since I saw his prick, and plunged my pego up her. Ah! my delight – to feel my prick up her and his sperm all round it. – H put her hand to feel, then clasping my bum, and heaving her arse. – 'Ohoo – fuck' she cried and glued her mouth to mine. Furiously our backsides oscillated, far too soon my sperm rose. 'Hurt me – shove hard,' she whispered, heaving her cunt up, and the next minute both were spending, her ecstacy as great as mine. then quickly back she went to him, her cunt full as before, her motte and thighs wet with our essence. – 'Make him fuck you in it.' – 'If I can, but he likes it washed before he does me again' were the last words.

She closed their door with a bang, cunningly giving the handle a turn so that it was left ajar, but so close that I could see nothing. To facilitate that a fortnight before she'd cut away, at eye height, a slip off of one edge, and painted it afterwards. We had arranged this together after the manner at the French lapunar. She laid down on the bed for *me* to see *her*, then I for her to see *me*, and we moved her bed a little to give the best view of those upon it, both delighted at the dodge. I couldn't see their heads when they were fucking, but saw all from their breasts downwards. – Now she took the side furthest off, and nearer the fireplace, and he turning to her had his back to me. – 'Ahem' – I pushed the door slightly open and saw them both well.

She began frigging *him*, then he felt *her*. 'You've not washed.' – 'No, how could I? – I will.' – 'My spunk's on your thighs.' – 'Yes, did you spend?' – 'My ballocks were damned full,' – said he with a coarse laugh. – Both laughed, and went on talking about some woman who had one of the smallst cunts he'd ever fucked, and about some swell Paphians she had known formerly, whilst she went on frigging him till, 'It's stiff, let's do it.' – 'Wash it.' – She got up, and holding the ewer, – 'There's no water.' – 'Ring for Sally and I'll show her my prick' – said he laughing and handling it. – 'I shan't – you'd better not – never mind washing' – getting on the bed again and frigging his tool. – In another minute after lewed chat he mounted her, she'd pulled her chemise off and tried to pull off his shirt. Saying it was cold, he refused but tucked it up to his waist.

They were fucking in an instant. Is the spectacle of even a handsome couple fucking beautiful or not? – Is the sight of a beautiful creature, all modesty and grace – whom one has walked, talked, and danced with, to be admired when on her back, heaving her buttocks up, her thighs high and round the man's while under is a thick gristly stem protruding from his belly, and going like a steam piston in and out of a bush of hair round her cunt – is it beautiful? – Both rumps jog, and heave, and thrust and meet, till with sighs and murmurs both are quiet. Is it a spectacle beautiful or not? – No. – Yet an entrancing one. – One that no man or woman would hesitate to look at, enjoy, and envy, none whose cunt wouldn't yearn – whose prick wouldn't stiffen at the sight. – Yet it's not beautiful, tho exciting, stimulating, entrancing to all the sense.

This was really a fine couple I must say, much as I disliked his vulgarity, but to know that that big tube, with its inner tube of discharge, was thrusting up *her* tube, with the intensest pleasure to both, made my prick, without frigging, stand till I heard their murmurs, knew that their pleasure was over.

He rolled off of her, she didn't hurry him. 'Get me a glass of whiskey and water.' – 'I shan't, you've had enough, get it yourself in the kitchen if you want it, don't make a noise, I don't want my sister to know a man's here.' The scout – Mrs **** – took care the man shouldn't know I was there. Hastily he put on his clothes and went off. 'Hush' said she as he went downstairs and she waited till he got to the kitchen.

In she came and I looked at her sexual treasure. Sperm is now to me clean, wholesome. It's the outcome of life – the issue and cause of the greatest human pleasure to giver and receiver. – I no longer mind my fingers being in it, but like to feel a cunt which is lubricated with it. – I opened hers, felt up it, wiped my fingers on my balls, and on her motte – the salacity of the act delighted me. 'You beast, you,' said she but

298

looking pleased with the lascivious act. Then up into her my prick went, and prick and cunt then revelled in the unction and the thrusts, and the lubricated friction of our movements, till both sobbed out our joy in the delicious crisis – her cunt discharged, my balls shot forth their sperm, and we mixed this essence of male and female life in her sweet channel – oh happy woman!

Pressing her sweet form to mine, her hand clasping my buttocks – in the lubricious conjunction we lay. – Slowly I still kissed her, our wet lips mingling moistures there as we lay conjoined – eyes closed – baudily thinking – vague visions of lust dreamily passing thro our brains. 'Aren't we beasts?' – the first words spoken. – 'Damn it, Helen – don't say that again – it's nonsense – nothing beastly about it – what beast could do or care about dong what you and I have done? – it's heavenly, divine – don't – I've often told you you annoy me by saying it.' She laughed, her belly jogged, her cunt moved, and out came my prick, and at once as many and as much as I could get of my fingers up her cunt I put there – lewed still.

This again was on a warm autumn afternoon, for it suited us both to meet at that time – the master of the house was then away. Soon Donkey Prick was got out of the house. I dressed, we had tea and toast, then I licked her cunt till she was exhausted with pleasure, then left.

I had now told Helen all the erotic incidents of my life. She, with her fertile brain, voluptuous temperament, and experience in amorosities, both approved, desired to emulate them, and herself to invent. She wasn't – as already said, – at first frank about her letches and lusts, hiding them somewhat and throwing the suggestion of the gratification upon *me* making *herself* but the complaisant partner; but the mask was now pretty well removed – tho probably women in all classes never quite tell their letches or the truth about their bawdy wishes – who knows? When guessing *her* desire, after talking about some luxurious fancies, I passed them over then finding I did not initiate anything, she referred to them again on other visits, and I met them by some such questions as 'Would *you* like so and so to gamahuche you' – or 'Like another man or woman with us?' – or 'Like me to see you fucked by another?' – 'Yes I should' came frankly at last. Then it was, 'Let's have a woman to gamahuche me, but *you* ask me to let her, I don't want *her* to think I wish her.' Singular modesty, it seemed to me.

Then we got our lascivious tastes gratified and to the full. That kept me from other amours, and to her almost alone, for she had youth, supreme beauty of face and form, was clever, conversable, voluptuous, and enjoyed every lewed device in body and mind – aye to the extreme. She agreed with me that every amorous trick might be tried, and we gratified our desires to the limits of possibility. I wanted no other woman, excepting when away from town, or on a sudden letch, or out of mere curiosity. These I nearly always told her of. Some of our amorous play I preserve in this narrative, some will never be even whispered about – the knowledge of it will die with us.

Helen soon had great pleasure in talking of her former tricks – would tell what she'd done or had heard of – reserve was utterly gone between us. She pronounced mine to be the most wonderful amatory career, when she had read a large part of the manuscript, or I had read it her while in bed and she laid quietly feeling my prick. Sometimes she'd read and I listen, kissing and smelling her lovely alabaster breasts, feeling her cunt, till the spirit moved us both to incorporate our bodies. Her sexual passion was strong, her strength great. I have fucked her thrice, and gamahuched thrice, yet seen her frig herself after that, and all in four hours, without showing a sign of fatigue.

Having now no harlot acquaintances, it was a real pleasure to her to have some one to talk with on these subjects. – Telling her of Camille one evening and talking of gamahuching, she said, tho the little servant whom I fucked had done it, it was a long time since a *woman* had gamahuched *her*. She liked a fine, fattish woman to do it to her and took a letch for Camille from my description of her. Camille was long past forty yet wonderfully well preserved, and one evening solely to gratify H I got Camille to visit her.

We had a lovely little dinner at Helen's, then adjourned to her bedroom, both women stripped and looked at each other's cunts – they were so quiet about that – and then Camille gamahuched. 'Fuck her, fuck her whilst she's licking me, let me see it,' H cried – But I wouldn't – I couldn't bear my sperm to go into any cunt but her own, and after she'd spent thrice under Camille's active tongue, I fucked her. Then after half an hour's rest Camille again licked H's quim till she screamed with the exhaustion of pleasure, and Camille could lick no longer. After repose and wine I wanted Camille to suck *me*, but she refused, telling H she'd never done it. – A lie, for she has many times minetted me tho she never liked it, and always wanting me to fuck her. – Poor Camille liked me to the last.

Again I then stroked H who excited by wine and lewd to her marrow made Camille feel my balls whilst fucking, she grasping Camille's motte, or feeling her buttocks whilst she was handling my stones. 'Why a lovely skin,' cried H as she felt Camille's buttocks. Indeed she had still that exquisite skin and her pretty, tight, deep cunt. Never were two more lovely skinned women together. I then fucked Camille at the request of both of them, which finished the night. Taking Camille home in my cab I paid her handsomely. She could do nothing but talk of the unparalleled charms of H I never brought them together again. H's letch was satisfied, and she did not want gay women.

I told her one evening how I had turned Nelly L's cunt into a purse, and she wondered if her own would hold as much. I had doubts, for it did not feel to me as large inside as the other woman's did, but I had H naked one day and tried. The silver brought was carefully washed, and the argental cunt stuffing began. I was so delighted and she also with the experiment, that I prolonged the work, not putting in five and ten shillings at a time as I did with the other, when my lustful curiosity was to ascertain a fact, but a shilling or two at a time only, feeling them of her cunt, then glorying in seeing her exquisite form promenading with the silver in her. When about forty shillings had disappeared up the belly rift, I put my prick up her, and felt with its sensitive tip the difference between a shilling which it struck against and the soft round compressive end of her cuntal avenue. She was as pleased with me at that trick as I was. I nearly spent, excited by my operations, and now with the idea of spending against a shilling up a cunt, but I didn't – wouldn't.

I resumed the silver stuffing, she her ambulations, and it is extraordinary that within a shilling or two, she held in her cunt the same number that Nelly had. She several times walked up and down the room with her cunt so full, that I could see the silver when I gently opened one lip. – The grip and tenacity of her Paphian temple seemed truly wonderful. – What muscular force, what a nut cracker! – But that indeed I knew, for her cunt was perfect in every way, a pudenda of all the virtues, powers and beauties for fucking, or doing anything voluptuous with – a supreme pleasure giver.

Then over the basin she squatted to void the argentiferous stream. It was beautiful to see her squat, her thighs then rounded into the fullest, loveliest form, it always delighted me to see her in that attitude washing her cunt or micturating. The silver tumbling out of her gaping hirsute cleft, with a clatter against the basin, made us laugh, some refused to quit the lubricious nook in which it found itself, I felt up for it, and she at last by muscular contraction of her cunt aided by her finger, got it all out. Then with a syringe she purified the receptacle, we went to the bed, and after a little mutual fingering, fucked, – the bawdy trick just finished enhancing our sexual delight.

The silver was washed and stored away. 'When you pay any one, tell them that the silver's been up your cunt.' – 'You beast, I will.' The servants and a female friend – for she had now a female friend – were told of this. We talked about it all evening, and she put one shilling well up for me to touch with my prick which I did, but did not spend whilst the shilling was in its lubricious receptable. [I wish now I had, it would have been something to remember.] Eighty-six or - seven shillings did her cunt hold.

NEXUS BOOKS

A LIBRARY OF THE FINEST EROTICA